LOVE &
ORDINARY
CREATURES

Love & Ordinary Creatures

A *novel by*

Gwyn Hyman Rubio

Ashland
Creek
Press

Published by Ashland Creek Press
Ashland, Oregon
www.ashlandcreekpress.com

ISBN 978-1-61822-031-8
Library of Congress Control Number: 2014936883

Printed in the United States of America on acid-free paper. All paper products
used to create this book are Sustainable Forestry Initiative (SFI) Certified
Sourcing. Cover design by Matt Smith (www.lilroundhouse.com).

To Tom and Debbie Hyman, both lovers of animals

In memory of
Katrena Hyman, who never met a bird she didn't like

O past! O life! O songs of joy!
In the air—in the woods—over fields;
Loved! loved! loved! loved! loved!
But my love no more, no more with me!
We two together no more.

— Walt Whitman, "Out of the Cradle
Endlessly Rocking," *Leaves of Grass*

One

When Caruso opens his dark eyes wide, he can will himself above the world. His pupils dilate as he soars back in time—seeing and remembering the Murray River, its muddy dark waters, thick as blood, snaking through the casuarina trees, the sun squatting like a gigantic monolith on their dangling, reed-like branches. He feels the heat, a volcanic blast of white, then senses the flurry of wings and the air currents above, below, and around him. With loud, raucous cries, the undulating wave of white breaks over the leafless trees. Yes, Caruso can remember these things, these primordial memories of his life before it changed.

The past disappears and the future becomes irrelevant the instant he focuses on Clarissa, lying white and still in the sunroom on the blue chaise longue in front of him. His pupils dilate and contract, pinning with pleasure, while he stares at her round, pink shoulder, free of the white silk robe.

"Claaa-risss-a." If she doesn't wake up soon, they'll run out of time.

She turns her head slightly. Her red hair parts to expose her white swan neck. On it, a few inches down from her left ear, is a mole, small and black as a papaya seed. The wooden blinds are open. A breeze wafts in from Silver Lake Harbor. Shafts of sunlight pass through the long, wide windows. Outside is the low thrum of a fishing boat as it slices through the water.

"Claaa-risss-a." He tries again, his voice more insistent. She promised to take him to the beach.

She mumbles and partially covers her face with the curve of her elbow. If he could, he would preen the white hairs on her forearm, then rub his body against the underside of soft pink flesh. She wiggles her dainty feet, and her brightly painted toenails catch his attention. They are orange, the same shocking color as the flowers of banksia, growing wild in the bush beyond the Murray River. If he could, he would draw his beak like a feather over those gems of orange.

He leans forward on his perch, lengthens his white neck, whiter than hers, and peers longingly through the bars of his home, catty-cornered from where she lies. He can stand it no more. How long has she been napping? Hours, it seems, and he's been patient thus far. If he dared, he would undo the snap hook and lock, steal through the cage door, and nest in her hair. If he dared, he would escape, not to the open sky but to her open palms. If he dared, if he dared, if he dared—but then if he dared, she would know that he is smarter than all the authorities of books on psittacids suggest he is—that he is smarter than the porpoise, the whale, the gorilla, and Ruthie, the four-year-old girl who lives next door. "Claaa-risss-a," he says a little louder.

He could pass the time rappelling up and down the chain attached to the top of his cage. Such ridiculous repetition, like a lazy mountain climber conquering the same slope again and again. Nor does he desire to jangle the yellow rattle she gave him last year. He is not her child.

Impatient, he maneuvers himself to the side of his cage and begins to clink his way down the bars in an effort to rouse her. He could release a siren-like shriek, so shrill it would send her lurching upward, wildly blinking her sapphire-blue eyes, but he must control himself, or else the thing he most fears could happen. He could lose her. He lowers his eyelids and looks inward.

Fear. There is danger all around. Prey, he is, and has been for more than twenty-six million years. In the bush of Victoria, he is constantly aware of predators lurking. He is vigilant when he forages for wheat seeds, when he plunders sweet papayas in groves that go on for miles. Damned as pests, he and his flock have been shot at and poisoned through the centuries. If not vigilant, he can be swallowed by a carpet snake camouflaged in a she-oak or hidden by a branch of eucalyptus leaves. If not careful, he can be seized by a saltwater crocodile, by a nighthawk, by a feral cat. He is a wild creature. Descending from the dinosaur, he has existed forever. Instinct and learning have taught him how to search for food, entice a mate, and defend his nest. He was born in a time before time—in an everlasting spiritual cycle when life was dreamed and formed. He was created in the distant past, in the present, and in the future, in the Everywhen, which the Aboriginal people call the Dreamtime. From the vast void of the universe, the Great Mother Warramurrungundji rose up from the ocean to create the land and the people. Soon thereafter, the spirit animals made the rocks, mountains, and trees, and it was the sacred duty of the Aborigines to protect the land and all the wild creatures. Is he a wild creature?

Curling his toes around the solid bars, Caruso performs a lively shimmy, shaking the cage even more. All he wants is to be paroled—from these four walls, this prison, this hole in a tree, this safe haven—in order to be near her.

"Caruso," she mumbles.

Does he dare?

"Caruso. Caruso," she says, pursing her lips, twisting her head one way, then another, her voice lilting and melodic. A blend of mountain twang and bluegrass drawl.

Does he dare?

"Caruso." She yawns loudly, before her body becomes still once more.

Fretful, he begins to throw himself back and forth, thumping the legs of the cage against the white linoleum. The yellow rattle scoots across the wire-meshed bottom. Water sloshes over the edge of his drinking cup onto the dog biscuit below. The framed photograph of her grandmother on the bookshelf topples over. The blue Wedgwood plate trembles on the painted chest. The wooden blinds, extending the length of the wall next to him, begin to clatter.

Her eyelids flick open. "Caruso!" she calls out, annoyed.

Like a child who has been caught doing something he shouldn't, he comes to an abrupt stop and timidly swivels his head toward her.

She eases herself upright, maneuvers her long legs over the side of the chaise longue, and plants her delicate feet, much too small for her height, on the floor. "Naughty boy," she scolds, wagging a finger at him. Her fingernails, unlike her toenails, are never polished. She vigorously shakes her head, her lax curls bouncing, as she rises. "Naughty, naughty boy," she says, "not letting me nap today."

Her bare feet make tiny sucking noises across the floor. She unlocks the cage door, pushes up the sleeve of her robe, and offers her left arm to him. "Up," she says, giving him the command, as though he would ever refuse to perch upon her alabaster skin. He lifts his foot, trying not to appear too eager, and—perfectly poised, with no need to use his beak for balance—steps up. She moves her arm forward slowly and steadily, all the while praising him. "Good boy, sweet boy," she coos, bringing him close to her face, breaking one of the cardinal rules.

He remembers when she used to read them aloud to him. They would be sitting in the sunroom—she on a Shaker-style stool beside his cage, he on his perch inside it. He can clearly recall the book because the profile of the Sulphur-crested Cockatoo on the cover was a reflection of him—with his headdress of yellow feathers, fluffed up, and his gray-black beak spread wide, revealing the dark-tipped knob of tongue. "Keep the bird away from your face at all times," she had read in her babyish, seductive voice.

"Kiss me," she says now. She puckers her wide, full lips. He leans forward and brushes his beak, strong enough to crack a Brazil nut, against her soft, moist flesh. She is not afraid because he has never bitten her, and he would smash his beak against a rock before he would. Light shoots through the prisms of colored glass, dangling by fishing line from the sunroom windows, fracturing the whiteness of her body into hues of red, purple, and blue.

Clarissa, his dazzling hen! His Eclectus with her sapphire-blue eyes and her velvet head of red. Clarissa! His chimera! His impossible fantasy.

"Up," she says again. He breaks another rule and ascends to her shoulder.

"Why can't you perch on my shoulder?" she had asked while they read the book together. Lifting her head, she crinkled her eyebrows in thought, staring right through him. "Oh, here," she said, her eyes on the page again. "If I let you perch higher than I am, you'll think you're the boss," she had read, giggling deliciously as she drew her finger beneath the reason.

How can he describe that giggle? It was the twittering of a hundred sparrows swooping down to feed. It was the sound of wind chimes tinkling in a gentle breeze. It was light skipping over raindrops during a summer shower.

She stands staring through the sunroom windows at the restaurant where she cooks. He knows that even on her day off, she is thinking about her work. He shifts around to look where she looks. If the light is right, not too sunny, he can get a clear view of her through the kitchen's wide glass panels, but most often she takes him with her. On those days, he watches her from an ornate cage positioned beneath the ancient live oak at the far end of the restaurant's terrace. "That cage is straight out of Victoriana," she often complains, but she keeps it anyway because the owner of Crab Cakes, an antique dealer who spends most of his time on the mainland—managing stores in Wilmington and Beaufort—was nice enough to give it to her when she confessed she couldn't afford to buy one.

Yawning, she heads for the kitchen, where the sunshine is splashing through the glass top of the door. Beyond the deck, he can see the deep pink pom-poms of crape myrtle fluttering in the breeze and can hear the little girl laughing on the rope swing next door. Clarissa goes behind the T-stand. He knows what to do. Moving off her shoulder to the plank of her arm, he steps up to the metal perch, keeping his eyes on her as she sways casually to the sink on the other side of the small, square room. Wrapping her fingers around the tap, she gives it a quick twist. Water pours from the rust-mottled spigot. She picks up a juice glass on the drainboard, fills it up, and drinks slowly, as though it is nectar from the gods and not warm tap water. She turns the flow off.

"Claaa-risss-a," he sings, making the most of his voice, but he's a cockatoo, and human speech is not his strongest asset. Leave this gift of mimicry to the African Greys, as a way to compensate for their homeliness, he thinks. "Caruso loves Claaa-risss-a. Caruso loves Claaa-risss-a," he croons, futilely trying to mimic the great Italian tenor for whom he's named.

It was Theodore Pinter who named him this. Caruso recalls the sound of the singer's booming voice on the scratchy vinyl records the old man had played. "Enrico Caruso was a large man," Theodore Pinter would say while he turned the disc over. "But his size was his greatest attribute because it gave heft to his beautiful, golden voice. Sing like the maestro," he'd ask Caruso. "Make your voice soar like his." And Caruso would struggle to imitate his namesake.

"You're certainly no Enrico," Clarissa says, pivoting back around, trailing her finger down the side of her long, flat nose.

A month ago, he'd overheard Beryl, her best friend on the island, saying, "If I had your strong bone structure and flawless skin, I'd never complain about my looks again."

"Cherokee bone structure and Scots-Irish coloring don't mix," Clarissa had shot back, unconvinced.

Her profile might be less than charming, Caruso thinks, but her full face—staring at him now—is enchanting. In truth, she has a handsome, captivating face. A face committed to his memory forever.

It was the old man's failure of memory that had led Clarissa to him. After a series of small, undetected strokes, Theodore Pinter began to lose track of his days. Algae would bloom green in Caruso's water bowl. Larvae would wiggle. Once, when the old man forgot to feed him, Caruso had escaped from his cage late at night and foraged for food in the kitchen. Eventually, Theodore Pinter was placed in a nursing home and Caruso in a pet store.

In the beginning, though, life with the old man had been calm and stable—if boring. A retired headmaster from an elite boys' school in Greensboro, Theodore Pinter believed there was a time and place for everything. Unlike Clarissa, he knew how to be firm and asserted his dominance over Caruso early on. Theodore Pinter was the alpha bird, the one in charge. "I was a competent headmaster because when I was a teacher I learned how to obey intelligently," the old man had told him. "Now, you must learn how to obey me." He ran his long, tapered fingers through his thinning hair. "I train you because I'm your teacher, because the more self-disciplined you are, the freer you'll be," he had said again and again, treating Caruso with the same wise, rigid civility that he brought to bear on his students as he taught basic obedience skills to his bird, and during the three years that Caruso had lived with him, he had grown to respect and like, if not love, the old man.

"I love you, Claaa-risss-a," Caruso warbles, staring into her eyes.

"I love you, Caruso," she replies.

Caruso wishes he had Zorro's gift of gab. If he did, he would say something special to her now, the way Zorro had responded to the customers at the pet store. "Pretty bird. Pretty bird," they'd say to the blue-and-gold macaw. "More than pre...tty. Beau...ti...ful," Zorro would rejoin.

If Caruso were Zorro, he could've imitated Enrico's singing, put a teardrop into his voice, and pleased the old man.

If he were Zorro, he'd fill Clarissa's ears with songs performed by the old timers. "The original stylists," she calls them, whenever she plays their recordings. If he were Zorro, he'd mimic Nina Simone's jazzy sound and the heartfelt blues of Billie Holiday before performing a rendition of "Is That All There Is?" in the sexy, honeyed voice of Peggy Lee. If he were Zorro, he'd echo the unique style of Frank Sinatra and Tony Bennett, then croon like her favorite—The Velvet Fog, Mel Tormé—whose mellow, rich baritone sounds as if his jaws are packed with wheat seeds.

"Mel Tormé. Mel Tormé. Mel Tormé," Caruso says suddenly.

"In your dreams," Clarissa teases, gliding toward him, coming to a halt in front of the T-stand. She spreads out her shapely arms, her white silk robe cascading, transforming her limbs into wings. Closing her eyes, she rocks from side to side and sings in a thin, pretty soprano not a jazzy tune but an old ballad from the highlands of Kentucky, her birthplace. He has heard it many times before. Today, she sounds a little more like her beloved Jean Ritchie. "'All in the merry month of May/When the green buds they were swellin','" she begins, her voice gently lilting. "'Young William Green on his death bed lay/For the love of Barbry Ellen.'"

He closes his eyes and tries to lose himself in the sweetness of her voice. He pays close attention to the lyrics, wants to lock them away in his memory, but much to his surprise, his mind begins to drift off, and before he knows it, his body is winging high above the earth. "Oh! there once was a swagman camped in the billabong/Under the shade of a Coolibah tree," he thinks, the old tune returning as he flies over the vast brown desert.

"'He sent his servant to the town/To the place where she was dwellin','" Clarissa sings on.

On the parched ground below, he spots the clusters of spinifex grass and the patches of turpentine bushes. He breathes in—the piercing scent of turpentine invigorating him. "And he sang as he looked at his old billy boiling/Who'll come a-waltzing Matilda with me," he remembers, his heart thumping out the words. Ahead, he notices a flock of pink Galahs roosting in a solitary wattle tree, dressed in yellow blossoms.

"'Sayin', "Master's sick and he sends for you/If your name be Barbry Ellen."'" She catches him in the net of her voice, pulling him back down to her.

"Matilda!" he cries out, confused, plinking his dark eyes open.

"And who's Matilda, you bad boy?" she asks him. "Are you two-timing me?" She giggles.

How could she say such a thing? he thinks, his yellow crest falling.

"Did I say something wrong?" she asks, reaching out to stroke his head.

He senses the love coming from her fingers, seeping through his feathers, her affection growing bigger and stronger with each caress of her warm flesh against his skin. Her love is so great now his small body can no longer contain it, and it oozes from him, filling up their cozy cottage, spilling from the windows and into the sandy yard. There, it flows freely around white oleander bushes and flagged red cedars before whirling down Fig Tree Lane, pouring into Silver Lake Harbor, and drifting out to sea—away from Ocracoke Island.

"Mama will make you feel better," she says.

Mama, he thinks, the insult jerking him from his reverie.

No, he objects, with an indignant shiver. She is not his mother. She is his goddess. His dazzling Eclectus Parrot, with her sapphire-blue eyes and her velvet head of red. She was his fantasy before the world was dreamed and formed—his chimera, when there was no word for yesterday, no word for tomorrow. She was his present on a huge continent, insulated by an ocean of water, that kept the language of regret and expectation at bay. She has been his beloved—now, always, and forever.

Two

PERCHED IN HIS CAGE, CARUSO CASTS HIS EYES through the long, wide row of windows and sees the green-striped tote bag bobbing in the wire basket above the bicycle's front wheel. He follows her breasts, rising and falling like buoys in deep water, as she pedals down the rutted driveway—her white, untanned legs an anomaly on Ocracoke Island during the hot blaze of July.

After her nap, she had bathed, her skin smelling of lavender and soap, then wiggled into a short, V-shaped white skirt and an Indian-print halter top of yellow and green amoebas. "Is it tied high enough?" she asked, slipping on a pair of orange flip-flops that matched the orange polish on her toenails.

"Beautiful Clarissa," he said, inhaling the perfume of her. Although his sense of smell is not as acute as his other senses, he can always detect her fragrance. "I don't trust you, Caruso. I don't mind looking like a hippie chef from the sixties, but I don't want to be jiggling around town." Whipping her deep red curls upward, she clipped them on top of her head. "I'm gonna get us some treats," she said. "Then we'll go to the beach." Giggling, she had dashed through the sunroom and out the kitchen door.

"Caruso, I love you!" she called out, blowing him a good-bye kiss over her shoulder, the silver clasp in her hair catching the sun, sending it back to him like a gift.

"Clarissa," he says wistfully, when she is out of view. He misses her already—craves her shimmering eyes, the color of the Tasman Sea; her bronze-red curls, the shade of the coppery-hued butterfly from Cairns; her luminous skin, as milky white as the pearls of Broome. And this deep yearning that swells in him just now makes him hunger for the equanimity he had felt during his years with the old man.

For back then, he had been a voyeur only, witnessing the vicissitudes of Theodore Pinter's obsessive love, not suffering, as he is at this moment, from his own obsessive love for Clarissa. On the perch in his cage near the study window, he had observed the real and surreal nature of the old man's world. "I moved back into my childhood home because from here I can see Olivia clearly," he had revealed. "She is my whole life again, same as she was when we were young, growing up in these two houses side by side. In those days, she filled the empty spaces in my heart, which my shyness with others had created. Years later, it was Greensboro Academy, with its tidy campus and ready-made community of friends, that made my life easier. And, oh yes, I would date other women," he said when Caruso puffed out the feathers around his face and cocked his head questioningly. "There was a private school for girls down the road from the academy, and I halfheartedly went out with a few of the teachers there. Trudy Fenton was one of them. She taught biology. A cute gal, she was, with strawberry-blonde hair and a mass of freckles. I liked her. Yes," he said, pensively nodding his head, "I can honestly say that. She had so many admirable qualities. Smart, sensitive, passionate. And she loved birds."

Caruso clucked softly at the old man. "In fact, she knew everything about them—could mimic their calls, describe their migration patterns in detail, could tell you what they ate, if they were monogamous, how they raised their young. She had an old crow named Merlin. When he was but a chick, she had rescued him—fallen from his nest, into the high grass, after an awful storm. His parents were nowhere. 'Probably dead,' she had said, 'because crows are good parents. They don't abandon their young.' So she took him home and raised him."

He paused for a moment, his eyes glazed in thought. "She's the one, Caruso," he said, his voice suddenly jubilant, "who introduced me to the joys and difficulties of owning a bird, and although I liked her immensely, I just couldn't love her the way she deserved to be loved. What does a man do when his heart simply isn't in it? A woman can intuit this lack of sincerity in him. Regardless of how hard he tries, she can see the truth. Trudy knew what I was doing—comparing her to someone else, concluding that she didn't measure up. Even in a lifetime of effort, she could never be the woman I thought Olivia was."

He grew quiet again for a second, rubbing the underside of his neck. "Poor Olivia," he said, with meaning. "To be worshiped, like I worship her, is a burden. What a heavy weight for a woman to carry. One false step, she probably feared, would send her tumbling down my mountain of idolatry into the flat land of ordinary folk. No woman wants to be a queen forever. Certainly not my Olivia. But I can't help the way I feel about her. She is royalty, my queen eternally, and I always hope she'll choose me to be her king one day. Choose me," he repeated in a faraway voice. "How can she not, when I so adore her? But look, Caruso," he said excitedly, cutting his monologue short, pointing at the long, narrow pane of beveled glass.

Caruso followed the length of the old man's strong, tapered finger—his gaze sailing over the shady side yard, twenty feet wide, before spotting a figure passing in front of the window of the house next door.

"Did you see her?" he asked, turning toward Caruso.

Caruso erected his yellow crest of feathers, rocking on his perch.

Theodore Pinter half-closed his bespectacled eyes and recited, tapping the air with his index finger every time he stressed a word:

> She walks in beauty, like the night
> Of cloudless climes and starry skies;
> And all that's best of dark and bright
> Meet in her aspect and her eyes...

Sighing, he shifted back to the window. "She's still beautiful, isn't she?" he said, grimacing as he leaned forward, pressing his hand firmly against the sill, pushing through the pain in his back, the result of a car wreck several years ago.

An old hen, Caruso thought, with a dismissive flick of his head, but seconds later, when she passed by the window again, he saw her in a different light. Her head high, her chin up, her back straight, she put him in mind of a proud cockatoo displaying, and he was enchanted by the sight.

"Olivia Greenaway taught ballroom dancing," Theodore Pinter continued. "You can see it in the elegant way she carries herself. Dancing was just one of the many things we had in common. Whenever I danced with her, I forgot about my shyness. I was lean, lithe, and graceful, just like Fred Astaire, but while dancing was only a hobby for me, it was Olivia's passion. She kept taking classes—through junior high, high school, and college, long after I quit—and she was a rising star in the ballroom scene before she married *him*," he said, bitterly stressing the last word.

Gracefully, Olivia lowered herself into an overstuffed chair facing them. Then, extending her long neck, like a Goffin Cockatoo's, she stretched sideways and retrieved a large book from off the end table to her left.

"What could she be reading today?" Theodore Pinter mused when she flipped open the pages.

Often, Caruso couldn't distinguish the old man's attempts at conversation from his spoken thoughts.

"I'll fetch the binoculars," he said giddily. Wheeling around, Theodore Pinter moved vibrantly across the pine floor, stepping not with overt energy but with an intensity fueled by his emotions, and Caruso knew that, despite the physical discomfort in his back, his legs remained strong and undefeated. For when he was young, he had played soccer passionately for a small neighborhood team, and his thighs and calves, even in old age, were firm and sturdy.

From off the top of a long row of white cabinets—surmounted by a high wall of bookshelves—he grabbed a pair of black binoculars, slipped off his wire-rimmed glasses and tucked them into his shirt pocket, and retraced his steps. He removed the eyecups from the lenses and placed them on the desk behind him. Positioning the apertures against his eyes, he covered the right lens with his hand.

"The left is clear and sharp," he pronounced after rotating the focusing wheel for several seconds. Next, he covered the left front lens with his palm and turned the right eyepiece. "Clear," he said, taking a quick step forward, tightly clutching the field glasses with both hands, holding aloft his pinkies. "It's *The Complete Poems of Emily Dickinson* again," he said. "Same as I, she feels a strong kinship to the woman in white. We read her poems to each other when we were young. Emily, too, had a secret love, and although she led a quiet life, she lived every moment of it loudly. Now, what poem of hers is she reading?"

He toyed with the focusing wheels some more, inched closer to the window, then stepped back. "Dammit," he said peevishly. "If she'd just lay the book on her lap, I could make out the number, even upside down. You see, Caruso, the poems have numbers instead of titles," he added, with a glance over his shoulder. He swiveled back to the window. "Sometimes, Olivia reads them aloud—so, sometimes, I just frame her mouth," he whispered, tilting forward.

Caruso heard his breaths coming in short, quick spurts, as he readjusted the focus. "She's licking her index finger..." he murmured. "Turning the pages. Please!" A high cry, like that of a cardinal whistling a glissando, emanated from his throat. "Please!" he groaned, the pinkies beside his face drooping with disappointment, but then they rose up again, like the wings of a finch in flight. "Ah, Caruso, we're in luck," he said. "At last, her lovely lips are moving."

Caruso's heart thumped restlessly against his breast. As he read her lips, Theodore Pinter paused between the words, savoring each of them.

Of Being is a Bird
The likest to the Down

"I know it by heart," he said, lowering the binoculars, closing his eyelids.

An Easy Breeze do put afloat
The General Heavens—upon—

It soars—and shifts—and whirls—
And measures with the Clouds
In easy—even—dazzling pace—
No different the Birds—

Blinking open his eyes, he stared longingly at Olivia Greenaway through the window.

Except a Wake of Music
Accompany their feet—
As did the Down emit a Tune—
For Ecstasy—of it

He finished, his voice circling high, like a raptor, in the passionate heat of Dickinson's words.

"Caruso, I'm home!" Clarissa yells as the back door slams shut.

Lost in thought, he'd missed her pedaling by the sunroom windows. He hears the tote bag plopping on the kitchen worktable.

"Pretty bird," she sings, sashaying beneath the archway toward him. He squawks with joy as she unlatches the cage door. He ruffles the feathers on his neck and bows his head. She obliges by scratching him there. "Did you miss me?" she asks, presenting her arm to him. At once, he is on her shoulder. She returns to the worktable. "Grapes from Styron's," she says, nodding at the tote bag. She taps her fingertips against the tabletop, and he descends. "Smart bird," she praises him. "Smart bird."

She doesn't have to tell him he's smart. He already knows it.

Before Clarissa took him home with her, he had shown the pet store staff just how smart he was. Every cage they locked him into, he broke out of. They timed him. In under five minutes, he opened a belt hook. Could even pick a combination lock because he remembered the rolling and tumbling sound of the clicks. Desperate, they wired his cage shut, but once more he broke out. *Houdini,* they nicknamed him, but he would only answer to Caruso. As a last resort, they had placed a metal plate over a wire-shield lock, making it impossible for him to escape.

"From California," she says, thrusting her hands into the tote bag, bringing up a bunch of white grapes. She plunks them in front of his feet and shoves in her hands again. "More," she announces, grinning flirtatiously at him. "For you—only," she states forcefully, setting down two pomegranates. "I don't like them. They're way too tart for me, like those baby gherkins Granny used to put up. Everything else she canned was tasty, but not those pickles. I pretended to fancy them, but I couldn't fool her. I'd crunch into one, my lips pulling downward, and she'd say, 'No blue ribbons for me, if you was the judge.' I prefer sweet, not sour," she says, screwing up her pretty mouth, looking so funny he can't help but screech. "Shush," she warns him, pressing a finger against her lips. "The neighbors."

Immediately, he silences himself.

"Some s...e...e...d...s," she says, the letters sizzling in her throat as she draws out the word. Holding up a small brown paper bag, she rattles the seeds inside it. He loves seeds of all kinds. In the wild, he was first and foremost a seed eater. She places the paper bag on the table. "And something special for you to gnaw on," she announces victoriously, a pinecone dangling from her fingers, "'cause I know how bored you get in your cage when I leave you here alone."

Pinecone in hand, she heads for the doorway. He chuckles like a
kookaburra while she's out of sight, gauges her distance from him by
the loudness of her flip-flops as they smack against the linoleum tile.
He does what the kookaburra does. He lets loose a chuckle that asks
her where she is. The click of the cage door, as she unlatches it, is her
answer. *I'm in here*, the click says. *In here*, the click repeats when she
closes the door again. He keeps chuckling to her and doesn't stop until
she returns to the kitchen.

"Are you pretending to be a kookaburra?" she asks.

He squawks softly, emitting another kookaburra call.

"Nope...I don't wanna hear that," she says, planting her large hands
on her hips. "I wanna hear the laugh song."

Two weeks ago, she'd read a new book about kookaburras to
him, sending him back to the first time he heard the kingfisher's
distinctive laugh. It was dawn, and his mother had just fed him when
the ear-shattering chorus began. How happy their song had made him!
So, from then on, he anticipated their singing in the early hours of
every morning and evening. One dusk, though, it was not music that
filled his ears but an angry cackling. Looking around, he spotted two
male kookaburras, teetering on a perch, fighting for dominance. With
their beaks entangled, they furiously punched the air with their wings.
Then, unexpectedly, another family of kookaburras, who lived in an
adjoining territory, burst forth with their evening chorus. At once, both
of them quit boxing. Reverently, they listened to the music as if they
had—at that very moment—been given the gift of awareness, as if they
finally understood that the spirit animals—the creators of the rocks,
mountains, and trees—were uniting them all in peace. As soon as their

neighbors' laugh song was over, the two opponents—with their heads thrown back and their beaks still locked together—began to sing, as did the other members of their family. Nevertheless, when the round of singing was finished, they resumed their sparring and fought as vigorously as they had before.

Displaying his yellow crest, Caruso belts out the boisterous laugh—beginning with its low chuckle of *ooos*, rising to the loud series of *ha-ha-has*, and ending with two chuckle notes.

Clarissa claps her hands and giggles. "Very good," she compliments him. "Would you like me to sing the kookaburra song for you?"

He rocks forward and bounces on the worktable's worn wooden top.

"Okay," she says, swallowing a mouthful of air before beginning. She sings:

> Kookaburra sits in the old gum tree.
> Merry, merry king of the bush is he.
> Laugh, kookaburra. Laugh, kookaburra.
> Gay your life must be.

When finished, she mimes him a kiss. "How about a bath before you eat?" she says, seizing the grapes and raising her lovely forearm. Eagerly, he steps up. "Down," she tells him when they come to the sink. The porcelain feels cool against his feet. She grabs a cobalt-blue bowl from the cupboard, sets it on the counter, and turns on the water. She rinses off the grapes, water tickling his toes. She nestles the fruit in the bowl, then uncoils the sprayer's hose and presses down on the lever.

"You're my sweet, smart boy," she says as the water showers over him, washing the powder dust off his feathers. "This is how my granny used to bathe me when I was a little girl," she goes on. "She'd set me in the tub and cut on the water. There was a rubber shower hose hooked to the spigot, and when the water was just right—as warm as milk from a baby's bottle—she'd shower me with it, then soap me down. She made her own soap and was proud of it. I remember how she'd lean over the side of the tub, pucker up her lips, and blow at the bubbles on my arm. Up, they'd fly, disperse, and disappear. Boy, did she scrub me hard! Probably why my skin is so soft now." With an infectious laugh, she douses his neck and crown of gold.

Playful, he fluffs out his cheek feathers and hoots back at her.

"I love you, too," she says as she twists off the water.

He flutters his wings and shimmies.

"I'm your guardian," she says, quoting from one of the parrot books she has read to him many times over. "Your patron, your mentor—not your jailor."

But you are my captive, he tells himself. When you had not yet come down from the trees of the ancient forests, I was a companion to you.

She holds out her arm, and he dutifully goes to her.

The instant his feet touch her silky skin, he realizes how self-deceptive he is, for there is no way he can own her when she wields so much power over him. A gift from Warramurrungundji, the Goddess of Creation, she is. But don't all pleasures come as gifts from the Great Mother? Wasn't the water that washed the powder dust off his feathers a gift, as well as his view of their backyard through the glass top of the kitchen door as she bathed him? The lacy foliage of the crape myrtles dancing like green-feathered hummingbirds in the breeze is a gift, along with the deep, fertile smell of the ocean and the shells scattered like strands of broken pearls upon the shore. Isn't the *wheep-wheep* whistling of the oystercatcher—winging low over the foamy waves—a gift also?

She retrieves the cobalt-blue bowl, and he rides her shoulder to the worktable. She puts the bowl on the rough wooden top, lowers herself onto a bench—positioned between the table legs—and with sturdy fingers pinches off a grape and offers it to him. He champs it noisily. She takes one for herself and sucks it into her mouth. She chews it luxuriously, every so often licking the juice off her bottom lip. She offers him another. He cradles it in his beak. Extending her long swan neck, she eases her head back and parts her lips in anticipation. He tilts forward, drops the white grape into the dark well, and follows the sensuous movement of her mouth and throat as she swallows. What he wouldn't give to be that grape inside her mouth!

"One for you and one for me," she says, now feeding him every other grape until she is snipping the last one off. It is the plumpest one of all, he notices.

He takes it from her fingertips, his heart exploding, his eyes hypnotized by her face, while he sups and swallows. Oh, how he yearns for the uncomplicated days with Theodore Pinter—when he was learning about love from afar and not caught in its throes—up close! Suddenly, he wants to go back to his life before the pet store, the old man, the net thrown over him, when he was but a young bird, nesting carefree in the hole of a gum tree, waiting for his parents to feed him. Both had reared him, but what he remembers most is his mother's touch. How gentle her beak was! How tenderly she had fed him! Everything she did spoke of love. Oh, yes, to be that lighthearted fledgling once more!

He trills to himself the beginning of "Summertime" and wonders where he first heard those words. Was Billie Holiday the one who had sung them, or was it Nina Simone?

No, they had danced off Clarissa's lips, he remembers, the day she brought him home from the pet store. The ride on the ferry from Swan Quarter, he recalls, had been long and hot, and she had rolled down the car windows to cool them off. He was crouched on his perch—nervously swaying from side to side, threatening her with hisses—but she had displayed no fear. Rather, she had unlatched the cage door, filled the empty space with her handsome face, and calmed him with the music of those words.

Three

WARY OF THE SUN, SHE NEVER GOES TO THE BEACH until late afternoon. Her grandmother, she once confided to him, who loved her more than anyone, had died from too much gardening and too much sun. *The cancer began as an inconspicuous spot on her shoulder, and before we knew it she was gone.* She always reminds him that she rescued him from a country scorched by the sun's harsh rays. "Thanks to me, your plumage is wrinkle-free," she likes to tease him. "Yes, Caruso, I rescued you from that horrid pet store," she then adds in a serious voice.

Whenever she says this to him, he wants to set her straight. It was the old man, not her, who saved him from the worst of fates—a long, miserable life in a parrot breeding mill. "But what bird, you silly girl, would not choose to fly free?" he'd like to say but never would, even if he could, because he loves her, because Theodore Pinter told him that words could cut as deeply as bites inflicted by a parrot's beak.

Caruso remembers how hot it was that August day when the old man taught him about the harshness of words. The Shasta daisies—as Theodore Pinter called them—were hanging their heavy heads in the heat. Blue jays, their voices *toolool*ing, were diving down to cool themselves off in the birdbath, and Caruso was envious as he watched them bathe. "Words can be as sharp as daggers," the old man had said out of nowhere as they sat in his backyard, surrounded by a high brick wall splashed with English ivy. After retiring early at sixty-two, Theodore Pinter had moved back into his childhood home, then immediately hired a brick mason to construct the privacy wall. When it was finished, he removed a brick toward the rear near the hydrangea shrub, another up front beside the gate, and a third from the center. "This way, I could see her drinking her Scotch and soda at twilight," he explained.

As Caruso listened, he tried to understand why the old man had erected a wall with peepholes in the first place. Why didn't he simply open his garden gate and visit with his love whenever she came out?

"You might be wondering why I built this barrier between us," Theodore Pinter said, as though reading Caruso's thoughts. "But just think about it, Caruso. What's a man to do when the love of his life chooses not to see that he still adores her? What's he to do when her husband watches her every move as if she, not he, is the one who has lovers?"

Caruso shook his head and fluffed out his feathers.

"I'll tell you what that man must do, my friend—wait. He must remain patient and love her from afar, though he lives next door to her. Sure, he steals the occasional glance and searches for any sign from her that it's time to make his move. Meanwhile, he hides his true feelings, waves nonchalantly if they should spot each other on the sidewalk out front, nods agreeably if they happen to run into each other in the post office or at the bakery around the corner. Sometimes, he speaks to her, but the words from his mouth are dull and nondescript, conveying nothing of real substance, as if he is hiding his true feelings behind a mask. They are words about the weather or simply mundane phrases like *How are you?*—for the man is biding his time, playing a role, until he can take his mask off. The woman never asks him over, and he never asks her. And whenever he goes out, it's with his colleagues from school, not with anyone who knew the two of them years ago. For there is something unspoken between them. Something he is afraid to hear should it not be what he hopes for. Something she might, at last, confirm—that she cannot love him the way he wants because no one could love him the way he loves her. Or it could be something more—the something he dreams of. The something she doesn't say, he thinks, because she's afraid of the truth—that he's the one she should have chosen all along. So, my friend, I exist in a solitary world, hoping that one day the something I've always wished for will come true."

Theodore Pinter rocked his glass of Scotch and soda, clacking the ice cubes against one another. "Still, there are some connections between us," he asserted softly. "I drink Scotch and soda now." He smiled wistfully as he brought the rim to his lips and downed a little. "I don't really like hard liquor," he confessed, taking another sip, the muscles in his face tightening as he swallowed. "I only drink it to feel closer to her. I've adored Olivia Greenaway my whole life," he went on. "We spent our childhood together. Whatever she asked me to do, I did. If she wanted me to pull taffy with her in the kitchen, I did it. We hopscotched on the sidewalk in front of her house. Skipped rope in the driveway. Threw jackstones and played Monopoly in her parlor. Everyone thought I was delicate. I wasn't. I was a boy and liked doing boy things. I was skilled at marbles. Many a classmate lost their prized cat's-eyes in a shooting match with me. Many admired my dexterity on a soccer field. Flexible and fast, I always was, but I gave those things up because I wanted to spend every waking second with her. You see, I had to be near her. I was obsessed. She was my heart—my heart," he repeated loftily, pressing his open hand against his chest. "In the end, all that I did, none of it mattered because she didn't see me as the boy next door who adored her but only as another friend."

He finished off his drink, teased out the twist of lemon with his fingers, and tossed it into his mouth. He chewed the rind thoughtfully and gulped it down. Removing his glasses, he leaned forward with his elbows on the wrought iron table. "One day when we were in her kitchen, snacking on pimento cheese sandwiches and drinking glasses of sweet iced tea, she cupped her hand against my chest and said, 'Oh, Teddy, you're as soft as a girl.' *Soft*, that seemingly benign word, was a dagger to my heart. What do you think, Caruso? Am I not hard enough to be a man?"

Caruso had survived hard. Hard was the hand of man that chopped down the gum trees in which the cockatoo chicks were nesting. It was the hand of greed that kidnapped the fledglings and sold them into captivity for life. Hard was the narcissism clouding man's vision, making him believe he was the only important species on the planet, while also pitting him against his own kind. Hard was the Englishman slaughtering the Aborigines for dog food, then countenancing their genocide.

Caruso knew Theodore Pinter wasn't hard, but he also knew he wasn't soft either. Theodore Pinter had the right balance of soft and hard inside. Theodore Pinter was tender. "You think I'm too soft, too. Don't you, Caruso?" Caruso ruffled his cheek feathers and squawked. He took three steps over the iron filigree top toward the old man, and they met crown-to-head, beak-to-nose. On the precipice of *Dreamtime*, they perched—intuitively understanding each other, yet unable to put this understanding into words. "Although her words hurt me," the old man had murmured, tears filling his eyes, "mere words are impotent to describe how much I adore her. Even now, I can see the lovely whiteness of her fingers pushing gently against my dark-blue shirt."

The violet-blue straps of Clarissa's bikini top look like petals of slender blue flag iris against her pale skin. Hugging a rolled-up beach towel under her arm, she presents her impeccable shoulder to him. He climbs up, and they head out the back door—never locked. She shuts it, then slams the screen door behind her. She is watchful of the harsh sun, but not of hard men who could be just as dangerous. As they descend the deck steps, Caruso makes note of the broom propped against the wall beside the door. His instincts of survival have crossed the Pacific Ocean with him, and if the broom has shifted even slightly upon their return, he'll know it. Have no doubt—he will defend her if he has to, the way his parents often defended him. When he was a chick, he had looked on in horror as a marsupial, the size of a rat with a bushy tail, crawled along a branch toward the hole in which he nested, but with an alarming screech his father had swooped down to protect him. Ramming his wings against the predator's back, he had pierced his furry body with his razor-sharp beak and sent him fleeing.

Clarissa squats, and Caruso crosses from her shoulder to the handlebars. After depositing her towel in the wire basket, she straddles the bike, flips up the kickstand, and pedals off. "It's a three-speed," she has said. "Nothing fancy." Caruso faces forward, trembling with pleasure as the ocean air whips over his feathers. Flinging back his head, he lets out a shriek, but this time she doesn't tell him to be quiet. They ride down the dusty lane and onto the narrow paved road bordering the harbor. She pedals easily—her legs strong and muscular below her shorts. "This is a birdwatcher's paradise," she had boasted when he first came to live with her two years ago—as if he would derive joy from watching the little birdies, too. Yes, he is a warm-blooded vertebrate with wings and feathers, he must admit this, but he is more intelligent and beautiful than the simple birds who make this island their home. He is no common seagull, no diminutive piping plover, no silly sanderling, his black legs racing to and fro, chasing waves futilely as they break against the shore. He is a parrot. A virile Sulphur-crested Cockatoo. A Cacatua galerita galerita, a full twenty inches long. He would fully unfold his wings to let the breeze show off his snowy plumage, but he doesn't, for then she—much too close to him for such a long ride—would see how much his wing feathers have grown.

They pass a fishing boat docked in the harbor and spot a motorboat cutting through the smooth water of the sound. He glances back at Clarissa, and she smiles. They take Highway 12 north for miles and miles.

Late in the day, the parking lot is empty. He hears only the rumble of the surf as it breaks against the shore and the lone cry of a seagull. Bike racks are to the left of the information board about riptides, but Clarissa never uses them. Instead, she stops at the bottom of the wooden steps, where she pushes down the kickstand and slides off the seat. Struggling out of her shorts, she places them in the basket and stands there—with her hands on her hips—before him, her hair flaming like ribbons of fire in the ocean breeze. He eyes her from top to bottom. In her vivid, violet-blue bikini, she is spectacular. His dazzling Eclectus Parrot!

She leans over, and he passes to her shoulder. Grabbing the beach towel, she follows the walkway, built protectively over the dunes. He spots pennywort, surfing the mounds like dark green sand dollars. The seaside goldenrod is in bloom, and it makes her sneeze. "Bless you," he says, and she answers, "Thank you." There's a Coke can lying next to a patch of wax myrtle, corralled by bunches of beach grass. The instant he spots it gleaming in the late afternoon sun, he screeches and flaps his wings to let her know it's there. She turns toward it. "I see it, Caruso," she says. "But we aren't allowed on the dunes. The park rangers will have to get it later. Why do we act like the planet is ours alone?" she asks him, touching his toes tenderly. In this way, they are allies. "Defenders of the earth," she calls them whenever they pick up plastic bottles along the beach.

Three weeks ago, they had noticed the most egregious filth. Perched on her shoulder, he was the lookout, same as always, when his eyes landed on a white plastic blob in the sand dunes to the right of them. Immediately, he swiveled toward it, unleashing a shrill shriek and flapping his wings, until she came to a standstill. "Dammit," she said, through clenched teeth. "Why didn't she toss that dirty diaper in the trash can? Don't you just hate people sometimes, Caruso?" He had thought about that for a second. He loved Clarissa. Yet wasn't she *people*, too? Still, he understood what she was saying. Birds did things differently. A blue tit, for instance, after feeding her chick, would nudge its rear, prompting it to lift up its rump and release its white sac of waste. Which she would then eat, thus keeping her chick safe from predators by eliminating any trace of her nest. The lyrebird of Australia would gather together her chick's excretions and release them into a nearby stream.

"Ocracoke is a fragile, thirty-foot lens of moving sand, as flowing as the sea," she quotes for the umpteenth time to him as she traipses over the weathered planks. "Don't take my word for it, Caruso. That's what the experts say." He makes a trilling noise to signal he's listening. "The barrier islands can't be stabilized, and shouldn't be civilized," she says, peeking back at the Coke can. "They shift freely and, like hurricanes, go wherever they want." She laughs, and he makes a laughing sound with her.

At the end of the walkway, she hangs her towel over the railing and tells him to wait for her on the post. "Don't fret. I'll be right back," she says, slipping off her orange flip-flops, her feet sinking into the white sand, her heels bobbing, as she sprints toward the water. A wave licks her toes, and she squeals. Twisting around, she waves gingerly at him and plows forward, the breakers crashing against her thighs. Lifting up her arms, she transforms her body into an arrow and vanishes into a blue-gray swell.

Anxious, he keeps his eyes on her. Though she's a strong swimmer, the riptides here are deadly—like saltwater crocodiles lurking beneath the surface—and he doesn't blink until he spots her white arms digging through the billows, her legs kicking up plumes of froth. Within seconds, she disappears again. He scans the waves on the purple-red horizon, a tight knot of fear in his crop. Soon, it will be too dark to see her. She resurfaces. Relieved, he slings back his head, flaps his wings frenetically, and screams, but she doesn't turn back to shore. At the first sign of trouble, he'll soar out to her. Swooping down, he'll snatch her hair in his claws and lift her head above the water. It will be then she'll know what he has kept hidden from her. She failed to clip his wing feathers short enough to keep his flight to a brief flutter.

He shrieks some more—so vehemently he feels his throat aching. Why won't she look his way? he thinks. He is leaning forward, his wings outstretched for takeoff, when he notices a dark figure riding over the swells. She waves, signaling she's all right, but the figure on the surfboard keeps rolling. Moments later, the two of them are paddling through the choppy surf toward the beach.

Together, they trudge through the deep sand. She is laughing, her white skin glowing like the inside of a conch shell in the fading light. "I wasn't in any trouble," she says, nearing the walkway, "but thank you for paddling all the way out to get me."

"My pleasure," the man says, stopping abruptly in front of the post. "What on earth is that?" he asks, pointing at Caruso.

That, Caruso thinks indignantly. He's not a *that*. He's a psittacid of importance.

The man takes another step, staring wide-eyed at him. Alarmed, Caruso sits upright, slicks his feathers down, and lifts a threatening foot.

"I wouldn't get too close, if I were you," Clarissa warns.

The man halts.

"Don't look at him directly," she says. "That's what predators do."

"Will it bite?" he asks, looking away.

It, Caruso thinks, no longer fearful. He's not an *it*, either. He and his kind have been written about and painted for centuries. As far back as 1250, the Saracen Sultan sent him to the Emperor of the Holy Roman Empire of German States as a gift. Insulted all over again, Caruso glares at the man.

"Okay, try again," she says. "But, this time, blink your eyes. Act shy, like you're the one who's afraid."

The man does as she tells him, timidly blinking both of his eyes at Caruso.

Appeased, Caruso cries softly at him, stretches out his wings, and gives them a gentle flutter.

"You see, Caruso's nice to people who are nice to him," Clarissa says, half-smiling.

"What can I say? I'm a bird pleaser," the man says. "Just can't seem to help myself."

"Well, thanks for trying so hard," Clarissa says. "Caruso's my best friend, and I don't like to see him scared."

"Your best friend's a parrot?" the man says, as though amused.

"Parrots are wonderful companions, especially cockatoos."

"He must've cost you a pretty penny."

"It took me almost a year to save up for him, but he's been worth every cent."

"How long have you had him?"

"Let's see," she says. "I got him Labor Day weekend of ninety-one, so almost two years now—but I feel we've spent a lifetime together." Leaning over, she plants a kiss on Caruso's forehead.

"He's a lucky guy." The man grins, his front teeth gleaming like opals in the dusk.

"I best head home, while it's still light out," Clarissa tells him.

"Yeah, I like to surf in the late afternoon, like to have the beach and waves all to myself," the man says. "I'd give you a lift," he adds, his tone apologetic, "but I drifted. My van is parked a couple of miles up."

"It doesn't matter," she says. "Caruso and I do this all the time."

"I wish I could be of more assistance."

"Why, you're quite the Southern gentleman," she says, with an enticing giggle.

"Joseph Hampton Fitzgerald, at your service." He presents his hand to her.

"Clarissa McCarthy," she says, shaking it.

Caruso follows the movement of her strong hand, firmly clasped around his, and a momentary feeling of jealousy knifes through him.

"Jo-seph Hamp-ton Fitz-ger-ald," he says, mimicking the man perfectly.

"Sounds just as pompous coming from him." His head thrown back, his mouth opened wide, the man lets out a boisterous laugh. "Why my parents did that to me, I'll never know. My friends call me Joe. You live here year-round?"

"Uh-huh. I'm the chef at Crab Cakes."

"I know the place," he says. "Across the street from the harbor. I've heard tourists raving about your food. Mind if I drop by tomorrow evening and say hello?"

"Please do," she says, smiling warmly, "and I'll thank you for your valor with a little taste of my cooking."

A little taste of her cooking, Caruso thinks, whipping out his cheek feathers, studying the man with disfavor. Dirty-blond hair. Brown irises, flecked green. Medium height. Neither handsome nor ugly. An ordinary Homo sapiens. Not worthy of comparison to any bird. Common, Clarissa would call him. No sooner does he think this than his gaze falls upon the man's arms, long and muscular with biceps round as coconuts, then upon his chest. Unlike Theodore Pinter's, it is broad, strong, and hard. Hard as the nut of an oyster around a pearl. Hard as the shell of a sea tortoise. Hard as the heart of a great white shark, he fears.

Four

SOMEHOW, SHE SEEMS DIFFERENT TO HIM TODAY, annoyingly chirpy, like a sparrow. He perches on the T-stand, returned this morning to its customary spot in the sunroom, and watches while she dons her white tunic, pins up her red curls, and squeezes into the black Reeboks she swears alleviate the discomfort of standing for hours in front of the stove. With hands on hips, she turns this way and that in front of the mirror above the chaise longue, stretching her swan neck so far out he fears her head might tumble off, then she takes a step closer to her reflection and licks her lips until they glisten. She bats her long eyelashes, deep red like her hair, winks at herself, and says, "Not so bad after all. Maybe Beryl's right." Spinning around, she saunters over. At once, he's on her shoulder.

They head out the kitchen door, but instead of taking the shortcut through the backyard to Crab Cakes, she makes a beeline for her bike and mounts it. Before he knows it, they are cycling over the driveway toward Fig Tree Lane, veering left, away from the restaurant, onto Silver Lake Drive. "I need to speak to Beryl," she says into the breeze.

Speak to Beryl, he thinks. About what? It's Tuesday. Time to get back to Crab Cakes. Time to get back to work.

She turns right at Biff's Dockside Store, where Beryl clerks for her cousin when not painting in her studio, and kerplunks over the warped, weathered planks. "Stay put," she tells him, braking in front of the entrance. "I'll be back in a jiffy," she says, pushing down the kickstand, sliding off the bike.

Back in a jiffy, Caruso thinks, hissing with irritation. Usually, she and Beryl Gaskill get together on Monday, when the restaurant is closed. Typically, they hang out at Beryl's house, where five generations of O'cockers have gathered on her family's screened-in front porch, drinking beer and telling tall tales with an exaggerated island brogue before enjoying a supper of spicy boiled shrimp, onion-laced hush puppies, french fries, and coleslaw. But seldom do they meet on Tuesday, when Clarissa must get to the restaurant early to prepare for the next six days of hectic work.

Moving toward the wooden pocket door, she slides it open, leaving him alone beneath the hot sun on a rickety dock above the splashing water. What is she doing? he wonders, glancing furtively around. Isn't she worried about what could happen to him, same as he worries about her? After all, he is an expensive bird. Someone could sneak up, hurl a beach towel over him, and steal him away from her forever. Doesn't she care? Even as he thinks this, he knows his fears are histrionic, for on this island of eight hundred residents, a thief of parrots would be quickly found out. Besides, the tourists who swarm here during the summer come to have fun—not to get into mischief.

The vague sound of their chitchat, drifting through the partly closed door, tantalizes him. Why didn't she take him inside? he puzzles. She knows how much he likes to listen to Beryl Gaskill talk. The first time he heard Beryl say *hoi toide*, he had laughed like a kookaburra. "High tide," Clarissa had translated for him. Then, a few days later, when Beryl came out with, "Don't mommuck me. I'm feeling quamished," Clarissa had immediately explained that *mommuck* was harassing a person, while *quamished* was being sick to your stomach.

Caruso aches to know exactly what they're saying. Swiveling his head, he checks to see if anyone is coming. The dock is clear. Using his beak for balance, he tightropes down the bike's crossbar, alights on the gray floorboards, and hastens toward the doorway. Staying out of sight, he cranes his neck and listens intently.

"When I saw him on that surfboard, rolling toward me," Clarissa is saying, "I didn't know what to do. I mean, he's so hot he's..."

Hot? Caruso muses. The sun is hot. If Clarissa stays outside too long in the heat, her skin feels warm beneath his feet. Yet yesterday, it was dusk when Joseph Hampton Fitzgerald came paddling toward her on his surfboard. The sun was no longer shining, and he was yards beyond her reach. So how did she know he was hot? Caruso thinks, just as Beryl says, "*Hunksome,*" finishing Clarissa's sentence for her. And although Beryl isn't in sight, the loud *thump* suddenly filling his ears paints a picture of her in his mind—plunking her rough elbows on the counter while clasping her paint-flecked hands. He imagines her short black hair shining bluish-purple in the sun-filled room. That is, if she hasn't already dyed it another color. It seems to Caruso that she is constantly molting, her hair falling out one shade before growing in another.

Two years ago, when they had first met, Beryl's unruly, clipped thatch had been yellow, the hue of a snowflake lily on a Kakadu billabong after a severe monsoon, but the next time he cast his eyes on her, it was wine-red. As soon as he adjusted to that, she changed it to sweet-potato orange, and then a few months later to wren-brown. Which he must admit didn't suit her. Now, it's crow-black. Her natural color and the one that looks best on her, she insists.

"That's right," Clarissa says, with an intoxicated sigh. "*Hunksome.* That's what he is. I've never seen anyone built like him before. I mean, his pecs are huge—Herculean."

Herculean, Caruso muses. The old man had often told him stories about Hercules and his great feats of strength. The surfer's arms were long and muscular. His chest was broad, strong, and hard—but *Herculean?* Caruso ponders this some more. No, he wouldn't go so far as to call his pecs that.

"Herculean pecs," Clarissa says again. "When he was paddling over the swells, with me beneath him, I felt his chest brushing against my back, and I tingled all over."

Tingled all over. From the heat? Caruso wonders.

"And then on the beach, as we were walking, I saw his stomach. He has a stomach like a washboard."

A stomach like a washboard. What does that mean? Caruso thinks with a befuddled shake of his head.

"No body fat at all?" Beryl says, her tone dubious.

"None that I could see," Clarissa tells her. "And the rest of him looked pretty good, too. Strong chin. Full lips. Brown eyes. Blond hair, and oh—the longest eyelashes I've ever seen on a man."

"But is he nice?"

Caruso can imagine the teasing smile on Beryl's face when she says this, as annoying as a sheath around one of his pinfeathers.

"Well, he paddled all the way out to help me."

"That was nice," Beryl says, with an ambiguous drop of her voice. "What's his name?"

"Joseph Hampton Fitzgerald," Clarissa replies deliberately.

Three big names to tattoo across his hard Herculean pecs, Caruso thinks.

"I don't know the name. He must be a *dingbatter*—not from around these parts."

"He's dropping by the restaurant tonight," Clarissa says. "Wants to say hello. I'll ask him where he's from then."

"Smooth operator," Beryl says.

"I offered to fix him a little something," Clarissa says, ignoring her remark. "'Course, I haven't decided what yet."

"Shuck him some oysters," Beryl suggests, her tone immediately helpful. "Hain't nothing better than oysters on the half-shell with some lemon juice and cocktail sauce for dipping."

"They're not in season now, not as sweet," Clarissa says. "Besides, anyone can shuck oysters and serve them on a bed of chipped ice."

"Hain't so," Beryl objects, in a voice gruffer than usual. "Ya gotta use your oyster knife, know your way 'round the mouth."

"But there's no cooking to it," Clarissa shoots back.

"Ya want an arrow through his heart, ya best shuck him some oysters."

"Beryl, honey," Clarissa says, sighing, "I want to cook him something special."

"Oysters are aphrodisiacs," Beryl argues. "Will put ya in the mood. Hain't that what it's all about, anyhow?"

"No."

"You know what *shucking* rhymes with?"

"I'm not serving him raw oysters," Clarissa almost shouts, just as Caruso remembers that Beryl is the five-time and still-undefeated champion of Ocracoke's annual oyster-shucking contest.

"I'm just trying to help," Beryl says with a pout in her voice.

"I know, sweetie," Clarissa says. She softens her voice before adding, "I know what I'll do. I'll fix him a plate of Oysters Rockefeller. Show off my culinary talent."

Will she feed him oysters like she feeds me grapes? Caruso asks himself, shifting sinuously from one foot to the other. Will she slip the plumpest one into his mouth?

"Might work," Beryl concedes halfheartedly.

Neither speaks for several seconds.

Caruso listens to the water lapping against the pilings and to the throaty gurgling of a motorboat idling nearby. Next comes the nasal twang of a country song blasting through an open window, then fading as the car rumbles down the road. All of a sudden, Clarissa blurts out, "I better get going. My God, it's almost one! Between deliveries and prep, you know how crazy my Tuesdays are."

"Too much work and too little time," Beryl says with a great big sigh.

Panicked, Caruso shambles over the dock and is halfway up the crossbar when Clarissa catches him. "Caruso!" she yells, dashing over. "What are you doing? Didn't I tell you to stay put?"

He lowers his head, refuses to look at her.

"Handlebars," she commands in a brusque voice.

He maneuvers himself to the top, curling his toes over the hot, curved metal, stubbornly keeping his back to her.

"I'm late," she mutters, mounting the bike. With a swift clack, she kicks up the stand. The tires thunk over the buckled planks.

Unlike the old man, she's forever running late, Caruso thinks, cutting her no slack.

Out of nowhere, an image of Theodore Pinter's grandfather clock looms up in his mind. Six feet tall, its design of boldly shaped curves had stood out against the sage-green wall in the study. A pattern of swirling birds was carved at the bottom of its mahogany case. The pendulum was brushed brass, he remembers, and with the arrival of each hour, "Ode to Joy" chimed. Large and easy to read, the numerals on the clock face had brought shape and form to the old man's solitary life. Every weekday morning at seven, he'd slip the custom-made cover off Caruso's cage and say brightly, "Let's hope the mail comes early." Whereupon he'd tread down the hallway toward the kitchen, only to return ten minutes later to stand by the window sipping strong black tea in a mug. As soon as the postman ascended the porch steps, Theodore Pinter would set the mug on the desk and step closer to the pane of glass, bouncing excitedly on his toes as Olivia passed by the living room window, then out of sight, on her way to pick up the mail. His eyes would flit over the exterior brick wall of her house, glide above the porch railing, and come to rest on her slender fingers, dipping into the woven basket tacked to the doorjamb.

The wire basket in front of Caruso's toes begins to jangle as Clarissa cycles around the curve of Silver Lake Drive. Bothered by the sound, he shifts his attention to the thick growl of the Cedar Island ferry coming in to dock, followed by the foghorn's low, deep tone. Inhaling the salty air, he takes in the scenery—the weathered storefronts advertising deep-sea fishing and day trips in small, open boats to the deserted island of Portsmouth, with its miles of pristine beaches and rare shorebirds, spotted whenever the flats are wet. He sees Ride the Wind—tourists in line for parasailing—the Slushy Stand on the opposite side of the road, and the picturesque Silver Lake Motel and Inn. They cycle past the Treasure Chest Restaurant, whose chef is Clarissa's main competitor. "Always sending out his spies to steal from my menu," she has complained time and again. It's true, for Caruso has heard comments from the patio diners: "I ordered this the other night at the Treasure Chest, but it can't compare to what I'm eating now." Every time she tried something new, the inferior "Chef Louie" version would be created a few days later. "When I was growing up, my brother stole all of my parents' attention," she often grouses to Caruso. "Chef Louie is the one stealing from me these days."

"Chef Louie! Chef Louie!" he shouts, trying to get back into her good graces by mocking the man.

"Don't push your luck!" she growls.

"Chef Louie!" he tries again, but she turns a deaf ear to him.

By the time they roll to a stop in front of Crab Cakes, she is winded, her breathing short and rapid. "Come here, you little brat," she says, banging her foot against the stand.

Compliant, he goes to her arm and ascends to her shoulder.

"Next time, you'd better stay put."

She makes straightway for the front entrance, which leads into the dining room, the long arm of the L-shaped bistro, and takes a quick left, rushing by the storage room and into the kitchen.

"You're late, Clarissa," Rick says, in his soft, effeminate voice. He is the head line cook, sous chef, and also the owner's nephew.

"I stopped by Biff's. Wanted to talk to Beryl," she explains.

"About what?" he asks.

"About a gentleman I met at the beach yesterday."

"A gentleman?" Rick says. "A...gentle...man," he repeats, as if each word were a sweet fig in his mouth. "Oh, hi there, Caruso," he says, his left eyebrow levitating, his right eye wandering the instant he acknowledges the bird.

Caruso loves it when he does this trick. In fact, Caruso is utterly intrigued by the way Rick looks. His wispy, silver-blond bangs. The thick black eyebrows below them. The lazy right eye of cerulean blue, the same blue as the feet of a Galapagos booby. Clarissa calls him an uninspired cook, says that she only hired him because he's the owner's nephew and she had to. Regardless, it seems to Caruso that he performs efficiently in the kitchen. Once, when Clarissa fell sick with a headache, Caruso had looked on as Rick took charge, issuing orders with decisive gestures while decorating dinner plates with his colorful palette of sauces. "Rick tries hard," Clarissa had given him later, "but, bless his sweet ole soul, he should've been a painter."

"I wanna hear more," Rick says, whisking eggs into a bowl of cream, raising his left eyebrow once more.

"*Un novio*," Jorge, the produce guy, hums, glancing up from the potatoes he's scrubbing.

"As soon as I deal with Caruso, I'll tell y'all about him. And he's not my boyfriend," she says, looking pointedly at Jorge as she brushes against Skeeter—the salad man—on her way to the door. Big, rumpled, and bearded, Skeeter steps promptly to one side, his eyes wide with amusement. Rick waves good-bye with a shimmy of his fingers. She draws open the glass door and lunges through, her stride purposeful as she crosses the patio with Caruso still on her shoulder. "Okay, you little monster," she says, unlatching his cage door, "now get inside."

He descends to her forearm and lifts his foot up to the perch. "Chef Louie, Chef Louie, he go. He go," he warbles over his shoulder, in a last-ditch effort to win her back.

She smiles, her irritation thawing. "I'll bring you a dish of treats as soon as I have a spare moment. But next time, when I tell you to stay put, you better do it. I worry about you, you know."

She worries about him, he thinks, instantly feeling grateful. She pulls a hairnet from the pocket of her tunic, eases it over her red curls, and leaves him—her footsteps landing resolutely against the bricks.

He knows her better than she knows herself, for he has studied her in action. A spare moment won't come anytime soon. She can never relax when she's cooking. At first, she'll try to stick to her supervisory role, but, within the space of ten minutes, her eyebrows will tent upward, her mouth will twitch, and her index finger will slice through the air as she points out someone's mistake. It's hard for her to delegate. Before too long, she'll lose all self-control and will be taking over completely—washing, peeling, and cutting produce for Jorge while helping his wife, Amelia, with the weighing, grinding, and slicing of meats, the washing of seafood, and later the tidying-up. Eventually, she'll be breathing down Skeeter's neck, checking on his salads, terrines, and cold desserts. Once, she even loaded the dishwasher for Manuel, the busboy, whose brown hands flit and quiver with the speed of hummingbirds. She's as driven and as focused as a crow.

Regardless, she loves her job and is forever reminding him of how lucky she is. Thank God she doesn't work in a factory, repeating the same mindless tasks every day, she says, or flipping hamburgers at Howard's Pub and Restaurant. She cooks not because she wants to make a lot of money, she insists, but because she likes to be creative. Even the caveman, she believes, was a chef of sorts, picking the ripest, plumpest berries to eat, hunting for the fleshiest nuts to complement them. "Cooking is a solid, stable, artistic profession," she constantly reminds him before adding blithely, "It relaxes me," making him doubt—in those three words—every word that came before, as no part of her is relaxed while she cooks.

Right now, she's spilling a large spoonful of tomato sauce on her clean jacket. Reaching behind her, she snatches a dishrag off the counter, her tongue and head wagging as she dabs at the splotch. Caruso glances away. From the corner of his eye, he spots Sallie, the patio waitress, ambling toward him with an armload of white tablecloths. It's her day to set up.

"Hi, Caruso," she says, plopping the pile on a glass-topped table to his left. With knobby fingers, she pinches up a tablecloth and whips her arms upward, then brings them down. Long and white as a stork's wings, the linen unfolds, floats in the air, and lands on the surface in front of him. "Say something to me," she says, circling the table, fiddling with the hem. "Say *Sallie*. Say *sexy Sallie*."

Will she give him a treat, like she would to a performing circus beast, if he says what she wants?

"Say *sexy Sallie*."

Can he say it and mean it? he wonders as he studies her from toe to crown. She reminds him of a hodgepodge bird with her cassowary feet, heron legs, emu neck, owlish eyes, and crow hair. She grabs more linen, going from table to table, her arms rising and falling, until she finally returns to where he is, picks up another stack, and repeats the process until every table on the terrace is covered. From a cart beside his cage, she seizes a small vase of zinnias and thunks it in the center of the table where she started.

"I love Catherine's zinnias," she says, glancing at him. "Can you say *zinnia* for me?"

Caruso recalls the last time he saw Catherine O'Neal at her greenhouse on Lighthouse Road, which is where Clarissa buys all of the flowers for the restaurant. As usual, Catherine was wearing her yellow polka-dotted bonnet. "Caruso should've been here an hour ago," she said, wiping her plump, dirty fingers on the bib of her coveralls.

"What happened, Catherine?" Clarissa asked.

"This dingbatter drove up in his fancy car from Ohio, said he heard we talked funny. He kept repeating, 'Say something. Say something weird and funny.' I took his head off. 'Look, mister,' I said, 'I hain't no stupid parrot.'"

"He sounds awful, but parrots are smart, you know," Clarissa reminded her.

Catherine nodded at Clarissa. "I'm sorry, Caruso," she said, idling toward him. "You're not at all stupid. Much smarter than that dingbatter, I'd say. Please accept my apology."

Her forthrightness was so refreshing. She didn't hem and haw. She knew she had spoken out of place and went right to the heart of the matter.

"I'm sorry, Caruso," she had said once more.

"Sorry, Caruso," Sallie says, bumping against his cage as she reaches for another vase of flowers. "I'm kinda clumsy. What do you think, Caruso? Am I sexy Sallie or clumsy Sallie?"

Caruso doesn't know. Clarissa is a woman, and she's sexy, he reasons. Does this mean that every woman is sexy? Maybe? But then he envisions the raven beside the crow. Though both are sleek and black and belong to the same family, the raven is beautiful while the crow is not.

"Okay. Okay," Sallie says. "I'll answer the question for you. My friends say I look like Olive Oyl. So it seems only Popeye and Bluto find me sexy."

Caruso knows who these cartoon characters are from watching Saturday morning kiddie shows in the living room with Clarissa. "Popeye..." he trills, mimicking Popeye's gravelly voice.

"You're way too much, Caruso."

"...sailor man."

"You're a hoot," she tells him.

A hoot, he thinks. He never hoots like an owl, but he'll do it, if she wants him to. He widens his eyes and hoots loudly.

"A scream," Sallie says, throwing back her long emu neck, laughing. "If Clarissa wasn't so crazy about you, I'd take you home with me."

She's crazy as a loon about me, Caruso thinks, whipping up his yellow crest of feathers.

"But I'm afraid you've got some competition," Sallie says, looking sideways at him.

Instantly, his crown plummets.

"Right now, she's back there in the kitchen raving about Joseph Hampton Fitzgerald."

Caruso snaps his beak angrily.

"Yep, she likes the guy, all right."

With a loud shriek, Caruso rears up on his perch, flapping his wings so fiercely that the powder dust on his feathers flies.

Sallie begins to sneeze—one sneeze after another—until she is wheezing and cupping her hands over her mouth and nose. "Did I upset you?" she asks, when the sneezing fit is over.

Caruso clamps his beak shut and snubs her with his back.

"Caruso, you okay?" she says, inching closer to the cage. "Don't be mad at me. Please. I was just kidding."

He makes a mournful, hooing noise.

"Bluto is always trying to steal Olive Oyl away from Popeye, but she's never unfaithful to him," she says reassuringly. "Still, though, I think you could do better than Betty Boop." Slapping her thighs, she guffaws loudly. "Listen to me," she says. "I'm talking to you like you understand me."

He hears her big feet shuffling over the terrace. He doesn't want Sallie, Olive Oyl, or Betty Boop. Whoever Betty Boop is. Doesn't Sallie know that parrots are monogamous? Yes, he is a one-woman cockatoo, as faithful as the goose, the crow, the swan, the cardinal. He gives her a full minute before he swivels back around. But what man would be faithful to Sallie? he asks himself. The sight of a heron wading through water is poised and graceful, whereas Sallie—vase in hand—resembles an albatross bumping down for a landing or a loon hopping clownishly on the shore. Definitely not sexy, he decides.

Five

THE NIGHT SLOW, THE DINERS GONE BY NINE, CLARISSA stomps across the terrace toward him. "Lots of leftovers for you," she says, unlatching the cage door. "Here," she barks as she dumps into his dish a healthy portion of fruits and vegetables, which he would have gobbled up earlier but refuses to touch now because she neglected his needs to prepare Oysters Rockefeller for a scoundrel who never showed.

"You, too, huh?" she says, with an edge of sarcasm in her voice. Unlike Catherine O'Neal, Clarissa finds it difficult to say she's sorry. "If you don't want it, then don't eat it...you selfish jerk."

Selfish jerk. He pivots with the insult, sparing himself the sight of her, the sound of her footsteps like thorns in his skin as she goes. Mosquitoes buzz in the oleander bushes beyond the snuffed-out torches, and frogs peep from an artificially constructed pond next door. A moonflower vine that Rick planted last spring is currently blooming, its white blossoms as round as Clarissa's crepes. The glass door shuts with an irritating clack.

Caruso doesn't have to look her way to know she's busy with those seemingly superfluous tasks that the others never think of and the perfectionist in her remembers. Those little touches that make her entrées more appetizing than Chef Louie's, that extra care she puts into everything, regardless of the expenditures of time and money. Her perfectionism is both a blessing and a curse. A blessing because it drives her to do her best and will make her a great chef someday, while Rick will still be experimenting with colors. A curse because she never feels she does anything well enough. She wasn't good enough to earn her parents' love, she often says, and most likely won't be good enough to sustain a healthy relationship with a man. So why does she take her failures with men out on him, the one who loves her as she is? Caruso asks himself.

Soon, the two of them will return to their less-than-cozy cottage on Fig Tree Lane, where he will ruminate alone in his cage for hours on the harshness of her words. "Words can be as sharp as daggers," the old man had warned him, and until now Caruso hadn't understood how much her words could hurt. "Selfish jerk," she called him. That gash is deep and wide. *Jerk*, his mind keeps repeating. *Jerk. Jerk. Jerk.* She must not love him at all if that's what she thinks he is, he decides. Stretching out his neck, he parts his beak—poised to pluck out a feather—but then, a conversation he'd heard years ago at the pet store prompts him to reconsider.

According to one of the clerks, a realtor—eager to impress potential clients—bought an expensive green Amazon parrot and put the cage in the waiting room of his business. For weeks, he worked patiently with the bird, teaching him to say, "Welcome, friend," whenever the front door opened. Unfortunately, the lesson didn't stick, and the bird shrieked at anyone who came inside. Soon, clients began to gripe about the noise and the mess on the floor around the parrot's cage. Instead of increased sales, as the realtor had expected, business began to drop off. Angry and disappointed, the realtor locked the bird inside a small, dark closet. Except for feeding him and changing his water daily, he never spoke to or touched the parrot again. Lonely and desperate for affection, the Amazon began to pluck out his beautiful green feathers. When the cleaning woman found him weeks later, he was gouging his beak deep into his naked flesh.

Better not go there, Caruso thinks, clamping his bill shut. Feather plucking is a dangerous, addictive habit.

"Shit!" Clarissa says loudly, as a crash thunders over the terrace toward him.

He spins around to see dozens of white porcelain fragments shattered upon the red-tiled floor. That's odd, he thinks when she does nothing, only stands there as though lost in thought, staring down at the pieces. A full minute passes before she begins to move again, heading for the light switch by the door. At once, the inside and outside lights blink off. The glass door opens and shuts with a snap behind her. The key complains in the lock. Footsteps clump over the terrace.

"Let's go, Caruso," she says as she throws the latch on his cage door. She wraps her fingers tightly around his torso and takes him out. Which—according to every parrot book she has ever read to him—is something she shouldn't do. Her grasp hurts him, and he squawks. "Don't give me any of your shit," she scolds him. "You guys are all the same. Selfish and egotistical." She presses him too hard against her chest, and he glares at her, but the truth is, he is both angry and pleased. *You guys*, she had said, lumping both him and Mr. Herculean Pecs together, implying that the same force crushing him now could turn into passion later.

Much to his surprise, they take the shortcut through the backyard, leaving the bike out front. "My Oysters Rockefeller were superb," she huffs, stomping forward, the parched grass crackling beneath her feet. "Shame he didn't get a chance to taste them. Men," she spits out, her fingers still taut around his body. "Lazy, untalented, no-count men."

"Mel Tormé. Mel Tormé," he says in protest.

She comes to a sudden stop, jabs his head up with her finger. "Didn't I tell you to back off?" Her voice scrapes against him like bike wheels scraping against a curve. With a quick twist, he frees his head and shoots her a wounded look. She ignores him, moving on, pounding her feet even harder against the sandy soil. Where the two properties adjoin, she halts again, staring glumly in front of her, not speaking. The stars, thick as whipped cream, light up the night. Lightning bugs blink in the darkness. He hears a humming sound, then spots an emerald luminescence winging toward them. The greenhead fly lights on her wrist and tips forward, ready to bite. Instinctively, he opens his beak and bends over.

"Be still," she barks.

Vengeful, he freezes.

"Ouch!" she cries, shaking her arm. "I hate this damn island," she says, storming forward. "Biting flies and *jerks*."

She climbs the wooden steps and crosses the deck, flinging open the screen door, then twisting the doorknob and shoving the other with her shoulder. She flicks on the globe light as she steps inside. "Another boring kitchen," she says, her gaze disdainful. She goes straight to the sunroom, where she drops him on the T-stand before yanking furiously on the ceiling fan chain above her. The blades *ca-chunk* slowly through the heavy, hot air while she tortures her Reeboks off, using the toe of one shoe to smash down the heel of the other. She unsnaps her white tunic. With an outward fling of her arm, she whips the tunic off and drops it on the floor.

Choking down a sniffle, she walks over to the chaise longue and sprawls out on top. It is then she begins to sob.

He forgives her. Whenever men make her cry, he can't help but feel sorry for her. She either comes on too strong with them or else gives way to her bashfulness. The result is always the same—a hot rush of her tears. Last summer, it was a burly, plain man with a bulbous nose and fat lips who had upset her. His name was Burt, but Caruso called him "Burrrppp," elongating his name, noisily gulping down the p's like tasty wheat seeds, pretending to admire the oaf, all the while detesting him. Adjust the mask. Play the role well; be convincing, he would remind himself whenever Burt walked through the back door. So much into character did Caruso delve that he actually forgot how he felt about the man. That is, until the brute screamed at her.

She had asked him to taste the new dish she was creating. "It's baked bluefish," she said, "with capers, Kalamata olives, fresh basil and oregano, some garlic, a splash of olive oil, and a hint of Madeira. I think you'll like it," she told him. "Please, just a little bite." She'd moved forward, holding up the fork of fish, inching it toward his mouth.

But instead of obliging her, he had yelled, "Stop it, Clarissa! I'm not a baby."

His words had hit her like a bolt of lightning. Her breathing became shallow, fast, and fearful as the fork plummeted from her fingers and clattered against the floor, splattering fish on the white linoleum. At once, Caruso reared back on his perch and screeched, spreading out his wings, flapping them in fury, and had he not been caged, he would have soared toward the man and taken a big chunk out of his puffy lips. As it was, he flew forward, grabbed the cage door with his claws, and savagely whipped his wings against the bars until Clarissa had asked the beast to leave.

"He frightened me," she confessed to him later. "When he yelled at me, I wasn't here anymore. I was back in Kentucky with my brother. My childhood was a battlefield, and Randall's fists were the weapons," she said with such sorrow that Caruso wished Burt had treated her better—but only momentarily, for he was thrilled with the outcome. Once more, she'd succumbed to her natural shyness and given up on men for a while. Burt faded from her memory, and, same as before, she was *all his* again.

She closes her eyes and releases a little moan.

Worried, he hurries down the metal stand and wobbles toward her. Her forehead is wet with perspiration, and he feels guilty. She is forever sacrificing her own needs for his. Because he can't tolerate the cold, she sets the thermostat high so that the air conditioner won't kick on. She tries hard to protect him not only from unpleasant boyfriends but also from his inquisitive nature—his attraction to bright colors, especially red; his craving for foods that are toxic to his system; his overall talent for getting into trouble. Curious, that's what he is. Therefore, she locks up poisonous household cleaners, keeps him away from suffocating pots of steam, closes the lid on the toilet to prevent his falling in; she never runs the overhead fan on high to protect him from its blades. The list of potential dangers is lengthy, but she remains as vigilant as the mother of the four-year-old child next door, except that he is not her offspring.

"Caruso," she says lovingly when she feels him against her stomach. She caresses the back of his neck with her fingers, following the grain of his pinfeathers—up, then down—over and over until they both drift off.

Thirty minutes later, she is wide awake. "I'm finished with men," she announces in an alert voice as she nudges him off her belly. Groggy, he tousles his feathers. "Love never pans out for me. No matter what I do, nothing seems to work. I give up."

She twists around and stands quickly. "From now on, cooking will be my only passion," she vows, weaving her fingers together as she reaches high for the ceiling. Bending her left leg up, she grabs her foot and presses her heel against her buttocks, then does the same with her right. "I need a shower before bed," she says, striding down the hallway toward the bathroom but, oddly, going past it. He waddles to the head of the chaise longue and curls his toes over the high curved front, leaning forward like an adornment on the prow of a ship. Nosy as always, he listens for her footsteps. Which unexpectedly come to a stop. There is a loud beep, followed by his rival's deep Southern accent.

"I hope 'C. McCarthy' is you, Clarissa. It's Joe Fitzgerald. Sorry I missed you tonight. Something came up, but I promise I'll be at Crab Cakes tomorrow. Can't wait to sample your good food. Bye now."

He hears another beep and braces himself. The message plays again.

"Something important came up. The reason he didn't come," she says, pattering gingerly into the sunroom. "Why do I always overreact?" she asks, squatting down low in front of him.

He takes a wary step back.

"Poor ole Caruso," she says, rocking forward. "You're the one who pays for my bad moods." She gulps down a mouthful of air. "I'm sorry, so sorry." She splutters into silence.

She never says she's sorry to him. So which *selfish jerk* is she apologizing to?

"Give me a kiss," she says.

Relenting, he teeters toward her, and she brushes her full lips against his beak. "My oysters weren't all that good, anyway. It's not the season for them."

She plants her large hands against her thighs and rises. He fixes his eyes on her as she sways down the hallway, but this time she veers into the bathroom. Seconds later, the hooks on the shower curtain are clinking, and her bare feet are thwacking against the prefabricated plastic floor. He listens to the whooshing and spraying of water, then to her sweet soprano, singing a jaunty little tune he has never heard before.

Six

FOR HOURS, CARUSO RUMINATES IN HIS CAGE, like a cave now because she has covered it.

"Good night, lovey-dovey," she had twittered before cheerily skipping off to bed. Never before has she called him *lovey-dovey*. A lovey-dovey is a bird he would never want or pretend to be.

Well, yes, he might be monogamous like a dove, but he is no ground feeder—no cooing, squatting target for lazy neighborhood cats. He's a fighter—a fighter and a lover. He'll fight to the death for himself and for the one he loves. "Lovey-dovey," she had said, but he was not the lovey-dovey she was thinking of. Mr. Herculean Pecs is her dove, he fears. But how—with his long, muscular arms and broad, strong chest—did he ever qualify for such a gentle nickname?

As soon as he raises this question, he knows what the answer is. It was her innate sweetness that named him this. He admires this quality of hers because despite the rage her brother inflicted upon her, his anger never took root in her nature. She is constantly saying that people can change. One day her brother will become a better person, she claims, and they'll be like any other loving family. Desperate to change herself, she clings to the inevitability of transformation.

He recalls a conversation she had with Beryl a few months back on the Gaskills' front porch. The discussion unfolded, same as always, with Clarissa insisting that Randall could change, if only he tried, and Beryl asserting that he was incapable of it. Back and forth, they had argued until they grew bored and moved on to their favorite topic—ex-boyfriends. Why did most relationships with men begin with sublime passion, only to end in unambiguous disappointment? they asked themselves before delving into a long-winded exploration of man's fragile ego and his gross inadequacies. At one point, after a jag of uncontrollable laughter, Clarissa's mood took a turn, and, in a thoughtful voice, she said, "Have I ever told you about Priscilla Pincushion?"

"I don't think so," Beryl said. "Sounds like a character in a children's book."

"No...she was real, all right," Clarissa said, taking a deep breath. "She was a classmate of mine, back when I was a kid."

"When you lived in the mountains?"

"Yeah, during elementary school, before we moved to the Bluegrass. I was a very shy little girl. Afraid of everyone. Didn't know how to speak up. Wallpaper, that's what I was, and Priscilla was shy, like me, except somehow I blended in, and she didn't."

"Why didn't she?"

"Her fire-engine-red hair, I think. It was the first thing about her that caught everyone's attention. No one could be wallpaper with hair that color. The students would stare at it first, their eyes invariably drifting down to her forehead, thick with freckles round as coriander seeds, every bit as riveting. Next, they would become mesmerized by the freckles on her eyelids, on her cheeks, and even above her lip. There were freckles, like swarms of gnats, on her neck. She had them all over her arms, at the tips of her fingers, and on the skin between them. The pigmentation of her legs made them look like those of a speckled cricket. When she wore sandals in late summer, you could see the flecks of brown on her toes. The boys in our class, young and foolish, didn't know how to act, didn't know what to make of her, and so they teased her. *Priscilla Pincushion*, they called her, day after day."

"Sad."

"Very sad," Clarissa agreed. "I mean, if they had focused less on her freckles and a little more on what was inside her, they would have realized how sweet she was, but they didn't really see her and bullied her instead. We can either fight with or flee from those things that frighten us. Fight or flight—the two choices we have, or so the experts say. Priscilla chose to flee. Strange, because I thought I'd be the one in that situation. Me—with these huge hands and these tiny feet. I was the freak. But I was spared. Why? I asked myself as I looked on, watching them taunt her mercilessly at recess every day, but then this epiphany came to me, and soon afterward, things changed for the better."

"She did some serious ass-whupping." Beryl grinned.

"I'm talking about something important." Clarissa huffed. "I'm talking about change. How people change, how attitudes change, how growth occurs." Annoyed, she nibbled her bottom lip. "And you start your ass-whupping stuff."

"A good ass-whupping is a powerful catalyst for change."

"Please," Clarissa moaned.

"Oh, go on." Beryl relented. "I'm intrigued now. Finish your story."

Clarissa cleared her throat and shot Beryl a reproachful look.

"I mean it," Beryl said reassuringly.

Clarissa drew herself up in the porch swing and began. "It was really cold that day at recess. I was pounding my boots against the walkway to revive the feeling in my toes when I caught sight of her standing beneath the pin oak at the far edge of the playground. She had her arm stretched out and her palm open. 'Ain't no food in it,' she had said, looking up at the bird feeder as I struggled through my shyness and walked over, 'but I got me some cornbread here.' She showed me the crumpled pieces in her cupped hand. 'I don't like any critters going hungry, especially birds.' On the branch above was a cardinal. 'I love redbirds,' she had said, gifting me with her smile, 'but I love people better.'

"'I love birds better,' I quickly said back. 'Birds come into this world perfect, but not people. They gotta work real hard to be as good as birds. So you shouldn't let those boys bother you. It ain't important what they think. Ya wanna hear something that might help you with them?' I asked her.

"'I reckon,' she said, in almost a whisper.

"'Whenever they tease you, just accept it. Act like you don't care.'

"She stood there, nodding her head, attentive to my words. The very next day, she did exactly what I told her. When the boys began to pick on her, she didn't turn and run but faced them head-on with a smile, and within weeks their teasing came to an end."

"Where is she now?"

"Married with kids, living somewhere with her musician husband in Nashville," Clarissa answered. "I don't know much more about her, but her predicament made me realize that we have more than fight or flight to choose from when we're scared. Sometimes, acceptance is the answer. Sometimes we have to accept the situation we find ourselves in and have faith that it will change. Then we are fearless in a totally different way."

"Riding out the storm with dignity."

"That's right, and we can do it if we believe in change," Clarissa had finished. "If we believe that nothing is static, that nobody—ever—stays the same."

Nothing is static. Nobody—ever—stays the same, Caruso muses, mulling over her words. It's true that birds have changed over eons from dinosaurs into the flying creatures they are today, but does this mean that he must continue to change? Hasn't he—in his short life—already changed enough?

The instant the net was thrown over him, he was forced to change, and he has continued to change through the years. Change shaped him into the sensual creature he is today, endowing him with his greatest asset—his capacity to appreciate where he is and with whom he is at the moment. In the bush of Victoria, he had loved his family of cockatoos as they flew haphazardly through the white-hot sky. Now, he loves the orderly V of Canadian geese migrating. As a chick, he was comforted by the strident tang of eucalyptus leaves around the tree hole where he slept. Today, he loves the soapy scent of lavender on Clarissa's skin when he sleeps beside her on the blue chaise longue. After he was kidnapped, he taught himself how to appreciate the harmonious singing of the birds in Greensboro, knowing full well that he would never again hear his parents' raucous song. He sharpened his ear once more and became entranced by the old man's Southern accent as he recited Emily Dickinson to him. Then, after that, he fell in love with Clarissa's twang and drawl. Years ago, he had loved the taste of papayas, mangoes, and pineapples fresh from the fruit groves of Australia, but lately he relishes the sugary white grapes that Clarissa buys for him at Styron's. Once, he was soothed by the softness of his parents' wings around him. Nevertheless, he was able to experience that sensation anew in the blanket of Theodore Pinter's words. Nowadays, it is Clarissa's thin, sweet soprano that sustains him.

He doesn't need to change anymore. From the confines of his cage, he has learned how to love those pleasures that Warramurrungundji has given him, and his ability to be grateful for each and every one of them is growth enough, he feels. He chooses to accept himself exactly as he is.

Seven

SHE LOOKS SEXY AND BEAUTIFUL TONIGHT, he thinks as he watches her from his perch inside the ornate Victorian cage under the live oak at the restaurant.

She had spent more than two hours primping for the evening—painting some thick, white liquid on her ivory skin to make it even lighter and following this with a whisk of peachy-colored powder across her cheekbones. She outlined her eyes in brown. "Mascara wand," she explained, holding up a stick with a brush at the end of it and sweeping her lashes until they were as thick as his wing feathers. After snapping up her freshly starched chef's tunic, she made a conch shell of her hair. "It's a French twist," she said. "Remember *The Birds*—Tippi Hedren? She wore her hair like this. Sexy, isn't it?" They had watched this unflattering movie about birds late one Sunday evening last summer, and throughout it, she had vehemently contended she was on his side.

As they headed out the back door toward Crab Cakes earlier, she had looked like an imposter to him, but now—as he regards her every gesture through the wide glass panels—he changes his mind. She is still his sexy, beautiful Clarissa, even though she made herself more beautiful for Joseph Hampton Fitzgerald, not for him.

"How beautiful she is!" the old man had said that summer morning while they were spying on Olivia Greenaway, her shapely legs crossed in the overstuffed chair that faced the window. "*Pascal Robinson* doesn't deserve her."

"*Pas-cal Rob-in-son*," Caruso repeated, dandifying the name the way Theodore Pinter had.

"He may be the mister to her Mrs. Robinson," he said bitterly, "but she'll always be Olivia Greenaway to me." Binoculars in one hand, lunch in the other, he took another big bite of his tuna fish sandwich. "It still hurts...right here," he said, swallowing, holding the sandwich over his chest.

"*Pas-cal Rob-in-son*," Caruso said again, his voice quavering with resentment, for he could list all of Theodore Pinter's grievances against the man.

"I never stood a chance. Not a snowball's chance in hell," he said, looking somberly at Caruso. "Pascal had it all. Born of a good, old Southern family. His father a well-respected judge." Rolling his lower lip between his teeth, he shook his balding head. "My father owned a bookstore, jam-packed with used books. A dreamer, he was, like I am. My mother's family had money. She bought this house. The facts speak for themselves," he said, sighing wearily.

Caruso eyed him from head to toe and trilled.

"You're a loyal bird," Theodore Pinter told him. "But I know the good and bad of me. Pascal, with his hard, impassive chest; I, with my soft, sensitive one. Pascal, with his law degree from Duke; I, with my master's in English from a state school. Pascal, rich and powerful; I, a retired teacher and headmaster with a small pension. Pascal," he said, with an exaggerated French accent. "Pascal Robinson. Exotic and melodic, isn't it? Teddy Pinter," he spat out, sharply stressing the *T* and *P*. "Puts me in mind of one of Gogol's fussy bureaucrats. Need I say more?"

Caruso squawked to disagree.

"Yes, you're kind, way too kind," he said, scrunching up his dimpled chin. "'Oh, Teddy, you're as soft as a girl,' she'd said that day, pressing her hand against my chest, as if my sensitivity were a flaw, as if it made me less of a man. Girls are attracted to guys they think they can't have. Olivia knew I was hers completely. There was nothing she could do that would make me turn away. Whereas Pascal...well, she had to win him. I was no challenge, you see, so she took me for granted, the way I take so many things for granted—food in my belly, a warm house in winter, clothes on my back, flowers every spring, the poetry of Emily Dickinson. Strange—since it is Emily's vision of the world that shakes me out of my complacency and makes me see that everything on this earth is a blessing, that nothing and no one should be taken for granted. Olivia's lack of regard for me back then still hurts."

Distractedly, he combed his neck with his fingers. "The instant we entered junior high, she set her cap on Pascal." He paused momentarily, seemingly to find the right words. "It disheartened me to watch her mooning over him, trying much too hard to catch his attention. At the time, I was her very best friend, and I felt it my duty to warn her. 'Olivia,' I said, 'open your eyes. See him for what he is. You can do better.' I could never understand why she failed to notice that crown of entitlement on his head, but she was bowled over by his exaggerated sense of self-worth, and my words fell silent on her ears. She began to avoid me soon after.

"Before Pascal came on the scene, she would stare right into my eyes while we talked. She trusted me, you see. She never flinched, never looked away, never refused to meet my gaze, even if she had something tough to tell me—but then, after she met him, she began to look slightly above my eyes whenever we spoke. I would lean into her, demand her attention, but as soon as I did this, she would pull away and stare past me, over my shoulder, and into a distant place where I wasn't allowed to go. Those glorious blue irises of hers would shut me out, alighting everywhere but on my face. At first, these little changes of hers were almost unnoticeable, and I was able to pretend them away. Yes, Caruso, I knew in my heart of hearts what was happening, but can you blame me for not wanting to admit it?"

Caruso rocked from side to side on his perch.

"Gradually, Olivia stopped coming over to my house after school. Whenever I rang her, her mother would answer. 'Olivia's too busy to talk right now,' she would say. 'She'll call you back later.' But, invariably, the time between those *laters* grew longer and longer until she quit calling altogether. After that, she ceased eating lunch with me at school and ate, instead, with her girlfriends. Next, she deserted them, as easily as she had me, to eat with Pascal. I ate alone, observing her with him, the worshipful way her fingers touched his shoulder, the way her eyes latched onto his, and at last I was forced to acknowledge the truth of how she saw me. I was an old friend whom she'd outgrown."

With rapt attention, Caruso watched as grief mottled the old man's eyes.

As a fledgling, he'd witnessed that same grief in his mother upon returning from a flight with her flock. They were scouting for mango groves on the outskirts of Coffs Harbour, abreast the silver-blue South Pacific, when they spotted a small roofless shelter beside a country road. The mangoes—stacked high on a wooden shelf inside it, along with a payment box for coins— signaled to them that the orchard was close by. Hungry and eager for the taste of mango, they kept flying. Within minutes, they caught sight of the bright red flowers circling the farmhouse, and then, on the steep hill behind it, the bull's-eye—the grove of fruit trees, heavy with the orange-red orbs. Oh, how they shrieked as they descended, swarming like locusts, squawking ecstatically as they bit into the luscious flesh! It was then the shots rang out, felling a dozen of them at once, their bodies plummeting downward, as if they—not the fruit—were being picked. Five more of them died before they clearly understood the danger. With a loud, panicked beating of wings, they rose upward, the curses of the farmers rising also, the blue steel of their shotguns gleaming in the sun's hot rays, the leaves of the mango trees trembling crimson with the blood of the flock, grief mottling his mother's eyes, the way it had the old man's that day.

"So I built a wall between us, kept my world small to avoid getting hurt," Theodore Pinter went on. Dutifully, he ate the last of his sandwich, dusted a bread crumb off his cheek, and shifted back to the window. In the house opposite them, Olivia Greenaway uncrossed and crossed her legs again, apparently unaware that they were looking at her. "Her blue eyes never fade. Her lips remain full. Her legs are still shapely. Ah, my beautiful Olivia!" the old man had gushed when she delicately pulled the hem of her dress over her knees.

Ah, my beautiful Clarissa! Caruso thinks from up high on his perch as she moves hypnotically around the kitchen—splashing wine into a sauté pan, whipping cream in a large bowl, shaking black olives in a jar of hot pepper seasoning.

When he glances around again, the patio is packed with diners, and he is cheered that Joseph Hampton Fitzgerald isn't there. Jazz is now undulating through the speakers, camouflaged behind the white oleander shrubs, and the mosquito torches are flaming orange-red. He smells perfume coming from the honeysuckle hedge beneath the elbow of windows along the dining room wall. With a loud pop, Sallie uncorks a bottle of champagne at the far end of the patio, while Manuel removes dirty dishes from the table beside her. Nearby, a middle-aged woman is praising Clarissa's famous crab cakes, and Caruso zeroes in on the tines gleaming toward her mouth. She chews and swallows and, leaning forward, asks the man across from her if he would like a taste. He nods, whereupon she scoops up a bite and passes the fork to him, sharing her food the way Caruso's mother did with him.

"Hi there, Caruso," Sallie says, startling him as she shambles over, her big feet slapping against the bricks.

"Miss!" a diner calls out, with a snap of his fingers.

"I hate it when they do that," Sallie says, ignoring the man. "Are you still mad at me, Caruso?"

He is, but he trills at her anyway.

From her pants pocket, she leisurely withdraws a pencil and spears her black mound of hair with it.

"Miss!" the diner says again.

Scratching her scalp with the pencil, she pretends not to hear him. "Joe hasn't shown yet," she says, leaning conspiratorially toward Caruso. "And I'm glad. I'm rooting for you, Caruso."

The man snaps his fingers three times in a row. This time, Sallie answers with a backward wave. "Don't worry," she says. "Clarissa's a man magnet. They come, they flirt, they go. They never commit. And why?" she asks, fixing her owlish eyes on him. "Because there's not much to her."

Not much to her, Caruso repeats to himself, mulling the words over.

"Hey, miss!"

"Okay...okay," Sallie says, returning the pencil to her pants pocket, weaving leisurely toward the man's table.

Not much to her, Caruso thinks. Why would Sallie say that? Clarissa has soft skin, taut muscles, and strong bones beneath her white jacket, and, best of all, a kind-hearted spirit.

Caruso feels air swelling to his left and shifts toward a white cloth, rising and falling upon the table usually designated for fresh linen. "*Reservado*," Manuel says, thumping down two place settings of silverware, next a bouquet of deep red zinnias, then a placard against the vase.

"*Re...ser...va...do,*" Caruso says after him.

Manuel glances up at him and laughs.

The melancholy voice of Billie Holiday singing "God Bless the Child" comes through the speakers.

Deftly, Manuel unfolds a small metal stand and angles it beside the table.

"Another bottle of wine, please," a man orders.

"Club soda with a twist of lemon," drifts a girlish voice.

Stars begin to appear like pinpricks in the veil of night. The outside lights flicker on. In front of Caruso's cage, white porcelain plates float by like cockatoos in flight. He breathes in the crisp, sweet aroma of shrimp—lightly fried in a batter of egg white, beer, and flour—then the salty, lemony scent of grilled mackerel. Haughty as a peacock, Sallie saunters across the patio, toting a tray with two entrées: shrimp and grits, alongside scallops in saffron cream over linguine. Five feet away, Devon, the new waiter, is delivering glasses of white wine to a table of three. "Appetizers?" he asks, flipping a thick rope of blond hair off his shoulder.

"Crab beignets," the young diners say simultaneously.

Caruso peers into the kitchen again, hunting for Clarissa. "Claaa-risss-a," he trills when he doesn't see her there. He swivels to his left, searching for gaps in the hedge of honeysuckle, yearning to catch a glimpse of her through the dining room windows, but the foliage is too thick. Next, he scans the bar through the long glass door. Not there, either. Maybe she's in the bathroom or in the supply room, he thinks, his feathers itching with panic. It's the same routine, night after night. He's trying to follow her every movement from the solitude of his cage; she's hard at work in the crowded restaurant, oblivious to his needs. He lets out a frustrated coo. Sometimes he would rather be elsewhere—with Theodore Pinter in his study, in the company of other birds at the pet store, or most of all with a wild flock of Sulphur-crested Cockatoos. "Claaa-risss-a," he says, relieved, when he sees her gliding back into the kitchen.

"My God, have you no pride, Caruso!" Sallie says, suddenly reappearing. "Do I have to draw you a picture?" she adds through clenched teeth, nodding at the table set for two beside his cage.

He glances down at her huge feet, then back up to her blue-tinged face. With each passing second, she reminds him more and more of the Australian cassowary—the gigantic, blue-faced, flightless bird with claws sharp enough to rip apart a man's stomach. Would Sallie, in a jealous rage, ever hurt Clarissa? he wonders.

"Maybe you should be pining over me," she suggests. "Why don't you say my name for a change?"

"Claaa-risss-a," he says stubbornly.

"She's making a cuckold of you," she says, taking an aggressive step toward him.

I'm a cockatoo, not a cuckoo, he thinks, insulted, as he scoots to the far end of his perch.

"Oh, come on, Caruso."

"Claaa-risss-a," he warbles in an unsteady voice.

"Why won't you say Sallie?" she asks, leaning forward, invading his space.

Crouching, he sends his mind back in time, remembering the sights and sounds that once calmed him—rose-breasted Galahs, like pink tutus pirouetting in the sky; pineapples ripening gold in the heat of the sun; deep notes pulsating from the didgeridoo—and, strengthened by these memories, he holds on to his courage. "Clarissa," he says defiantly.

"Be that way. But remember, three's a crowd," she says, wheeling around, her big feet spanking the brick patio as she storms toward the kitchen, flings open the door, flashes by the glass panels, and disappears from view.

The bar door snaps shut, and Caruso pivots around to see Pops, the maître d', moving sprightly down the walkway, dressed as usual in his white linen suit from the sixties. A retired jewelry maker from Wilmington, he is a member of the Ocracoke Art League and one of Beryl's closest friends. "This way, sir," he says to someone behind him. "Your table is over here by the oak." Pops steps aside, and standing there in full view is Joseph Hampton Fitzgerald.

Caruso shrieks in dismay.

"Hello again, Caruso," Joe says, sauntering toward his cage.

Caruso stares at his faded brown shirt and frayed blue jeans. Where is his suit and tie? he thinks, for if he really liked her and wanted to impress her, he would've worn them. Even Burt donned a coat and tie that night he took her out to eat. Shiftless as a seagull, he thinks, deliberately changing his focus to Devon, who is energetically delivering the three orders of crab beignets to his table.

"Don't you remember me?" Joe persists, but Caruso continues to dismiss him.

"Don't take it personal." Pops jumps in. "Sometimes he can be persnickety."

Caruso doesn't know what persnickety means, but it sounds offensive.

"Chef McCarthy has asked me to take care of you," Pops says. "She's prepared an extraordinary meal—off the menu—and hopes you don't mind."

"Certainly not," Joe says. "I'm honored to be placed in her hands. And what has the chef cooked for me?"

Unable to control his curiosity, Caruso steals a peek at the man.

"A delightful meal influenced by Spanish cuisine," Pops says ardently, his Adam's apple rising like a yo-yo in his throat. "We'll start with a refreshing sangria," he continues, "and follow this with an appetizer of fried sardines." Forming a tent with his fingers, he rocks forward on the base of his toes. "Then comes a spicy gazpacho. After that, a salad of tropical fruit." He pauses for a second, releasing little puffs of air, before resuming in a fervent voice: "Your entrée will be a wonderful seafood paella, stuffed with snapper, crab, scallops, and shrimp—most of it caught fresh around here—except for the mussels, that is. To top the meal off is a flan beyond your wildest expectations. Now, how does this sound?"

"Terrific," Joe says.

"Relax and enjoy this lovely evening," Pops tells him. "I'll be right back with your drink."

"Caruso," Joe tries again, as soon as Pops leaves.

What to do? Caruso thinks. Ignore his rival or face him—bird to man?

"Remember? I'm the fellow with the ridiculously long name—Joseph Hampton Fitzgerald."

Undermine his strengths, or play to his weaknesses?

"Joseph Hampton Fitzgerald," the man repeats.

Play to his weaknesses, Caruso decides. "Jo-seph Hamp-ton Fitz-ger-ald," he mimics.

"Or just Joe," he says with a grin.

"Joe," Caruso relents, locking eyes with him.

"That's right," his rival says. "Joe. Short and sweet. Really, Caruso, I'm not so bad once you get to know me."

Once you get to know me. Which means he plans on staying around awhile, Caruso understands him to be thinking.

A glass pitcher in hand, Pops passes through the barroom door with the ruby-red drink, his footfalls staccato against the walkway. With each step he takes, the orange slices and lime wedges in the sangria bob like exotic, tropical fish. "Would you like some now?" he asks. Joe nods, and Pops fills up his goblet.

"Very good," Joe says after taking a healthy swallow. Caruso notices a red-wine mustache, like a thin smear of blood above his lip, and lets loose a squawking laugh.

"Now, the appetizer," Pops says, thunking the pitcher on the metal stand before making a beeline to the kitchen.

Minutes later, Joe is devouring crisp sardines smelling of olive oil and garlic. Next, he's tearing off a wedge of crusty Cuban bread, baptizing it in the gazpacho, and ripping it apart with his big white teeth. If Clarissa were hand-feeding him now, he'd bite off her fingers, Caruso thinks.

In the background, Mel Tormé is crooning about lost love. Caruso hopes this is not an omen, hopes that this won't be his fate. Nearby, a portly woman savors her last spoonful of Clarissa's best dessert—her chocolate bread pudding—while a young mother, breast-feeding her baby, dips a fried shrimp into a container of freshly mixed aioli and pops it gingerly into her mouth.

Joseph Hampton Fitzgerald has now started on his fruit salad. Caruso glances down at his feeder of parrot pellets. Short shrift for a bird, he thinks as Joe enjoys chunks of papaya and pineapple, two of Caruso's favorite fruits. Is there no justice? he asks himself, remembering the apple-cantaloupe flavor of papaya that his mother would regurgitate into his mouth. The Velvet Fog's voice rises to a crescendo, reminding him that the past is the past.

"Mel Tormé," Caruso says longingly.

"Who?" Joe asks.

"Mel Tormé. Mel Tormé. Mel Tormé," Caruso repeats.

"Oh, yeah. The singer. I like him, too." Joe props his fork against the inside edge of his plate and raises his goblet of sangria. "To Mel Tormé," he toasts, taking a big gulp.

Mel Tormé belongs to Clarissa and me only, Caruso thinks, contemptuously flapping his wings.

"What's wrong, buddy?" Joe asks, setting his goblet down. He forks up some more papaya, slips it between his lips, and chews. "Why all the fuss?" he says, swallowing. "Are you hungry? How about a piece of this?" he asks, pushing away from the table. He picks up a sliver of the yellowish-orange fruit and walks over to Caruso. "Here," he says, poking his fingers through the bars, dropping the papaya into the feeder. "Try it. You'll like it."

Caruso flattens his feathers against his body and liberates a hiss.

"Okay...okay," Joe says, holding up his hand, backing off.

"Better not feed him," Pops warns. "One bite of something like avocado can kill him. Clarissa has read us the riot act. We don't feed him anything."

"Sorry," Joe says, moseying back to the table and reclaiming his seat. "Last summer, I lived with a family in Mexico. They had a parrot named Lorito—original, right? A dog called Perro and a cat called Gato, but for some reason, their rabbit was Roberto." He laughs so wildly that it makes Caruso blink. "Anyway, I fed Lorito papaya every day and he lived, so I figured it wouldn't hurt Caruso either."

"Well, Clarissa's awfully protective of that bird."

"I won't do it again," Joe promises.

"The chef will be taking care of you now," Pops says, putting a bottle of white wine and two fluted glasses on the table. "I'm resuming my job as maître d'. Are you finished with your salad?"

"Yes, sir. It was mighty tasty."

Pops bends over and retrieves the empty plate.

"Thanks for everything," Joe says warmly.

"It was my pleasure, sir, serving you this evening."

Clarissa passes Pops on his way to the kitchen. Like a goddess with an offering, she is carrying a large, round, shallow container, her fingers wrapped around the red handles. His eyes crackling with resentment, Caruso watches her place the carbon steel pan on the table. "Seafood paella," she announces. Caruso sniffs the briny scent of shrimp, the honeyed aroma of crab, and the musky odor of mussels.

"It looks delicious," Joe says. "You're a great chef," he adds in a voice so unctuous Clarissa could grease her paella pan with it.

"Before you say that, you should taste it first," she teases. "Have you ever had paella?"

"Only once," he replies. "In Charlotte, but the rice was too gritty."

"Mine, I hope, will be perfect," she says, reaching for two stacked plates on the metal stand, depositing them in front of her. "I use Bomba rice—what the chefs use in Spain," she says, "but I've toyed with the traditional recipe. Authentic paella Valenciana has no seafood in it, but in these modern times you can do what you want. So I decided to stick to seafood, most of it caught fresh—today. Paella Clarissa, made just for you," she says, making her voice even softer than usual.

Listening to her, Caruso flinches with suspicion. He stares resentfully at the asparagus tips, pimientos, and peas decorating the circumference of the pan—at the mussels and shrimp fanning out like bicycle spokes from the center. She has never made this dish—not for anyone, not ever.

With large spoons, she plucks up a mound of yellow-tinged rice and lowers it to a plate, and next she tops the rice with mussels and shrimp, along with some of the vegetable garnish. After giving this plate to Joe, she fixes the other one for herself. She pours wine into both glasses and sets the bottle down.

"To the chef," Joe says, standing, lifting his glass up high.

"To my rescuer," she counters. Then, like a gorgeous angelfish, she undulates above the tabletop and taps her wineglass against his. They take several slow sips, staring at each other.

Reaching behind her, she curls her fingers around the top of a chair and slides it over. They put their glasses on the table and lower themselves down. Joe forks up a mouthful of rice and eats it slowly. "How is it?" Clarissa asks, eating some, too.

"Definitely not gritty," he says, breaking into a smile. "What gives it that yellow color?"

"The smoked paprika," she tells him, "but mostly the saffron."

"I know saffron's an herb, but where does it come from?"

"From the yellow-orange stigmas of little flowers that look like crocuses. It's very expensive, you know, and a rice dish can't be called paella unless there's saffron in it. It's one of the secret ingredients."

"Seems not much of a secret," he says, laughing, his big teeth gleaming in the dark like those of the Saturday-morning cartoon character Dudley Do-Right of the Royal Canadian Mounted Police. "No one but me knows the secret to my scrambled eggs and tuna," he says. "I'm not going to tell you what it is."

"Why not?" she says, leaning forward. "Don't you want me to be a better cook?"

"It might have the opposite effect," he says with a mischievous grin. "Might undermine your self-confidence."

"Nothing could make that dish sound appetizing," she says, giggling.

"It sounds worse than it tastes," Joe says, stabbing a shrimp and nibbling on it. "Best not judge a dish by what's in it."

"Okay...then the next time I cook for you," she says, "I won't mention beforehand that the mashed potatoes are laced with peppermint oil." He looks amused as she tweezes a mussel from its blue-black shell and slips it into her mouth. "Needs lemon," she says, taking a wedge off the side of her plate, squeezing it over her shellfish.

Simultaneously, they lift their glasses and drink.

Caruso ruffles his feathers in indignation.

They eat and drink some more—taking their time, relishing the different flavors, not speaking.

"Thank you, Clarissa. This is a real treat," Joe says, breaking the silence at last. "I've been trying to watch my money, staying at Blackbeard's Lodge, subsisting on crackers, Vienna sausage, and canned sardines."

"No thanks necessary," she tells him. "Cooking is what I do."

"Do you cook like this for yourself?"

"Nothing this fancy. I have simple tastes."

He raises his eyebrows and crooks his mouth in disbelief.

"No, really. I'm a country gal from Kentucky. I like plain, simple food—ham biscuits, pinto beans and cornbread, fresh sliced tomatoes, fried chicken with cream gravy and mashed potatoes. Anything home-cooked with plenty of salt, pepper, and lard."

Chicken, Caruso thinks with distaste. No self-respecting raptor would be proud of such a kill. But then, a raptor is a bird, too, isn't he? Same as a chicken. Same as Caruso. Same as the blue-faced cassowary, who long ago lost his ability to fly. Wings are just one of the many traits they have in common. Wings let them soar into the sky with the grace of a parrot, the power of a bald eagle, the speed of a hummingbird. So what is the difference, he asks himself, shuddering, between fried chicken and fried cockatoo served on a plate?

"A heart-healthy diet." Joe laughs loudly, bringing Caruso back.

"Exactly," she says, laughing with him. "But my favorite dishes are those my granny made for me. Pork chops, fried up crisp and tender, mustard greens simmered for hours with fatback, vinegar pie."

He wrinkles up his nose. "Vinegar pie? Sounds even worse than my scrambled eggs and tuna."

"Believe me, it's good," she says, grabbing her wineglass, sipping.

"Granny's vinegar pie always brought the highest bid at the county fair. Butter, sugar, eggs, raisins, boiling water, and, of course, the vinegar. Plus her secret ingredient, but I won't tell you what it is. Don't wanna undermine your self-confidence."

He grins, digs out a lump of crab, and opens his mouth. "Mmm," he says as he chews and swallows.

"Tell me something about yourself," she says in her most solicitous voice.

"Well, I like to surf," he says. "It relaxes me, especially here in the Outer Banks. You know, island hopping from one beach to the next, wherever the waves are best."

Lazier than a seagull, a beach bum, Caruso thinks, eyeing Joe disdainfully.

"Waves are waves, aren't they?"

He nods and says, "Most often, I stay right here on Ocracoke. But sometimes I head out, take the ferry to Hatteras Island, ride the swells at Salvo, Waves, or Rodanthe. For some reason, the surf is better there."

"Is that all you do?" she asks.

"Beg your pardon?" he says, turning his ear toward her.

Caruso detects a hint of peevishness in his voice.

"I mean, what do you do for a living?"

"Right now, I'm in school," he says.

"Oh, so you're a professional student," she says, teasing him.

He's a beach bum! Caruso wants to yell.

"I don't understand," Joe says, catching his lower lip under his huge top teeth, biting down.

He's thin-skinned, Caruso thinks gleefully. Lucky for me, there's a little chink in his hard Herculean chest.

"I'm kidding," Clarissa says, meaning it.

"No problem," he says after a second. "It's just that Mama's been riding me for taking the summer off. She wanted me to come back home to work, but I wanted to do something for myself. I've been studying really hard, and I needed to unwind."

"School, where?" she asks.

"Third year law at Chapel Hill."

Law. Caruso almost slips off his perch when he hears the word. A lawyer, just like Pascal Robinson, he thinks, his mouth filled with disgust.

"What kind of law?"

"Environmental."

"Good!" she says emphatically. "And your family?"

"Dad owns a chain of medical supply stores in Raleigh. Mom has turned professional volunteer. The big issue," he says, rolling his eyes, "is that I'm supposed to inherit the family business. After all, I'm Joseph Hampton Fitzgerald the Third. Rightful heir to their hard work and fortune, but the operative word is *their*. It is *their* hard work, *their* fortune, not mine. Everyone deserves to choose his own pathway in life, and my decision to go into law is not sitting well with them."

"I chose cooking," Clarissa says. "And no one really cared one way or the other, except for Granny. She's the force behind me, told me to do what I had a passion for."

"You're lucky to have her."

"Had her," she says. "She died five years ago at eighty-two."

"Sorry."

"Don't be," she says. "I had her for a long time, and I thank the good Lord every day of my life for that." She picks up her glass of wine, taps her fingers against it, and sips. "Any allies?" she asks him.

"Huh?"

"Siblings."

"Five," he replies, elevating his hand, spreading wide his fingers. "I'm the second oldest and the only boy."

"I bet those girls spoil you rotten."

"Not all of them," he says. "My big sister, Jo Ann, bosses me around because she thinks she knows what's best for me, but the others hang on to my every word, like I'm some mystical guru, spouting pearls of wisdom. But, yes ma'am, I'm spoiled, though not one of them can cook like you do."

"I'm a skilled enough chef right now," she says, digging up a scallop and biting into it. "I hope to be great someday."

"I'm not sure what makes a great chef, but this meal"—he sweeps his hand over his plate—"is five diamonds in my review."

"Thank you, kind sir," she says coyly. She stabs an asparagus tip with her fork and sucks it into her mouth, her lips glistening as she chews.

"And what about your family?"

"There's not much to tell. My father teaches high school chemistry. My mother stays home to take care of my brother. He's much younger than I am, although he should be out of the house by now."

"Only the four of you?"

"Yeah. We moved from the mountains to the Bluegrass to get help for Randall when he was a little boy. He has big emotional problems. Started early on. Major ups and downs."

"Is he doing better now?"

"A little, I guess," she says, "but he's still a handful. Can't manage by himself. I love them all, but I keep my distance. For some reason—and

I don't understand it—Randall takes his anger out on me. Always has, but..." She pauses. Closing her eyes, she trails her fingertips along the underside of her arm, as if she's yearning for her grandmother's touch. "But..." she says again, her voice faltering. "I...remain...hopeful."

She opens her eyes and looks into Joe's. Caruso cringes. "Let's just say my parents continue to spend most of their waking hours worrying about my brother, but things could change. He could get better. I believe people always change, even if they don't want to, don't you?" she says, downing the rest of her wine.

"If someone's pointing a gun at them, they do."

Clarissa's blue eyes darken. "So you're a cynic," she says.

"Me and Flannery O'Connor."

"Who?"

"A famous writer from Georgia—long since dead."

"Other than cookbooks, I'm not much of a reader," she confesses to him.

"Reading's a habit," he says. "I was ten when the reading bug bit me, and I read everything I could get my hands on. Boy stuff. You know, Huckleberry Finn and Tom Sawyer, even Louisa May Alcott's *Little Men*. Can you believe it? My father had his own library. One wall was nothing but books for kids, and as soon as I finished one, I grabbed another off the shelf. I loved all the swashbuckling classics, then graduated to horror, mystery, sci-fi—anything to relieve my boredom. But it was Thoreau's *Walden*—I was thirteen when I read it—that pointed me in the right direction. I began to read more and more about the natural world—books by Wendell Berry, Annie Dillard, and others—and these writers showed me how to see the flora and fauna just outside my door. They taught me that some things are worth fighting for, that compromise can destroy some things forever. You could say that books led me to environmental law."

"Cookbooks did it for me. M.F.K. Fisher led me to my two passions—cooking and Caruso."

"She writes about food, doesn't she?"

"Uh-huh," Clarissa says with a nod. "But she garnishes her recipes with beautiful essays. In my favorite essay, she argues vehemently for the rights of pets—insisting that pets, like human beings, want to experience a variety of tastes. She gladly feeds leftovers to her dogs, she says, and feels that it's just and right to do so. The more I thought about what she said, the more I began to agree with her. Imagine how boring it would be to eat the same food day after day as long as you lived! M.F.K. Fisher is the reason I find cooking so important. Caruso eats better than I do," she says, giggling.

She rises abruptly from her chair. "Time for dessert," she announces. Joe opens his mouth to speak, but she is already wheeling around and heading toward the back door. Caruso follows her with his eyes as she goes inside, then checks out the patio.

Toward the rear of the terrace, near the kitchen, Sallie is perched between two tables, delivering cocktails to one before jotting down the orders of the other. Devon's three young people, he notices, have been replaced by a well-dressed couple in their forties, while Pops leads a mother and her toddler to seats on the opposite side of the oak.

The stars, visible through the top bars of Caruso's cage, are gummed together like the sleep in Clarissa's eyes when she wakes up in the morning. The breeze has died down, and the air feels soft and wet against his feathers. He can hear the buzz of mosquitoes beyond the torches, the scattered laughter of a handful of diners as they eat. Soon the night will be over, he thinks with relief.

"First, flan. Then, port," Clarissa says, approaching minutes later. She is holding a dessert dish in one hand and a long, slender glass in the other.

"Ah, flan," Joe says as she sets the creamy mound, with its dark cap of caramelized sugar, on the table, then puts the glass of amber-colored liquid beside it. "Aren't you joining me?"

She gives Joe a pouting look—familiar to Caruso—and shakes her head. "I'm sorry, but they need me in the kitchen."

She apologizes easily if it's not to her feathered friend, Caruso thinks.

"But Caruso will keep you company," she says brightly.

"How?" Joe says. "He doesn't understand a word I'm saying."

"Trust me, he does," Clarissa tells him. "It's not just mimicry with parrots. He uses language correctly."

"Then he's smarter than some of my drinking buddies," Joe jokes.

"I won't be long," she says. "I want to hear more about your studies. I want to learn more about the law."

The law, Caruso thinks, with a testy flap of his wings.

"The l...a...w," Joe says grandly, drawling out the word.

"Ah! The l...a...w," Clarissa says, imitating him.

"L...a...w," Caruso squawks angrily.

"He doesn't like to be ignored, does he?" Joe says, glancing up at Caruso.

"Absolutely not," she says.

"*Law!*" Caruso screeches.

"He wants my undivided attention," she says.

"I could discuss that with him while you're gone," Joe says. "Do you think he'll mind if I see you again?"

"The choice is mine, and I don't mind at all," she says, in her sultry Peggy Lee voice.

Caruso feels a knife-point of agony in his chest as their fingers inch over the table toward each other and touch, her silky skin feasting on his.

Eight

THE DARK NIGHT DISAPPEARS INTO THE LIGHT OF MEMORY—his deliverance when he cannot sleep. Hours before, she had covered his cage, and, besotted, floated off to bed. Even though he's wide awake, he knows she is sleeping soundly, dreaming about the evening she spent with him. *Him*. Caruso doesn't want to think his name, for thinking it would make him real, would will him into being. This must be jealousy he's feeling, Caruso reasons, the same jealousy Theodore Pinter had felt toward Pascal.

"To hope is to risk disappointment," the old man had told him one wintry day as they kept warm in the study. Caruso remembers that the gas logs were lit and that Theodore Pinter had pulled up a chair in front of the fireplace. "My life, so far, has been riddled with setbacks," he said. "Still, I wouldn't change a thing. Only cowards refuse to try because they fear frustration, and, for all my shortcomings, I am not that. I will keep hoping and fighting to win Olivia back until the last breath I take."

With a fervent cackle, Caruso rocked to and fro on his perch.

Theodore Pinter blew on his cup, then took a sip of his Earl Grey. "But years ago," he said with a swallow, "I must confess I was tempted to give up the struggle."

Caruso's rocking came to an abrupt stop. Tilting forward, he stared into the flames, listening intently.

"The temptation came in the form of another woman," the old man said solemnly. "Esmé was her name. She sat across the dining room table from me on a Yugoslavian freighter—the *Tuhobic*. I had boarded it with my fellow teachers in Savannah, Georgia, and we were sailing to Savona, Italy. The Atlantic was as smooth as glass the whole trip. For twelve days, I got to know her, mesmerized by her sea-green eyes over breakfast, lunch, and dinner. You see, Caruso, once assigned to a table, you weren't allowed to leave it. Which—due to her presence—bothered me not one bit. I was in my forties then; Esmé was younger, in her late thirties, I remember. She told me that she was meeting her husband in Florence. For over two months, he'd been away on a business trip, and she couldn't wait to see him. With trembling fingers, she opened her billfold and showed me his photograph. He had a bulldog face, like Winston Churchill's, and I couldn't, for the life of me, understand what she saw in him, but then I don't often understand what a woman sees in a man. In spite of the love she had for her husband, she showed an interest in me. At dinner, she wore long, flowing chiffon dresses, anchored over one creamy shoulder, and I instinctively knew that she had me in mind when she wore them. If I said something meaningful, she'd look into my eyes, reach out, and touch my hand. Whenever she found me witty, she'd laugh out loud. She was not timid. With a flick of her head, she'd toss back her sable curls and laugh so uninhibitedly that every head would turn toward her.

"She both confused and intrigued me, and I feared I was falling for her, like I had for Olivia. She was bolder and freer than Olivia was. Strange, because she was also a Southern gal, born and bred in Savannah, but she possessed none of the Southern woman's charm, that faux helplessness used to her advantage. Esmé was quite the opposite, in fact. Life had made her feisty and resilient, and we would argue about all sorts of things—politics, racism, books, and movies. You name it—we discussed it passionately. A liberal, she was. A new type of Southern woman. Very appealing to me.

"One night on the deck after dinner, as we admired the sunset—aflame with red, orange, and violet—I forgot myself, slipped my arm around her smooth shoulder, and gave her a kiss. I was taken by surprise when she kissed me back, her tongue flicking flirtatiously inside my mouth. Had I pushed, I could have made love to her that evening, but something told me not to, and it wasn't the immorality of sleeping with a married woman that made me stop but an awareness that she might be using me, in much the same way that I had used Trudy Fenton. Not from any calculated meanness, mind you, but from a kind of childish greed, wanting to fulfill a need without thinking of the consequences. Unconscionable, it would have been for me to let her do this, and so I removed my arm from her shoulder and left her standing there beside the railing, the wind blowing those sable curls against her cheeks. Later on, back in my cabin, I congratulated myself for acting honorably while also hating myself for not behaving like Pascal—for not being the bad boy that women want men to be—but I'm not a goody two-shoes, if that's what you're thinking," he said, fixing his gaze on Caruso. "I am no virgin."

Caruso had heard him use this word several times before, knew it had to do with love and loving, but its full meaning still eluded him.

"Are you listening to me?" Theodore Pinter asked, his voice insistent.

Puffing out his cheek feathers, Caruso cawed.

"Good boy," the old man said.

Caruso had been listening, all right, but he disagreed with what Theodore Pinter was saying. It's fine to act honorably, he thought, if you're willing to embrace a lesser life later. A life of dreaming, of regretting what you never did. Esmé wanted him. Theodore Pinter wanted her. So why did he restrain himself? What was so dishonorable about a romance between them? A night of pleasure would have yielded no negative results, only a few hours of bliss for the old man to treasure. Afterward, he would have resumed his longing for Olivia, and Esmé would have reunited with her husband. No harm done, Caruso had thought.

"Honor," Caruso squawks derisively into the quiet of the night.

Maybe his species of cockatoo is monogamous, but the Seram cockatoo hen of Indonesia is not. She cheats on her mate whenever she chooses but never suffers any consequences for her infidelity. He always welcomes her back with open wings. Perhaps the female Homo sapiens is more like the Seram cockatoo hen than one of his own kind. If this is true, Clarissa will continue to flirt with men, even date them, but she will inescapably choose Caruso, and he will—without fail—forgive her. But what if...what if? Caruso thinks, his heart knocking anxiously against his chest. What if they aren't fated to be together? What if she should forsake the touch of his wings for the touch of a man's fingers? What would become of him then?

Nine

FROM THE MOMENT SHE UNCOVERS HIS CAGE, dumps a handful of pumpkin seeds in his feeder, and checks his water, he senses her cheery mood. She sings out the door, doing a little dance across the deck and over the grass, not once glancing back at him as she quick-steps past a patch of nettles. Usually her Reeboks make impressions in the sand, but this morning her footsteps are as light as pixie dust. She foxtrots through the backyard toward Crab Cakes, lindy-hops up the steps, and jitterbugs through the glass back door.

The kitchen is empty. He wonders why she went in so early, when the staff doesn't arrive until two. She twirls from one place to another, opening and closing the refrigerator, unwrapping three sticks of butter, easing them into a stainless steel skillet that she grabs from a pot rack hung from the ceiling near the Viking stove. She sets the skillet on a burner and turns the flame down low, her hips swaying as she stirs the melting butter. He could watch her, working like this, for hours. Only if there are no human eyes on her—when she is cooking for herself alone—does she move loosely and effortlessly over the red-tiled floor, with no tension in her bones.

Once, long ago, in the sky above Deniliquin, he, too, as a fledgling, had flown freely and easily for himself—alone—even as he was alighting with the rest of his flock in the trees along the bank of the mighty Murray River.

She turns toward him, as though she has heard his thoughts. In front of the glass-paneled door, she throws him open-palmed kisses, and he feels secure in her love once more. But then, he remembers last night. He had not imagined it. It was real—the rose capering on her cheek, her bodice rising and falling as their fingers touched and lingered, as her skin feasted on Joe's—and within seconds Caruso's newfound confidence disappears. Does she love him for the bird he is, or has she simply been using him to fill the emptiness in her heart until someone of her own species came along? Right now, Caruso would do anything to know *how* she loves him. He would give up bathing in the shower with her, dropping white grapes into the crevice of her mouth, letting her feed the plumpest ones to him. *How* does she love him? Does she love him the way she loved her pets when she was a child? Is he no more to her than the dog, cat, or parakeet she once took care of?

No, she loves him more than this, he argues.

Why? he asks himself. Because he is as loyal as a dog, but not servile; as manipulative as a cat, but not cruel; as pretty as a parakeet, but not common. Because he is affectionate, gregarious, and playful. Because— like Mel Tormé—he is an original. Because, above all, he adores her, would do anything for her, and ask her for nothing back. Isn't this selfless, disinterested love?

Yes, he has become much more than a pet to her because *he is her family now*. And rightly so, for he has loved her as much as her grandmother did and much more than her parents, who lavish all of their love on her brother, and, naturally, more than Randall, who only loves himself.

If Clarissa and Randall had been born baby coots and not baby human beings, her life would have been different, Caruso muses. After hatching from his shell, the dull coloring of Randall's head would have indicated his weakness, and, rather than catering to his needs, his mother—determined to ensure the survival of the species—would have abandoned the sickly chick, leaving him alone to starve among the reeds, while feeding the extra food to Clarissa.

But human families allow their damaged offspring to rule with their powerful weakness, much like Randall had—always blaming his bad behavior on his mood swings. Whereas Clarissa had to assume responsibility for her mistakes. Maybe she resists apologizing to him for the very reason that she calls him *her family* now.

If she *anthropomorphizes* him, why can't he *psittacomorphize* her? he wonders. After all, fair is fair. Why must he accept her as a woman for his love to be real?

He knows that he is a parrot, a cockatoo, a white cockatoo, a Sulphur-crested Cockatoo, a Cacatua galerita galerita. He can readily list the physical traits that distinguish him from the Cacatua galerita fitzroyi. He is bigger than this subspecies, his ear coverts are not as yellow, and his eye rings are naked white, not pale blue. He is not delusional. If he can differentiate between himself and a cockatoo that is almost identical to him, he most certainly knows that he and Clarissa are not the same. Clarissa is a woman, a Homo sapiens, and he accepts her as she is, even though he will never forget the day when another Homo sapiens ensnared him in a net, as if he were catching a butterfly for his collection; as if he were robbing Caruso of just a few days of life and not the long life span predicted for him; as if Caruso wouldn't miss his parents, his flock; as if only human beings could suffer such pain. This appalling memory of man's cruelty—not some craziness inside him—is what drives him to psittacomorphize her, the way she anthropomorphizes him.

Clarissa takes a step forward, coming even closer to the glass-paneled door, and stares across the long expanse of yard at him.

Before last night, the two of them could often surpass the limitations of their species—he, a cockatoo, one of several species of parrots distinguished by their elegant, high crests—she, the one and only living species of the genus Homo. Whenever this happened, he would become her Ayers Rock, the heart of her universe, her sacred Uluru, her firm ground, while she would become his Great Barrier Reef, his largest, living mystery. Before last night, she allowed only Caruso to see her secret self, but last night things changed forever when she opened herself up to Joseph Hampton Fitzgerald and revealed the million coral polyps shimmering inside her.

"Caruso! Caruso!" she calls out, her lips silently mouthing his name. He would risk it, unlatch his cage door, and fly to her, except she has trifled with his feelings.

"Olivia drinks her Scotch and soda to feel good," the old man had explained to him one late summer day at the wrought iron table in his backyard. "As the heat of the drink warms her stomach, it also warms her mind, and she feels a sense of well-being. Whiskey doesn't hit me like that. Rather, I am affected by the sole act of drinking it. Knowing that we are imbibing the same thing, at the very same time, in backyards adjoining each other—now, this is what gets to me. This little connection between us gives me sublime pleasure, although I'm never able to forget that she isn't truly mine. My heart desires what it can't have," he had said, sighing as he glanced down at the cocktail glass in his hand.

My heart also desires what it can't have, Caruso thinks gloomily as he fixes his gaze on Clarissa, who is now pressing her full lips against the glass door. A few days ago such an intimate gesture would have numbed his doubts and sent him streaking his beak across the bars of his cage. Today, though, he is unable to bridge the distance between them, unable to glean any pleasure from their shared orbit. Let her heart desire what it can't have, he thinks, turning his back to her.

"HI THERE, LOVER BOY," Clarissa calls out as she bustles back into her own kitchen. She whips by his cage and down the hallway. Wire hangers rattle in her bedroom; drawers bang. After a while, she reappears in front of him, wearing a chartreuse sundress tied around her neck in back.

"Joe invited me to lunch last night," she tells him. "That's why I went in so early. Wanted to take a little time off now." She pinches the flesh beneath her upper arm. "See that. I've put on a bit of weight. It's snug around the waist, too," she says, sucking in her stomach. "Maybe I shouldn't wear this," she murmurs, checking herself out in the mirror above the chaise longue. "What do you think, Caruso? Does this make me look fat?"

He eyes her from top to bottom. Sloppy, she looks, like a not-quite-congealed mold of lime-green Jell-O. "Everything that deceives may be said to enchant," the old man said whenever he spoke of Pascal Robinson. Caruso wonders if he should wear a mask of deception right now. Aren't human beings forever changing masks? he rationalizes. A mask of politeness at work, another of regret at the end of a relationship, one of devotion in church. If she can wear a mask whenever it suits her, why can't he? So, opting for deceit, he shakes his head.

"Are you sure, Caruso?"

"Bar-bie doll," he lies.

"Bar-bie doll?"

"Bar-bie doll," he lies again.

She begins to giggle.

"Bar-bie doll," he says, a little louder.

"Will you quit it?" she says, all of a sudden giggling uncontrollably.

He wants to push the lie further. Not hard for him to do. After all, he is an Australian bird, a pretender by birth. So many birds of his native land are pretenders—the kookaburra pretending to be a stick so as to avoid becoming the hawk's prey; the male lyrebird mimicking every birdcall in the forest, pretending to be the best crooner to win a mate; the cassowary roaring, pretending to be a lion when he fights with a male rival. Therefore, Caruso will make the lie even bigger. The heart must fight for what it desires, he decides, throwing back his head, pretending to be a construction worker, wolf-whistling.

"Stop it, please," she says, giggling so hard she loses her balance and stumbles against the sunroom table. A vase of zinnias topples over. Water splashes across the wooden surface and spills on her dress. "You're incorrigible," she says, still tittering as she hurries down the hallway.

At last, he's the one in control, he thinks. Time to relax and enjoy his moment of triumph. Spotting the pinecone at the bottom of his cage, he rappels down to get it and then carries it back up to his perch. When she comes back, he is greedily gnawing the husk.

"Joe will be here soon," she says with excitement.

He glances up, his eyes falling on the delicate white silk blouse and the long blue peasant skirt. She has changed clothes. Immediately, his sense of control wavers, and his beak drops open, the pinecone plummeting to the wire-mesh floor.

"I finished what I needed to do at Crab Cakes this morning. The staff, I think, can manage without me for a while." Her hair is pulled back into a ponytail. Her lips are painted soft pink, the color of the pink dogwoods that bloomed every spring in Theodore Pinter's backyard. "He's taking me to the Treasure Chest," she says. "What do you think about that?"

He puffs out his cheek feathers and cackles incredulously.

"Oh, don't worry," she says, rolling her big blue eyes at him. Anchoring her hands on her kneecaps, she lists forward—her pink lips close to his cage—and whispers into his ear coverts, "I promise not to make a scene. This time, I'm gonna steal a dish off Chef Louie's menu. What's good for the goose is good for the gander, isn't it?"

Another bird aphorism, he thinks dismally.

"Does this outfit look nice on me, too?" she asks in a breathy voice.

For a second, he wonders if he should lie again, but then her mouth, so close to him, draws him in fully; and, no longer listening to her words, he takes another sidestep toward her, losing himself in the pink valentine of her lips. If he could replay this scene in his mind, over and over, to keep her forever with him, he would.

All of a sudden, a series of knocks punctuates the air, like firecrackers popping.

Light-headed with worry, he wobbles on his perch, then steadies himself by hoping to catch a glimpse of her lips again, but she is pattering down the hallway.

"How's my favorite chef?" Joe says, in his tar-heel drawl, the instant the front door snaps shut. "Nice place," he adds quickly, followed by the muffled sound of his sandals on the sea-grass rug. "Where's my buddy?" he asks her.

His buddy, Caruso thinks, offended.

"This way," Clarissa says.

He listens to their footsteps down the hallway floor.

"Hi, Caruso," his rival says, trudging toward him.

"Jo-seph Hamp-ton Fitz-ger-ald," he forces himself to say.

"Hear that, Clarissa?" Joe says. "We're already good buddies."

Like Popeye and Bluto, Caruso thinks, with a flutter of his wings.

"Caruso's a friendly guy," Clarissa tells him.

The mask must be doing its magic, he thinks.

"Would you like a glass of wine before lunch?"

"Sure. We've got some time," Joe replies, glancing down at his wristwatch.

"White wine for us and some white grapes for Caruso," she says in a sunny voice.

"She spoils you, too," his rival teases, poking his middle finger through the bars of his cage.

"Go easy, Joe," Clarissa says as she turns to leave. "That's his home. His safe place."

Joe eases his finger out and stares beyond Caruso at Clarissa, her hips oscillating through the doorway.

Several minutes later, she returns from the kitchen with a tray, which she puts on the table by the sunroom windows. After giving him a glass of wine, she takes the other for herself. Locking eyes, they press the rims to their lips—seeing only each other as they drink—before she sets her wineglass down, throws the latch on the cage door, and offers Caruso her arm.

He ascends, and she moves him through the empty space. He climbs up to her shoulder, and they sit down at the table. Winking at Caruso, she pinches off a grape and tenderly feeds it to him. Whereupon she tweaks off another and eats it herself—her lips appealing, her eyes half-closed as the grape travels down her throat.

Unexpectedly, Joseph Hampton Fitzgerald opens his lips, crooks up his arms, and flaps his elbows like wings. Laughing, Clarissa takes a grape and drops it into his upraised mouth.

Mocking me, Caruso thinks, his cheek feathers hot with fury.

"Watch this, Joe," she says, nipping off another grape. "Feed me," she says to Caruso, who parts his beak as she slips the fruit between his upper and lower mandible. She shuts her eyes and slants back her head. At once, he curves his neck to relinquish the white fruit to her mouth. Yet before he can savor this victory, his rival is out of his chair, picking off a grape, inserting it between his teeth, and tilting toward Clarissa.

Fake indifference, Caruso reminds himself as Joe brushes the champagne-colored rind against her trembling pink lips.

LIKE A BIRD GONE MAD, Caruso clings to the bars of his cage, rocking it with such ferocity the water in his drinking dish sloshes over onto the pinecone below, but the bothersome questions keep coming. What is she doing now? he wonders. Is she feeding him spicy, peppery shrimp with her fingers? Does she blow on his lips when he complains that his mouth is burning? Are they munching on island figs, just now coming into season? Are they sipping on glasses of wine? What are they saying to each other? Has she shared with him more secrets about her family? Has she told him that Caruso is her family now? If he were a human being, he would drink a shot of bourbon to soothe his frayed nerves.

This was what Clarissa had done last Christmas. In a moment of weakness, she had relented and called her parents, and Caruso had been privy to their loud voices seeping through the receiver, frantically discussing Randall and his woes. In the background, he heard her brother screaming, "Hang up the goddamn phone!" while Clarissa had just stood there, saying nothing, the receiver shaking in her fingers. After hanging up, she went straightway to the kitchen, where she had swigged from a bottle of bourbon to calm herself down.

Calm—this is how Caruso wants to feel.

"Claaa-risss-a!" he cries out, shaking the cage even harder. He remembers the old man quoting Sir Walter Raleigh to him. "'Hatreds are the cinders of affection,'" he'd said.

I'd rather hate her than love her like this, Caruso thinks, coming to an abrupt standstill.

"I could never hate her," Theodore Pinter had said as they snacked on carrots in the kitchen. "My love for her was always greater than that." He was peeling a carrot, the orange curls piling up on a paper napkin. Caruso recalls that the ornamental pear tree beside the kitchen window was in full bloom and that its heavy fragrance erased the smell of everything else. "She paid no attention to me through most of junior high, but during our very last semester, I breathed in a mouthful of courage and asked her to the Saint Valentine's Day dance. I invited her in January—ahead of time—because I wanted to act before Pascal Robinson did."

The old man cut off some carrot for Caruso, and after that a piece for himself, and they munched and swallowed. "I wasn't sure what Pascal would do. He might ask her, or he might not. You see, they clearly liked each other, but they weren't official yet." Removing his glasses, he huffed on the lenses and wiped them off on the tablecloth's hem, but instead of putting them back on, he slipped them into his shirt pocket. "What I'm trying to say is, he had lots of girlfriends. Wasn't a one-woman man back then—isn't one now, from what I hear."

He tentatively pinched the bottom of his earlobe. "And lo and behold, Caruso," he said grandly, "she said *yes*. As the date drew near, I rented a white tux from Moberly's and ordered an expensive purple orchid for her pink dress." Clucking, Caruso rocked forward. "Yes, Caruso," he said, sighing, "I know what you're thinking...that we were just kids, that I was going overboard, as usual...but I wanted to show her the stuff I was made of. I wanted her to perceive me as the better man."

He sliced off another circle of carrot and offered it to him. "For two months, I daydreamed about us—waltzing like Fred Astaire and Ginger Rogers across the gym floor. I had such great expectations," he said, shaking his head, "but they were dashed the second we stepped through the wide double doors and saw Pascal slow-dancing with Olivia's best friend, Suzanne Winters. Next, he tapped Carl Hinton's shoulder, and off he went with another one of her girlfriends. Dateless, he danced with every girl there. Every girl but Olivia. 'I don't care a fig about him,' she kept saying, her eyes brimming with tears, 'and if he taps you, Teddy, let's ignore him.' Of course, he never did. Pascal Robinson was born with a gift for manipulation," the old man had finished, "and by June's end, Olivia was all his."

"Clarissa!" Caruso cries, his legs quaking from the memory, his body shivering with fear. His belly hurts. The feathers on his breast itch from worry. Dread claws at his throat. Lowering his head, he parts his beak, isolates a pinfeather, and jerks it out. At long last, relief burns through him like a shot of bourbon.

Ten

THE CLOUDS IN THE SKY ARE AS TRANSLUCENT as a convergence of jellyfish, Caruso thinks, glancing up from Clarissa's shoulder while they sit at a wrought iron table in front of Iris's Coffee Shop, the scraggly pine beside them providing little shade from the sun.

"I like your bird," a teenage waitress, in cutoffs and a yellow tank top, chirps as she hurries over. "What kind is it?" she asks, setting down Clarissa's Very Berry smoothie.

"Caruso's a parrot. A Sulphur-crested Cockatoo," Clarissa explains, taking off her floppy cotton hat, hanging it by its strap from the back of her chair.

"Does he bite?"

"He's never bitten me," she says, smiling, sucking Very Berry up a large purple straw.

"I'd like to have a bird like that."

"Parrots are a lot of hard work," Clarissa tells her. "You've got to feed them the right foods, give them baths every day, and spend time with them, or else they'll get sick."

"He's beautiful," the girl says dreamily. "You must take really good care of him."

"I try to."

"Does he like fruit?"

"Uh-huh." Clarissa places the straw on the table, nudges the glass against her lips, and gulps.

"I could cut up some fresh pineapple for him—free of charge."

"That'd be awfully nice of you," Clarissa says, licking purple froth off her mouth.

"Might take me a while, though. We're pretty busy."

"There's no hurry," Clarissa says as the girl turns to go. "I'm waiting for someone, and I'm here a little early."

Waiting for someone. These words resound ominously in Caruso's ears. "I've been leaving you alone too much lately," Clarissa had told him before they took off this morning, "but I promise to spend more time with you."

Then, to keep her promise, she took him for a stroll down the dusty, winding lanes to Iris's Coffee Shop. Perched snugly on her shoulder, he listened intently to her as they walked. "That fig tree over there is pregnant with fruit," she said, pointing at it. "Look at the leaves on that crape myrtle. They're already fainting in the heat." And he had felt more hopeful about their future together, until he heard her say those words. *Waiting for someone.*

Anxiously, he surveys the premises. A line of diners, waiting to be seated, snakes out the entrance and onto the weather-beaten deck. Beside the road, six feet away from their table, are three huge garbage cans overflowing with soiled napkins, Styrofoam cups, and plastic water bottles. A common sparrow, with a dark-brown shield of feathers on his breast, hops toward a solitary french fry lying next to a paper napkin. Another sparrow, the feathered insignia on his chest much smaller, sees it also and flutters over. They meet, beak to beak, the french fry between them, and anyone else observing this scene would expect a skirmish, but Caruso knows there will be no conflict, for the sparrow with the largest patch of brown is the colonel, while the other is the lieutenant. True to form, the lieutenant flies away. The flock life of sparrows is one of rank and order.

"Here we are," the girl says, depositing a plate of pineapple chunks on the table.

"Thank you," Clarissa says. "Caruso adores pineapple."

"Enjoy yourself, Caruso," the girl says, clapping her eyes, round as tortoise eggs, on him. Her mop of short-cropped brown hair and her pug nose put him in mind of a cuddly koala bear, and he squawks with amusement at her. Startled, she jumps back and then begins to giggle—not deliciously, like Clarissa, but artlessly, like a teenage girl.

"My friend should be here any minute," Clarissa tells her.

"I'll keep an eye out," the girl says over her shoulder as she starts for the deck.

Caruso tightropes down Clarissa's arm to the table, tweezes up a piece of fruit with his toes, brings it to his beak, and eats it. *So sweet,* he thinks, remembering the pineapple fields of Australia upon which clouds of cockatoos would descend, then devastate.

"Over here!" Clarissa shouts, waving her arms high above her head.

Apprehensive, Caruso looks where she is waving and is relieved to see Beryl, zoom-zooming over the scanty grass.

"Ya said *ten-thirty,*" Beryl says defensively, whipping out a chair the way she'd whip out a wet sheet to hang on a clothesline. She plunks herself down, slamming her coin purse on the table.

"You're not late," Clarissa says. "I'm just early—wanted to spend some quality time with my main man."

My main man. Caruso feels reassured again. He grabs another morsel of fruit and takes a bite.

"You're lookin' gooooood," Beryl says, drawing out the word.

"I'm feelin' gooooood."

"I don't have to guess why," Beryl says with a grin, the dimples in her cheeks as deep as toe prints in wet sand, her spiked hair like the steeples on sand castles. "I saw ya two the other day at the Treasure Chest," she says, pitching forward.

"Well, what do you think?"

"He's Mr. Herculean Pecs, all right," she says, whistling through the crack between her two top front teeth. "That's what bothers me. I'm happy for you, but I'm also worried."

"Worried?" Clarissa says, widening her eyes. "I'd rather hear the *I'm happy for you* part."

Caruso detects a pixel of irritation in Clarissa's voice.

"Don't get your underwear tied in a knot," Beryl teases her. "Something worrisome came to me last night. That's all."

"You think I've erred again."

"Did I say that?" Beryl says, wrinkling her brow. "Anyhow, we've been on this *I met a man* roller coaster before. By now, you should know I have your best interests at heart."

Clarissa clamps her hands on the edge of the table. "Okay," she says, breathing in deeply through her nose. "Just give me the highlights of the bumpy road ahead."

Beryl juts out her chin and tightly presses her lips together, as though daring Clarissa to interrupt her again. "You've heard a hundred stories about Savannah," she says, moments later, "about my years in art school there."

Nodding, Clarissa rat-a-tats her fingertips impatiently against the table.

Beryl ignores her. "Because I was graduating from SCAD, my roommate wanted to treat me to dinner. Anywhere, she said, so I picked The Crab Shack on Tybee Island. I had never eaten there before. You need a car to get there, and she had one."

"Her name was Pansy, right?" Clarissa says, bringing her strumming to a stop.

"Uh-huh," Beryl says, stubbornly quiet again. A peevish silence between them follows, their chests rising and falling. Caruso imagines their exhalations bumping into each other, refusing to move, producing a thin vibration of tension, until Beryl pushes through, her voice calm and unflappable. "The Crab Shack is celebrated for its—"

"Eccentricities," Clarissa says wearily. "'Eat at The Crab Shack, and get your photo taken with the alligators.' I've heard this story. Spare me, please."

"Tell you, or spare you," Beryl says. "Choose."

"Okay. Tell me, but skip the mossy oaks, the dining rooms like boxcars on the edge of the swamp, the plastic plates, the hole in the center of the table, the trash can below it."

"Skip the food, too?"

"Not the food," Clarissa says. "I can't ever hear enough about good cooking."

Beryl lowers her long lashes until they cuddle her cheeks, thinking, then whips them open and says politely, "Well, Chef, if ya insist."

"Of course, I do."

"The freshest seafood," Beryl begins.

"From the dock to the table."

"The shrimp are perfect."

"Hot and spicy."

"The oysters *plumpsome*."

"Divine."

"And the fish is extraordinary."

"Manna from heaven."

"Ambrosia from the gods."

Bored, Caruso flaps his wings, for he has heard this routine before and wants Beryl to hurry up and get to the *worrisome* part.

"But wait! We're talking about Southern cooking," Clarissa announces grandly.

"What's wrong with this picture?" they ask in unison, casting their gaze on him. There is a beat of five seconds before they sweetly harmonize, "Nothing is fried."

"Only boiled, broiled, baked, or grilled," Beryl adds.

"A health-conscious bistro," Clarissa says, with an amused twinkle in her eyes, "tucked into a moccasin-infested, alligator-ridden swamp."

Speechless, they are, basking in their performance, as Caruso looks at Clarissa, then at Beryl, wondering which one of them will finally talk.

It is Beryl. "Only it wasn't the food I thought about last night."

"What was it?"

Time for the *worrisome* part, Caruso thinks with an eager wiggle.

"The Little Madonna..."

"The Little Madonna," Clarissa repeats. "Are we talking here about a great painting or another one of your bizarre encounters with crazy folk?"

"No, Claaa-risss-a," Beryl says, elongating each syllable of her name, exaggerating the sound of it before dropping it off, as if each were a rung on a ladder she's descending. "I'm not talking about a velvet Elvis painting or a weirdo in a gunnysack doing penance in front of a church. This was a real young girl who broke my heart. The Little Madonna of Tybee Island and her birds—"

"Birds?" Clarissa says.

Birds, Caruso thinks with interest.

"Uh-huh, *birds*," Beryl repeats. "You're a-listening to me now, hain't ya?"

Clarissa nods thoughtfully and teeters forward in her chair.

"Yes, the Little Madonna and her parrots were what affected me the most, and I know I've never told you about that."

"Not a word," Clarissa says, "but I'm all ears now."

"Ya sure?"

"Absolutely," Clarissa says, meaning it.

"It was still light out when Pansy and I drove up," Beryl begins, slowly pacing her story, "and when we were finished eating, it was a splendid dusk. The sky, I remember, was awash in rose, deep purple, and gold. The colors—so brilliant—you could see them shining like a rainbow on the surface of the swamp. As soon as we paid our bill, the shrieking and screeching started. Our curiosity up, we followed the racket, and it led us to the gift shop. The Little Madonna was just beyond the door, behind the cash register. Young and pregnant—in her late teens, I guessed—with a cockatoo perched on her forearm. The bird was half the size of you, Caruso," Beryl says, looking at him, "and nowhere near as handsome."

A Cacatua galerita fitzroyi, Caruso thinks, with a supercilious cheep.

"She was so busy talking to that bird, she didn't see us. 'You're not alone anymore, Ollie,' she cooed at him. 'You're ours now, and we're the ones

LOVE & ORDINARY CREATURES

who love you.' She ran her ring finger gently down his neck. There was no wedding band on it. She had swept her hair back tightly in a clasp. Her skin was drained of color. Her brown eyes, lusterless. Fragmented, she seemed, as if she harbored some harmful force that was ripping her into a thousand different pieces, with loneliness being the only trait they had in common, the only thing that kept them glued together. She never ceased caressing the bird's neck while she spoke to him, and I swear to ya, Clarissa, the affection she lavished upon him was both discomforting and consoling. It was not until I cleared my throat that she finally glanced up.

"'This is Ollie,' she said when she saw us. 'Only a mindless lowlife would toss a bird out like a piece of trash.' She lifted up one of his wings and pointed to a bald patch beneath it."

Paranoid, Caruso checks to see if there's a featherless spot on him that they can see—but, no, he's been careful.

"'Feather plucking is a parrot's way of grieving,' she explained, her tone so grim it made me shudder. She drew her lips into a thin, tight line, but the next second she was smiling as she showed us the new pinfeathers growing back in. After that, she introduced us to three other parrots in the gift shop. In the cage beside her was an Amazon named Peter Pan, willed to the owners by a longtime customer who had recently died of cancer. And in the next cage over were two red-fronted macaws that the local humane society had given them.

"Afterward, we followed her and Ollie to a large back room with more cages. I remember a rainbow lorikeet, named Sylvia Plath because of her high-strung temperament; a conure with a loud, piercing voice called Ethel Merman; and Bogart, an African Grey. I can't recollect the names of all the others, just that she kept calling them her babies.

'Every one of them has a story,' she said whenever she paused in front of a cage. 'Every one of them has felt abandoned and betrayed. But now they belong. Now they feel safe. Don't you, Ollie?' she asked him.

"After a while, Pansy got bored and wandered off to see the alligators, but the desperation in the girl's voice held me, and although I felt uneasy, I stayed. She went on and on about the birds, as if *they* were her real babies, not the one she was carrying inside her. Not once did she touch her stomach or acknowledge her pregnancy in any way, and I instinctively knew not to either. In all this time, she had not dealt with the other customers, and I noticed that another woman was now willingly working the register. Still, though, I couldn't bring myself to leave.

"Trailing her fingertips down Ollie's neck, she would lean toward me and stare into my eyes, as if I—alone—had the power to save her, but she never shared with me what she needed saving from. Never uttered a word about herself. Just spoke relentlessly about the birds in a kind of enigmatic code that transformed their heartache into hers. It was disturbing.

"'I better go find my friend,' I made myself say.

"For several seconds, she didn't speak. Then, righting her shoulders, she said earnestly, 'Come back soon, please!' Words she must have uttered again and again to customers but said with such anguish to me that I left quickly. I never asked her—her name," Beryl says, slumping forward.

"That's sad," Clarissa says, reaching over to touch her fingers, "but what does that poor girl have to do with me?"

"Why—can't you see it?" Beryl says. "This is the worrisome part."

At last, the *worrisome* part, Caruso thinks, taking a step closer to them.

"You're obsessed with Joe, the way the Little Madonna was obsessed with her birds. You're paying more attention to him than to the bird in your life," Beryl explains.

Caruso tilts his head to the side and cackles, confused as to whether he should feel consoled by Beryl's words or concerned.

"Obsessed?" Clarissa says, arching her eyebrows.

"You're not the abandoned little girl you once were. You've got Caruso and me and your staff at Crab Cakes. We love you and support you. We're your family now. Look, I know ya want a beau. I do, too. Just take it easy and go with the flow this time. If you do this, you'll be able to accept whatever happens between the two of you." She swallows hard and adds, "Isn't this the other choice, the acceptance you talked about?" A smile spreads over her face. "Ah, come on, Clarissa," she blurts out. "I don't wanna worry about you."

Clarissa is quiet for a moment; then, without a trace of meanness in her voice, she says, "So let's worry about you and your love life for a change."

"I hear ya," Beryl says, tossing back her head, letting out a laugh. "I shouldn't be going on and on about your *roller-coaster ride with men* when I got my own *lonely trail of tears* dogging me. Maybe I should quit obsessing about men, go with the flow, too, and be grateful for you, Caruso, and my own big mess of a family. But—what can I say—I like the opposite sex, and right now I've been without a fellow so long they all look yummy to me. Even Pops, who's old enough to be my granddaddy. It's scary."

"Well, Pops is a good-looking, David Niven type of man."

"David Niven. Who's he?" Beryl asks, ironing a spike of black hair with her fingers.

"A famous film star from the nineteen-fifties."

"Poodle skirts and slicked-back hair," Beryl says in a voice that is decidedly unimpressed. "I don't mind older men. President Clinton gives me a little thrill when he does that State of the Union thing on TV, but mid-fifties is as old as I'll go—although Pops is nice, always bragging on me."

"He likes how you paint—the colors you use, the way you play with the light."

Beryl nods. "Yeah, that's what he tells me." She flashes Clarissa a toothy grin, thrusts out her hands, and says, "See these fingernails. They're all *begombed* with oil paint."

"Cobalt blue," Clarissa murmurs, touching the tip of Beryl's thumb. "Hot pink." She nudges the pointer. "Vermilion," she says when she comes to the middle one. "Lemon yellow. Lime green," she finishes, tapping Beryl's pinkie with her own. "Gosh, Beryl, they're all Frida Kahlo colors."

"I can't help myself," Beryl says with a shrug. "I love the woman's work."

"You're not from Mexico," Clarissa states. "Not from some island in the Caribbean but from Ocracoke, and this is a landscape of whites, blues, and grays."

"I live on the isle of my dreams, and it's *prettysome*," Beryl says, weaving her fingers together, pushing them away from her small breasts with a crack.

Clarissa makes a face. "That'll make your knuckles big."

"They ache from too much painting," she says. "I saw this doctor on TV, and he said that popping your knuckles releases the lactic acid in them, and that's why you feel relief. Hain't nothing wrong with it, he said."

Relief. A crack of the fingers, a pluck of the feathers, Caruso thinks, tweezing up another bit of pineapple, retrieving it from his toes with his beak.

"Now back to your roller-coaster ride. Is this thing with Joe serious? Is it Deborah Kerr and Burt Lancaster in *From Here to Eternity*?" Beryl asks. "Is it like that incredibly hot kissing scene between them on the beach, with the waves breaking against their bodies? I know some film stars from the fifties, too."

Serious. Is she seriously kissing him on the beach? Caruso thinks with a quiver.

"When I saw you two, eating lunch—outside—on the *pizer*, you was holding hands," Beryl says, pressing Clarissa hard with her eyes.

"So?"

"So—is this a strong case of physical attraction, or is this something more?"

"Beryl..." Clarissa says, sighing.

"I'm sorry," the girl says, dashing over. "I got waylaid in the kitchen. Do you need a menu?"

"No," Beryl says with an upward glance. "All I want is a cup of coffee to go—black with no sugar."

"Small, medium, or large?"

"Small."

"Hey, haven't I seen you painting at the beach?" the girl asks.

"Most likely," Beryl says.

"I really like the way you paint."

Beryl slides her eyes up, then down, the girl's body. "If you model for me," she says, "I'll paint a couple of portraits and give you one."

"No kidding?" the girl bubbles. "My name's Sam, and I'm off on

Thursdays and Sundays."

"Modeling's hard work," Beryl warns her.

"Kind of like owning a parrot," Sam says, nodding at Clarissa. "One small black coffee coming up," she says, the toes of her sneakers digging into the sand as she spins around.

"Now, where was I?" Beryl says, thinking for a second. "Oh, yeah, I was worried that Mr. Herculean Pecs might morph into your new *puck*."

"My new boyfriend?" Clarissa says. "You, of all people, know my track record with men. Hot or cold, I manage to scare them off. But I must admit this feels different. There's definitely something going on between us."

"Ya fixed him that big fancy meal, didn't ya?"

"Where did you hear that?" Clarissa asks.

"There hain't no secrets around here."

"Pops told you."

"Maybe," Beryl says coyly. "I hear our Oysters Rockefeller weren't on the menu."

"*My* Oysters Rockefeller," Clarissa corrects her. "The night I made them he didn't show, but he came back the next night."

"And ate that fancy paella of yours."

"It wasn't that fancy."

"You don't think you went just a wee bit overboard?"

"What if I did?" Clarissa shoots back. "I don't care. He bragged on me all evening, said about a zillion times how delicious my paella was. He made me feel special, and I don't get enough of that."

Shocked, Caruso drops the pineapple he is eating. Hasn't he been making her feel special for years?

"My family treats me like a sounding board for Randall," she goes on, "but Joe listens to me. He gives me his full attention."

Don't I always listen to her? Caruso thinks, his crest collapsing.

"Now, for the million-dollar question," Beryl says with a naughty grin. "Did you, at any point during the meal, put your big foot in it?"

"I thought we were going to focus on you and your love life for a change?"

"Come on," Beryl persists. "I know you said something. You always do. Tell me what it was."

Clarissa takes another swallow of her Very Berry, and, in a soft voice, says, "Nothing too bad this time."

"Out with it."

"I might've insinuated he was a beach bum."

"Dumb."

"Yeah..." Clarissa says, fidgeting in her chair. "But not as dumb as what came out of my mouth next."

"What?"

"I called him a professional student."

"Doubly dumb," Beryl says, shaking her head.

"But when I told him I was kidding, he was fine with it."

"You still hain't answered my question. Is Joe your new beau?"

A cold tingle runs through Caruso's body.

"No, my main man's right here," Clarissa stresses, lightly touching his crown of feathers. The warmth of her fingertips soothes him.

"Caruso, are you Clarissa's main man?"

Caruso dubiously bobs his head.

"Black with no sugar," Sam says, all at once reappearing beside them. "Anything else?" she asks as she sets the Styrofoam cup down.

"No, we're just fine," Beryl says. "Meet me at Biff's Dockside Store next Sunday around twelve-thirty, and I'll take you on a tour of my studio. Tell you what you are letting yourself in for when you model."

"Great! I'll be there," she says. "Holler if ya want anything else," she adds before heading toward an old man in a green Speedo, sitting on the edge of the deck with his skinny, blue-veined legs dangling over.

"What is Mr. Herculean Pecs studying?" Beryl wants to know. She snaps the plastic cap off her coffee and sips.

"You're not about to let up, are you?"

"Nope."

"Okay, okay...I give up."

"So?"

"Law at UNC in Chapel Hill," she answers.

"An ambulance chaser, huh?"

"No, a defender of the environment."

"I like the sound of that," Beryl says, "but it's already too late for Nags Head."

"Hopefully not for the mountains back home."

"Is he out surfing now?" Beryl asks, taking another sip of her coffee.

"I reckon."

"Did ya hear about the shark that washed up yesterday?"

"No, where?"

"Up the beach, across from the wild ponies."

"Was it a big one?"

"A sand shark, I heard."

"I worry about Joe," Clarissa murmurs.

"You're supposed to be worrying about me and Caruso," Beryl reminds her.

"I worry about the riptides."

"My Lord, girl, either you're playing with me, or you're smitten."

Clarissa sucks on her bottom lip, then asks uncertainly, "You think I like him more than I think I do?"

"Naw, you're just horny," Beryl says, downing the rest of her coffee in two noisy gulps. "Don't ya know that love is the greatest aphrodisiac?"

"In love with love, right?"

"Right," Beryl says, looking up at the sky. "I best get going. The light's not too bright, perfect for painting." Leaping to her feet, she seizes her coin purse from off the table and unzips it. "For my coffee," she says, sliding several rumpled dollar bills toward Clarissa.

"I'm feeling generous today," Clarissa says, pushing the money back.

"Love makes you a big spender, huh?" Beryl says, with dimples of merriment in her cheeks. "Now, bring that boyfriend of yours by the store."

Boyfriend, Caruso thinks, his spirit sinking. Boyfriend—the sound of it weighs as heavy as a soaking rain on his feathered soul.

Shifting away from the village and Silver Lake Harbor, he stares meaningfully toward the Atlantic, where deep in the cold darkness the riptides form and grow. *Puck* or *pet*? What is he to her? How does she love him? Does she still love him as much as the Little Madonna of Tybee Island loved her birds? he wonders. Does she see him as her pet or—even worse—as her baby? The thought of either makes him queasy.

He breathes in the salty air, hears the waves rumbling. He is just a small, helpless bird on this large planet. His chest is not Herculean. His wings are not muscular like a man's arms. He is no match for the likes of Joseph Hampton Fitzgerald. He yearns for some power greater than he is to help him. So spurred on by jealousy and possessive love,

Gwyn Hyman Rubio

he asks the invincible Warramurrungundji to do what he can't do for himself—to send him a riptide, powerful enough to suck a surfboard beneath the swells and smash it into shards against the ocean floor.

Eleven

UPON LEAVING THE COFFEE SHOP, they meander down the dusty streets of the village and end up in front of the walkway that leads to the lighthouse. The sun is now high in the sky. Most of the tourists have gone inside to escape the heat or else are baking in it at the beach. She looks, as does he, at the white, rocket-shaped cone gleaming in the distance. The lighthouse property is one of their special places.

She believes the historic lighthouse has a soul, like Ayers Rock in Australia or the Appalachian Mountains of Kentucky. "It is the oldest mountain chain in America," she has told him, "much older than the Rockies, a fact most folk don't know." She insists that the fire tower she once climbed as a girl has a soul also, same as the animals, the trees, the stones, the grass, even the plastic bottles that litter the landscape.

So whenever the stress at home became too much for her, she would visit the fire tower in the deep woods behind her grandmother's house. Her hands on the railings, she would plant her feet firmly on the rungs and mount the steel staircase, climbing and climbing, until she reached the parapet at the top, where she would lower herself down, swinging her legs over the edge as she absorbed the sights, sounds, and smells above and below her: clean-scented creeks gurgling in ribbons around large rocks, furry creatures scurrying amidst dense hardwoods, turkey vultures circling above the stench of death, reminding her that life was brief, that every moment lived was precious. She wanted to swim with the bream, run with the red-tailed fox, and ride the warm air currents with the raptors. Her awareness of the soul-filled land brought her peace. Yet the instant her eyes fell upon the strip mines—those naked white scars on the mountain face opposite her—her sense of tranquility ceased. She would trace the defacement all the way down to the pond of greenish-black sludge at the bottom. If the slurry overflowed, it would poison the topsoil, the plants, the animals, the insects, the streams, the fish—the soul of every living thing in its pathway—much as her brother had poisoned the peace of their home with his outrage. *Save us from soullessness*, she would pray.

If Caruso could, he would endow her with wings. Like Peter Pan and Tinker Bell, they would fly up to the lighthouse parapet—its beacon, like a torch, above them—and from this vantage point they would marvel at the fish, animals, and birds of Ocracoke Island—free of coal, strip mining, and soullessness. But, alas, he is a bird, not a boy, and she is a human being, not a fairy, and they must be satisfied with what they are doing now—sitting on a wooden bench on the lighthouse grounds, following the ripples of heat rising from the sleepy asphalt street in front of them.

Perched on the back of the wide bench, Caruso curves his neck down and brushes his beak against her cheek.

"What a sweet kiss," Clarissa says, pushing her floppy hat back, glancing up at him.

Pretender that he is, he chirps like a sparrow.

"Oh, look at that," she says, suddenly jolting upright as a couple on a long bike with two seats pedals by. "I've never seen the woman in front and the man in back. Must be a feminist statement. We are equals, she's saying. Proving it by taking the lead."

Caruso regards the woman, built like a ferry, then the man, small as a dinghy behind her, and thinks he knows the reason for it. She is simply stronger than he is.

Only a Homo sapiens female, like Clarissa, would suggest that the woman's position on the bike was a declaration of her equality. For in a bird's world, Caruso thinks ironically, it is the cock, not the hen, who does the proving. When he was a fledgling, he had witnessed a male satin bowerbird clearing away brush for hours to make an entrance to his nest. After that, the bowerbird had stacked twigs into walls along the sides of his passageway and later spent days decorating both ends of it with an array of shells, berries, and bones. All this to win the fickle heart of a female!

Even more pathetic is the African masked weaver bird, Caruso thinks. Henpecked long before he is hitched, he is expected to build in the same tree as the other members of his colony, exposing himself to their ridicule as he seeks out the best spot for his nest—which must be woven tight enough to hold eggs and sturdy enough to handle the weight of growing chicks if he is to impress a potential mate. Should he fail to dazzle her, to command her respect, she will leave him there, dangling upside down from his cone-shaped nest, fluttering his golden wings, shrieking for her approval. A sniveling specimen of a bird is he.

Is instinct the force behind his own struggle? Caruso wonders. Does instinct compel him to plot and scheme to earn Clarissa's approval? Is he working his wings to the bone because he is a cock, driven by instinct to win a female, while she is a human being, given a choice instinctually to please or not to please a male? He should let her do some of the pleasing for a change, he thinks haughtily.

Unexpectedly, she starts to sing, and her lovely soprano recaptures his attention. Did she read his thoughts? he asks himself. Is she trying to please him?

The song is one of the old tunes her grandmother taught her when she was a girl. As soon as she comes to the last line—

But you'd look sweet upon the seat
Of a bicycle built for two

—he is ready to answer the first: "Caruso, Caruso, give me your answer, do," which she always returns to.

"Ye...s, mar...ry...you," he warbles.

"Caruso, I give my heart to you, too," she says sweetly, batting her eyelashes at him, moving on to other old songs—singing, humming, singing some more—while he plays the role of her grandmother, singing back to her on cue. In this way, they keep the memory of Granny alive, she has told him, and he gladly plays along because he wants to be as important to her as her grandmother was.

It was Granny who had taught her that fresh produce tasted best and that next best were the vegetables from her garden, lined up in Mason jars in the root cellar. During the summer, the two of them would spend hours harvesting tomatoes, green beans, peas, corn, and cucumbers for canning. There were rows of stewed tomatoes in quart jars and pints of cucumber relish. They turned corn into chowchow and picked the peaches off the tree out front and pickled them in a sweet-sour brine spiced with cloves. From the gnarly old fruit tree in the backyard, they made gingery pear preserves. Her grandmother showed her how to gather ripe blackberries without getting scratched and bake them into a lemony, sugary cobbler. It was Granny who insisted that nothing edible be thrown away—transforming watermelon rinds into sweet pickles, making wine from dandelions, using the petals from her roses to garnish their plates. Granny was the one who influenced Clarissa the most because she took the time to see what her granddaughter needed, whereas her parents, so obsessed with her brother, wouldn't.

Competing with Joe is onerous enough, Caruso thinks, but how can he, a simple bird, ever compete with Granny? To Clarissa, Granny is no longer flesh and blood but an otherworldly being, radiating selfless, disinterested love. Saintly—that's how Clarissa describes her. Still, when she forgets to edit herself, Caruso hears the real story. Her grandmother was a compilation of people: a seductive, calculating girl when she set out to catch her husband; a tough mountain woman when she chased strip mine operators off her land with an iron skillet; a passionate cook when she stewed a kettle of burgoo in the kitchen; a shrewd businesswoman when she bargained a price for her jam and eggs at the country store; a loving mother and doting grandmother whenever her girls needed her. Inside her lived all the selves she ever was. She was a woman of many masks—nothing less and nothing more.

These days, he is the one who must take care of Clarissa. These days, it is his time, not Granny's, to love her. Does loving her mean always putting her dreams before his? he questions. Does unconditional love demand that he do this? If so, how many more years will he need to sacrifice before she chooses him? Will he, desperate to win her love, become as foolish as the male satin bowerbird or as pathetic as the African masked weaver? Will he eventually lose the soul of who he is?

UPON ARRIVING AT CRAB CAKES, Clarissa doesn't take him straightway to his cage, as usual, but heads for the supply room. He casts his eyes over the refrigerator and freezer on the back wall and the floor-to-ceiling metal shelves on either side of him. The shelves to his left are stacked with cans of food, jars of condiments, and large tins of various kinds of cooking oil. Dry goods line the other wall—boxes of dried fruit along with bins of rice, flour, and cornmeal.

She lowers him onto the stool just inside the doorway. After whipping off her floppy hat and blouse, she drapes them from hooks on the antique coatrack in the corner. Wincing, she readjusts the straps of her bra, which are digging into her shoulders, then grabs a fresh undershirt and chef's tunic off the rack. After pulling the undershirt over her head, she puts on the tunic, takes a hairnet from one of its pockets, and slips it over her curls. "Do you think I'm getting fat, Caruso?" she asks, zipping the tunic up.

He swings his head—no.

"That's my guy. A chef has to taste what she cooks, and I gladly taste a lot," she says, holding out her arm to him.

They walk down the hallway and veer into the kitchen, where she flips on the overhead lights. Breathing rhythmically, she stands there. Centering herself, he knows, for the hours of preparation ahead. "One day," she says, "I'll be the executive chef of a five-diamond restaurant with a big budget." He has heard this speech many times. "Where there'll be enough money for five line cooks. Where I won't have to ask Rick to double as my sous chef. Or hire someone local to prepare the extra desserts. Or buy bread from a bakery. I'll have my own pastry chef, sommelier, my own restaurant director, my own chef de partie, and will feel confident that the restaurant will run smoothly if I want to take a few days off."

She gulps down three mouthfuls of air before stepping through the back door and onto the terrace with Caruso surfboarding on her shoulder. He spreads out his wings and balances on one foot, then the other. Mr. Herculean Pecs can't do this, he thinks, proudly holding up his head. For Caruso has mastered the arts of both flying *and* surfing, whereas Joseph Hampton Fitzgerald is accomplished in only one. Long before the evolution of ape into man, Caruso and his kin were taking to the skies, but Joe can manage flight only if he boards an airplane. If Caruso were free to do as he pleases, he would show Mr. Herculean Pecs just how special he is. He would hover inches above his rival's surfboard as he rode the waves, then would surf alongside him on the frond of a palm tree, thereby outshining him again. Crouching down on Clarissa's shoulder, Caruso extends his wings, listing from side to side with the rise and fall of her gait.

She lets him into his cage. "Let me get things started," she says after he settles on his perch, "then I'll come back out here to see you."

She never once complimented him on his surfing technique. In truth, she took no notice of him at all. She is harder to impress than any hen of any species of bird. His cage door clacks shut, and he waves good-bye with a fretful flutter of his wings.

Her demeanor changes on her way to the kitchen. With each step, she forgets a little more about Caruso. Out of sight, out of mind, he thinks while he watches her Reeboks land purposefully against the terrace bricks. She draws open the glass-paneled door and passes through. Deserting him for her own special world of stocks and sauces, condiments and marinades, hors d'oeuvres and stuffings—a universe of flavors distinctly foreign to his provincial tastes. He watches her from his perch while she twirls around the kitchen, her hands as fast-moving as the great dusky swifts of Argentina jetting through the thick curtains of Iguazu Falls to nest on the rocky ledges behind it.

She glides over to the refrigerator, from which she scoops out a handful of cilantro, jalapeño peppers, scallions, and limes, and deposits them on the worktable. Then, she moves to another brace of shelves, just off the hallway next to the inside door, where she seizes a bottle of hot red-pepper sauce. Retracing her steps, she sets the bottle down, leans over, reaches beneath the worktable, and comes back up with two ripe red tomatoes and a bulb of garlic in her large palm. A flash of sunlight, reflected off the stainless steel stove, beams through the extensive glass panels and blinds him. Just as he is about to look away, a mass of dark clouds snuffs out the light to reveal Joseph Hampton Fitzgerald, sidled up beside her.

Betrayal! Betrayal! Caruso thinks, his heart racing, pumping jealousy through his feathers.

"Envy and jealousy are the death knells of happiness," the old man had said. "Envious and jealous, Iago convinced Othello that his beautiful, loyal wife was being unfaithful to him. Finally, Othello strangled her in a green-eyed rage. I confess that I envy Pascal and that I'm jealous of Olivia's love for him, but I could never hurt the woman I adore," he added thoughtfully. "Only the one who hurts her." Still, Caruso had never seen him wound Pascal in the name of love.

Slipping her hand into her pocket, Clarissa takes out another hairnet. Tiptoeing upward, she arranges it meticulously over Joe's blond locks. Her throat quivers with the onslaught of a giggle—that delicious giggle, once reserved for Caruso. She smiles, her teeth gleaming in the light. Placing her hand on Joe's shoulder, she directs his attention to the Viking stove and to the rack of stainless-steel cookware hanging from the ceiling near it. Never before has she given a *date* a private tour of her kitchen. Not even fat-lipped Burt, who—for reasons Caruso still can't fathom—lasted longer than the others. Not even pretty, artistic Oliver, who would have appreciated its design.

Quivering, Caruso follows the trajectory of her finger as she points out the sturdy counter, the three-basin sink, and the commercial refrigerator along the adjoining wall. "Claaa-risss-a!" he cries, strangling the perch with his toes as she leans toward Joe, gently tucking loose strands of his hair beneath the fine-meshed net.

Grinding his beak, Caruso closes his eyes to the sight of them.

He is sailing above Kakadu National Park, dipping his wings to the tiny bee-eaters, finches, flycatchers, and ducks. He admires the floodplains, streams, and billabongs and envies the nesting birds. He spots an Australian stork, with whom he would gladly trade places, then—in the distance—a wedge-tailed eagle flying toward him. Panicked, he veers in the opposite direction, heading for the Timor Sea, with its serene turquoise water. He inhales the soothing breeze and tastes the salt on his mallet-shaped tongue. He shoots over the swells toward the shoreline, where Clarissa, her red hair ablaze in the sunlight, is wading through a shallow tidal pool. His eyes scroll down her creamy body, from her handsome face to her small feet, and fixate on her toenails, flashing bright orange in the water like tiny tropical fish. Instantly, he catches sight of the stonefish lurking in the sandy bottom. Her heel sinks into its lethal spine, and, terrified, he whips his eyelids open to the two of them again.

She is holding up a metal whisk while Joe is slanting forward, flicking out his goanna-like tongue, licking the salsa off it. They speak, their lips shifting silently. She sets the whisk on the worktable and turns around. He pushes his face against her long swan neck and begins to kiss it, nuzzling upward to her papaya-seed mole. That is Caruso's mole. He is the one who is first and foremost a *seed lover*, not Joe.

His eyes smarting, Caruso pivots away from them in the direction of Clara's Bakery, where a tall, stout man is emerging from the back entrance, happily whistling a tune, shambling over the dusty lot toward a blue delivery van. Is his joy justified? Caruso wonders. Is his cozy cottage really the happy home he believes it is?

He hears footsteps behind him. Next, their voices. He freezes, afraid to face them. But then she giggles coquettishly, and instinctively he pivots around and is confronted by the spectacle of them passionately kissing—billing and cooing—with closed eyes and lips pressed hard together.

Those lips are his, Caruso thinks. That is his mouth, his neck, his mole.

Clarissa takes a small step back and smiles raptly at Joe. They talk some more, so softly Caruso can't make out their words. Again, she giggles, tilting her head charmingly to one side, before they move on, her hips brushing against his legs as she sways over the terrace. She, with a brimming basket of tortilla chips. He, with a red clay bowl.

Seized by a sudden impulse, Caruso lunges off his perch, yanks up the latch, and swoops out the open door, keeping his flight low to feign clipped feathers. His crest is like an Indian headdress, his shriek a cry of war, as he slams against his rival's chest.

"Shit!" Joe says when the bowl flips up and over, flinging red salsa into the air and breaking into fragments against the bricks.

"Caruso!" Clarissa yells as the basket plummets from her fingers.

Caruso lands in an avalanche of tortilla chips.

"Bad bird, escaping from your cage like that," she scolds him. She pulls a dish towel from the waistband of her pants and comes toward Caruso, crunching the chips beneath her Reeboks. Squatting, she wraps the dish towel around his torso and carries him back to his cage. With brusque, jerky movements, she secures the door and double-checks the latch. "Why, you've got salsa all over you," she coos, and for a fleeting instant Caruso thinks the concern in her voice is for him. That is, until she shifts slightly and bends toward Joe. "I hope you're sorry, Caruso," she says sternly while she—ever so tenderly—dabs the salsa off his cheeks with her finger.

Sorry. Sorry only that the salsa isn't the scoundrel's blood, he thinks. Crooking up his leg, he tucks his beak into his back feathers and slips into a deep, unrepentant sleep.

"I STILL CAN'T BELIEVE IT," Sallie says, her loud pitch startling his eyelids open. She is wildly waving her hands, speaking to Devon on the walkway outside the barroom door. "There he was, right smack in the kitchen, salsa all over him, talking to the staff like they were his best friends. I mean," she says, in a voice that could grate peel off a lemon, "what would the health department think? Thank God he's finally gone."

"It was an accident. What's the big deal?" Devon says with a lopsided grin.

"The deal is, I work very hard."

"Clarissa works harder than any of us," Devon says. "Besides, they cleaned up their mess—every speck of the salsa and all of the chips."

"Well, she didn't clean up last Tuesday." Sallie sniffs resentfully. "When I came in early the next morning, Rick had me picking up broken pieces of porcelain on the kitchen floor. Clarissa did the breaking, so she should've picked them up. Anyhow, that's not the point. The point is Joe's not supposed to be here while she's working."

"It's her kitchen. He was wearing a hairnet. What's the problem?"

"Excuses, excuses...I bet you have a crush on her, too," Sallie harrumphs as she wheels around, her cassowary feet thumping toward the linen table near Caruso's cage. "You see?" she says, her eyes like X-rays piercing through him.

Caruso stiffens.

"I warned you, didn't I?" she says. Grabbing a tablecloth, she unfolds it with a flap of her arms. It parachutes, alighting on the glass top in front of her.

He ducks his head under his wing.

She clumps over to where he is. "Are you hiding from me?" she asks, dipping down to look up at him.

He peeks out. She's clearly not sexy, he thinks.

"I told you she was fickle," she says, still crouching. "Loves *you* one minute but can't stay away from *him* the next 'cause he's one of the *bad boys*. Believe me, I know."

Caruso lifts his head. Not all of them have been bad boys, he thinks as Oliver fills his mind. Before he met Oliver, he had always been able to tell the difference between a male and a female Homo sapiens. It seemed so obvious, as opposed to differentiating between a Sulphur-crested Cockatoo hen and cock. That's because they look identical, the color of their eyes being the only trait that distinguishes them. But therein lies the problem. The eye color in each gender is so diverse that it's impossible for humans to use it as a way of sexing them. The first time Caruso saw Oliver, he was as confused as any person trying to determine the sex of a cockatoo.

A man or a woman? Caruso had pondered while he stared at Oliver, who was sipping iced tea on the blue chaise longue in the sunroom. First, he checked out the skin, smooth as a woman's. The yam-colored curls were girly, too. Small gold loops hung from both earlobes, and little yellow flowers were embroidered along the outside edges of the jeans. Beneath the pink knit shirt, the chest was flat, meaning nothing really, since Beryl's was flat also.

"Oliver, this is Caruso. Caruso, this is Oliver." Clarissa introduced them as soon as she liberated him from his cage. Still flummoxed, Caruso wobbled along her arm to get a closer look. That was when he clearly saw the Adam's apple, small as a wild plum, and the peachy fuzz on the chin and cheeks, but instead of feeling threatened, he had felt relieved. Oliver was many things, but a bad boy he most definitely wasn't.

"I'm still rooting for you, Caruso," Sallie says, rising to her full height. He stares hard at her, and she stares back. "You're wondering *why*, aren't you?" She stands there, speechless for several seconds, then says, "'Cause we're the same—me and you. We both get hurt real easy. Clarissa might dump you for a bad boy, but I always get dumped for a pretty girl. I feel pain like you do. What pain has Clarissa ever gone through?"

How about all the hurt her brother heaped upon her? Caruso thinks.

"She doesn't know what pain is because she's never felt it," an exultant Sallie says. "And why? Because she's pretty, and pretty girls have it easy. If you were my bird, I'd never toy with your feelings. I would have already sent Mr. Joseph Hampton Fitzgerald packing. I would get rid...of...him..."

Rid...of...him, Caruso muses, no longer mindful of her words.

Twelve

HOURS PASS BEFORE CARUSO HEARS THEM pecking good night on the deck, the darkness through the windows as thick as chocolate icing on a cake. She almost never takes him with her to Crab Cakes anymore and comes home every night a little bit later than the night before.

Joe's sandals clunk down the deck steps; her Reeboks squish through the kitchen and into the sunroom. Caruso squawks at her, but she says nothing back. He tries again. "Hello, Caruso," she answers in her miles-away voice as she switches on the overhead light.

She walks over to him, and he instinctively lowers his head. Sticking her ring finger through the bars, she caresses his neck, but her touch feels cold and mechanical. A few weeks back, she would have released him from his cell and spent some meaningful time with him before heading off to bed, but not now. It isn't fair, he thinks; she's punishing him for being bad, although she loves the *bad boy* in Joe.

"I'm tired," she says, withdrawing her finger. She yawns loudly, opens the bottom drawer of the painted chest, and removes the baby blanket. She wishes him *sweet dreams*, in a tone so impersonal he could be a hamster, before draping the baby blanket over his cage. The light clicks off. Her feet pad down the hallway.

Restless with thoughts of her, he knows he'll be wide awake all night, while she'll continue sleepwalking in a lovesick dream. He hikes up his leg and burrows his beak beneath his back feathers. Where did they go tonight after Crab Cakes closed? he muses. Did they take a leisurely walk through the quiet streets of the village, or did she have a glass of wine with him in his room at Blackbeard's Lodge? Is their relationship—as Beryl had asked her—serious? He shakes his head, rejecting the notion. There was no ring on her finger when she rubbed his neck. The two are only friends. And after Joe returns to law school, she will forget him, same as the others.

He listens to crickets scritching beyond the window, to waves breaking against the shore, to a wild pony neighing in the distance. A night bird cries out, and he counts the calls. One. Two. Three. Four. Five. Six. Seven. His way of counting sheep. His way of not thinking about her. Eight. Nine. Abruptly the calls cease. He jerks his head up and opens his eyes to silent darkness. Will he ever be able to sleep again? From now on, will insomnia chase him, the way it had often chased Theodore Pinter?

"I can't sleep, Caruso," the old man had said, removing the coverlet from his cage with one hand and tugging the lamp chain with the other. Startled, Caruso blinked into the intrusive light. "I can't sleep," he repeated, rubbing his eyes, murky-looking without his glasses. "I can't sleep because my mind won't let me. All night, I've been agonizing over those missed opportunities when I let Olivia slip through my fingers. All night, torturing myself, playing the Monday-morning quarterback." He coughed wearily. "I've been berating myself like this forever," he went on, "punishing myself for those times I let her get away, but, just minutes ago, it came to me. Only two of them really mattered. After

Pascal transferred to Groton, then twenty years later when Olivia taught ballroom dancing."

Caruso sidestepped toward the lamplight to see the old man better. "The day Pascal left for boarding school, I was beside myself with glee," he said, his face suddenly lively. "It was my first big chance to take her away from him forever, and believe me, Caruso, I gave it my best shot. She'd come over to my house after school, and we'd gossip for hours, like we once did. In some ways, Olivia was as lonely as I was. We didn't have siblings, but we had each other to be with. She shared so much with me—trivial thoughts but important ones, too. Said she wanted to be stronger than her mother. Vowed she'd never let any man dictate to her. 'Oh, Teddy,' she'd tell me, 'you're so easy to talk to.' And it wasn't a one-way conversation, Caruso, if that's what you're thinking." Caruso vehemently shook his head. "She asked me questions also. Wanted to know if I got on well with my parents, if my mother was as passive as hers, if I liked reading poetry.

"I can see the question in your eyes, Caruso. Yes, it was Olivia who introduced me to Emily, even though we were much too young to understand her poems. Still, we discussed them as if we did. For months, everything was great between us," he said in a pensive voice, massaging the back of his neck with his sturdy fingers. "On the weekends, she and I went to the movies, ate popcorn from one bag, sipped Coca-Cola through two straws in the same bottle. We took hay rides, bobbed for apples at Suzanne Winters's Halloween party, celebrated Thanksgiving at my house, finished it off with sweet-potato pie at hers. I invited her to the fall dance, and we danced together all evening. That night on her front porch, I kissed her for the very first time. Just one kiss, but I still remember the sweetness of her lips. For days afterward, I was ecstatic, but a few days later I came crashing down when Pascal finally wrote her. He was coming home for Christmas.

"I endured the holidays like an alcoholic swearing off liquor. I craved the sight of her. I longed for our daily talks, but she was with him. That was when I began to watch her. Each time she crossed in front of this window, I would feel connected to her again. As soon as Pascal left for Massachusetts, I worked even harder to win her back. The months passed quickly. On April seventeenth, her birthday, I gave her a bouquet of her favorite flowers—not daisies, her birth flower, as you might expect, but a dozen long-stemmed pink roses. 'I want to put them in water,' she bubbled girlishly, her face glowing as she held them up to her nose and breathed in. Cradling them against her chest, she started for the kitchen. Within seconds, she was back, carrying a vase with the roses in it. After setting it on the coffee table, she smiled warmly and came toward me. I anticipated another tender kiss. She held out her hand. 'Look, Teddy,' she said, wiggling her ring finger. 'Pascal sent me this. Now we're officially going steady.' I gazed at the ring, a diamond chip in it, the bitter taste of defeat in my mouth."

Theodore Pinter was quiet for several minutes. "They caught me off guard," he said at last. "Ironical, isn't it? He managed to stay only a year at Groton. Couldn't adjust to the cold climate. Couldn't handle the school's austerity, its muscular Christianity, its strict rules. Returned wearing that silly blazer, with a hint of New England blue blood in his voice, and latched on to Olivia like a magnet. Six years later, they were married in the Duke Chapel, and I knew I'd lost her for good. Then, after twenty years, I was given another chance.

"She was teaching ballroom dancing at Arthur Murray's. Suzanne Winters told me she had lost another baby and wanted to dance her grief away. Arthur Murray's," the old man repeated nostalgically. He began to pace in front of Caruso's cage. "Immediately, I signed up for all of her classes. The American Smooth dances were her specialty, and the Argentinian tango was the one she loved best. As we tangoed across the floor, I unleashed my pent-up passion. With each push and pull, I felt some relief.

"During those months, she opened up to me bit by bit, like she had when we were young. She told me that Pascal desperately wanted a son. With each miscarriage, he grew a little more distant from her. But the last one, from which she almost died, changed everything, she said. She woke up and saw him beside her hospital bed, silently weeping, and for the first time in a long while, she knew he cared."

Theodore Pinter looked straight at Caruso and unloosed a snuffle of laughter. "He cared," he repeated in a tone that was both sad and acerbic. "He cared...when I absolutely adored her, when I was the one doing the tango with her, pressing my cheek against hers, jerking it away as though she'd just slapped me, but loving her enough to forgive her and hold her close again.

"And then she was pregnant. Quitting her job, she said. She wished her students well, and they wished her well back, but I refused to let her off that easy. Foolish idea it was, but it was my time to act. Damn politeness. Damn friendship. For once, I would embrace passion—totally. Not only my passion for her but also for her baby, if it meant I could have her. I was determined to make the three of us a family. I would hold on to hope—meld *her* hope and *my* hope into *our* hope at last. So I asked her to tango. She put on Carlos Gardel, and we glided over the floor, performing the intricate movements, sustaining the poses of lust and caution like we had so many times before."

The old man held out his arms, dramatically moving to and fro, as though he were dancing with Olivia. "When she tried to pull away from me, in that choreographed interplay of fire and ice, I clutched her close—pressing her breasts against my chest, tasting the honey of her breath—until our bodies were needle and thread. At that moment, I caught sight of him. His hands were cupped around his face as he glared at us through the studio window. He banged a possessive fist against the glass. Startled, she turned around, saw him, and broke away from me.

"I watched him as he argued with her on the walkway. The muscles in his thick neck were straining. His mouth was spread thin with indignation. But then she brushed past him, her heels clicking rapidly toward the entrance, choosing me...choosing me finally. With hope and courage, I rushed toward the door, but he must have said something to her, for just as I drew it open, she pivoted quickly and went running back to him, leaving me there—alone.

"Later on, I heard that she lost that baby, too—it was a boy—even though she carried it longer than the others. The depression that hit her afterward put her in the hospital for months. Eight years passed. Her parents retired to Roanoke Island. She and Pascal moved into her childhood home, but I stood my ground. She had really hurt me. I didn't follow her then. Rather, I began my own healing process. I started to date again."

Theodore Pinter closed his eyes and bent his tall, thin frame over. "Still, though, I kept up with her through Suzanne." Plinking open his eyes, he brought himself back up. "Oscar Wilde was right. 'Memory is the diary we all carry about with us,'" he quoted, his tone reflective. "If not for my memories of her, I would have sunk into despair."

Memories or despair. Where is the choice in that? Caruso thinks, staring wild-eyed into the darkness. He wants neither. To hell with misery, he thinks. To hell with those significant sufferings that build character. To hell with the acceptance of defeat. Damn hope! He will not wear it like a life vest. For the word itself acknowledges the possibility of failure. No, he wants certainty. Only victory for him, he vows.

Thirteen

BABY STUFF, CARUSO THINKS, scooping the yellow rattle between his toes, flinging it out the cage door. It rolls beneath the table, the ugly yellow out of sight. A blight on his bower, an insult to his love for her. But what does it matter, he thinks, since she spends all of her time in Joe's lair—an ordinary room at Blackbeard's Lodge.

When a prism of red hues shoots through the doorway and seizes his attention, he knows what he must do. Rather than fruitlessly pining over lost love, he will do what the bowerbird does. He will transform his plain cage into a nest of beauty and win her back. Beryl once said that red was passion. Embrace passion, embrace red, Caruso thinks, flying into the kitchen. He opens his beak, takes hold of the scarlet glass marble on the windowsill above the sink, glides back to his cage, and sets it on the brim of his feeder. Sunlight strikes it, and it explodes into a rainbow of reds. Yes, this will be his path to victory.

He pivots around, searching for another color. On the floor beneath the blue chaise longue is a deep purple plume from her feather duster. Purple is the color of royalty, he says to himself as he wobbles over to it. Red is wild passion, he thinks, while purple is suppressed desire. He considers which is worse: a hedonistic life of pleasure, or one in which all pleasure is denied. Both are equally unattractive, he decides. He plucks up the purple feather, rushes back, and plunges it into the mound of pellets in his food dish. When the purple plume brushes seductively against the red marble, he is entranced by the sight.

He makes straightway for her bedroom. From her dressing table, he selects a plum ribbon and drapes it artfully through the bars of his cage. Minutes later, he spots a string of ruby-and-wine Mardi Gras beads beside her jewelry box on the dresser. He loops them from the cage's high ceiling to create a canopy over his bower of love.

Back in the kitchen, he tears the leaves off purplish-red basil in a jelly jar of water on the worktable and lines his nook with their pungent smell and alluring color. After that, he pries open a vial of saffron threads and sprinkles a runway of them over the white linoleum in front of the stand upon which his cage sits. On top of this, he empties a box of purple bath-oil beads, which he found in the bathroom vanity.

He thinks long and hard about the finishing touches. Inside his cage, he arranges and rearranges a scrap of violet cellophane, a magenta eraser, two cherry-red jawbreakers, and a vermilion barrette, until he has created a harmonious flow of purple and red shades.

It is almost there, he thinks, surveying his handiwork from the T-stand perch. Still, he should add one last flourish. Scanning the sunroom, he dismisses a crimson leather bookmarker on the table because it is too vulgar, too coarse for her refined taste. What he needs now is something delicate and beautiful—his pièce de résistance that will take her breath away. It is then he remembers the Tyrian-purple orchid in the living room. She had bought it in Wilmington last year.

She had been cheerful that day, her steps springy as they strolled down the sidewalk, bougainvillea flourishing in large clay pots along the street. Behind them, the river was coppery in the bright sunlight. Every so often, she would hoist up his carrier cage to afford him a better view of the square. "Isn't it fun to get away, Caruso?" she would ask him, and he would answer her with a squawk. Without warning, she came to a halt in front of a flower shop window, exploding with orchids of every type and color. She stood there staring at them, her mouth agape. "I want that one," she had said in wonder, pointing at a stem of Tyrian-purple flowers, "to remind me of the exceptional woman I hope to bloom into one day."

Today he will refresh her memory, he tells himself as he teeters down the hallway, rounds the corner, and casts his eyes over the orchid's bluish-red petals shimmering—fine as gossamer—on the end table. She had blossomed because of him. She had blossomed for him, Caruso thinks, ascending without hesitation to the marble top. Gently, he snips off the stem of flowers, flies back to his cage, and places it in his water dish. Floating there, it is his Venus rising from the sea. It is the exceptional woman she wishes to be.

Perched on the T-stand, he waits eagerly for her footfalls. Before long, he hears them on the wooden deck. How delighted she'll be when she beholds his handiwork and realizes he's an artist, same as she!

"Caruso!" she says, widening her eyes when she sees him on the T-stand.

"Clarissa," he coos, holding his head up high.

"How did you get out?" she asks, taking a step toward him.

"Claaa-risss-a," he coos again.

She shifts toward his cage.

Finally, she'll see it, he thinks, his chest feathers puffed up with pride.

"I know I locked you in." She moves across the floor, the purple bath-oil beads popping beneath her sandals, but she doesn't hear them. Leaning over, she peers through the open door. "What on earth have you done?" she asks him.

"Is he in trouble again?" Joe says from the kitchen doorway.

"I don't understand," she murmurs, shaking her head. "All this mess," she says, touching the basil, the beads, the royal purple feather from her duster.

"Claaa-risss-a," he tries, but she ignores him.

"Oh, no!" she suddenly moans, the distress in her voice slapping him hard in the face. "My beautiful orchid," she says, caressing its silky petals with her fingers. "It was...so...beautiful, and now..." Her voice trails off. She draws in a long sigh of disappointment and wheels toward him. "How could you?" she says through clenched teeth.

"Claaa-risss-a," he pleads.

"What's that sound, that smell?" Joe says, walking over.

"Bath-oil beads," she says, glancing down. Squatting, she presses her index finger against the floor and holds it up to her face. "And about twenty dollars of saffron," she says, slowly rising.

"I'll be damned if that's not color-coordinated!" Joe says, peering into his cage. He turns toward Caruso. "Hey, buddy," he says with a disbelieving grin, "you are one smart bird—maybe even a smart gay bird."

Mocking me again, Caruso thinks, hissing.

"Both of you, knock it off," Clarissa warns them. "Come here, you," she says, bristling with recrimination. She stomps over the floor toward him.

"Go slow," Joe says. "He seems upset."

"Well, then," she says, "he can calm down in his tacky, fucked-up cage."

Words like daggers, Caruso thinks.

She reaches out and tries to catch him, but he quickly flees to the far end of the T-stand.

"I said, *come here*," she says and is about to grab for him again when Joe comes up behind her, seizes her arms, and yanks them back.

His crest flared in outrage, Caruso swoops off the T-stand, determined to protect her. Screeching, he scurries across the floor, aims his sharp beak at Joe's big toe, and bites down.

"Shit!" Joe yells, yanking his foot back, revealing a splotch of blood on the white linoleum.

With his beak wide open, Caruso moves menacingly forward, poised to bite once more.

"Caruso—no!" Clarissa cries.

The anguish in her voice lassoes him, and he is brought to a standstill—the feathers on his cheeks stained a passionate red.

Fourteen

CARUSO CAN STILL TASTE JOE'S BLOOD on his black-knobbed tongue, filling his crop with nectar. Victory is sweet! he thinks, the lingering thrill of the fight making him shiver. Impulsive, his reaction was. He didn't think about it. Didn't waffle. The instant Joe grabbed her arms and jerked them back, Caruso attacked. Like the hand of Warramurrungundji, he had struck decisively, defending her against the bully.

As a fledgling, he had been too terrified to fight the men who threw the net over him. Later on, at the pet store, he had almost gone to battle with an Umbrella Cockatoo over a pinecone, but, in the end, he had not wanted it enough to exchange blows. Many times, he had watched his parents risking their lives to protect him from snakes, marsupials, and once from a hawk who tried to snatch him from the air while he was learning how to fly. With beaks agape and wings extended, they had targeted the hawk like a missile and chased him off. Not until yesterday was Caruso's *cockhood* tested, and he had prevailed—attacking hard and fast, unlike Theodore Pinter, whose endless analysis of every situation diluted the fuel of his fury before it could combust. How satisfied Caruso feels, having reacted spontaneously without thinking of the consequences!

His chest pumped up with prideful feathers, he sits for hours on his perch, reliving his moment of glory. It had been a pitched battle, marked by the penetrating smell of adrenaline, the spine-tingling cries of war. What a fierce creature he was as he erected his gold crown of feathers and let forth his piercing screech! He replays the scene in his mind and distinctly remembers Joe saying, "Go slow. He seems upset," turning Caruso into the enemy, but he had not bought into this fiction. His wings spread wide and tail fanned out, he had dived off the T-stand. Scuttling over the floor, he had zeroed in on Joe's big toe and wielded his beak like a knight with a sword. I'm her bird-at-arms, he thinks, closing his eyes, dizzy with visions of his courage.

Bird-at-arms, he dubs himself.

Caruso. Houdini. Main man. Human names, given to him by humans. Did his parents have a name for him also? he muses. Did they coo it when they fed him? Did they cluck him to sleep with it at night? Who and what is he anyway? he wonders. Is he a bird, pretending to be a man who loves a woman? Or is he a man living inside a bird's body, in love with a red-headed Eclectus hen? Does he adore Clarissa, or does he only want to possess her? Is he, not she, the pet owner, trying to turn their cozy cottage into her cage? Neither bird nor man is he, he thinks forlornly, but some bewildered creature caught between the two species, as grotesque as a griffin, unable to bark with his beak.

Fifteen

THE DAY AFTER WHAT CLARISSA WOULD ONLY REFER to as *the incident*, Joe had wrapped thick wire around his cage door and looped it to the metal frame, wounding Caruso's pride, making him feel no better than a prisoner. He could cut through the wire with his beak and escape, but he doesn't dare. For two days now, he has been plucking out the feathers on his body beneath his wings to mitigate his grief, then hiding them among the preened ones on the cage's wire-meshed bottom. Not that she would even notice them, he thinks, as the back door bangs and the sweethearts waltz through, nodding at him but not speaking, making a beeline for the living room, away from his prying eyes. Yet every word they say drifts down the hallway to him.

A pang of self-doubt rakes through him as she giggles at another one of Joe's lousy jokes. Caruso grinds his beak in pain. She giggles again before beginning her litany of grievances against him.

"It's about trust," she is saying. "Ever since *the incident*, I've lost my trust in him."

Lost her trust in him, Caruso thinks, all at once so vulnerable he fears he will disappear. Jerking up his left wing, he parts his beak, aims, and plucks out a feather. First comes the initial sting, followed by blessed relief.

"I'll be limping for a month," Joe says with a laugh.

"Spoiled rotten," she says.

Caruso buries his head in his wing feathers and flattens them against his ear coverts in an effort to block out her voice, but her words worm their way in.

"He did it out of jealousy," she says. "For two years, he's had me all to himself. Now he has to share me, and he can't stand it."

"I didn't realize he could be so aggressive."

"A spoiled-rotten little brat," she insists emphatically.

Such betrayal, Caruso thinks.

"I'm a threat to him lately," Joe says, "but hopefully he'll change his mind about me."

Never, Caruso vows. The old man had never changed his mind about Pascal.

"He'll never change," Theodore Pinter had said, pointing at Pascal opening the door of his black Mercedes. "See that suit he has on."

Caruso had tilted forward on his perch and looked at the enemy's gray armor. "He bought it in Hong Kong last spring. Went there on a business trip for his law firm and returned with half a dozen of them—European cuts in silk and linen—but he brought nothing back for her," he said, making a zero with his thumb and index finger, holding it up high for Caruso to see. "Zilch," he said, his eyes flashing scornfully. "Not even one of those designer handbags you can get over there for half price, not even a silk scarf or a delicate comb for her hair. That's because he didn't think about her. Out of sight, out of mind. Suzanne Winters told me that Olivia was really hurt about it."

He had paused for several seconds, tapping his foot against the hardwood floor, and then in a sour voice he added, "The man is as thoughtless now as he ever was. He's a narcissist, Caruso. Obsessed with his own needs, oblivious to the needs of others. Totally unaware of how much he hurts her, and I'll never forgive him for that."

"I wonder if *you know who* remembers *the incident*—if he might be feeling a little guilty," Joe says.

"Of course he remembers," she tells him, "but I don't think he's eager to apologize to us."

Please, enough of this *you know who* stuff, Caruso huffs. He remembers, but he refuses to show any sign of weakness. Be more like Clarissa, he tells himself. Never say you're sorry.

"It's scary, really, how much he remembers," she continues. "And how he ends up using it."

"What do you mean?"

"Ruthie, the little girl next door, had a dog."

"Had?"

"She became allergic to him, so her parents gave him away. But he was a cute little mutt. Had a touch of beagle and terrier in him—a Heinz 57 mix. I liked him. His name was Tick, and he was a mellow fellow. That is, until Caruso stepped in."

"Bit him?" Joe says, with a grin in his voice.

"Oh, no," Clarissa says. "It was much worse. Pure, unadulterated mental torture. That's what it was."

"Torture. Really?"

"Really. I'm talking Chinese water torture, maybe worse."

"More aggression from the White Avenger? Please, go on."

"Well...it was a Monday, steaming hot, and I had raised all the windows to let in a breeze off the harbor. I wanted to take a cold shower to cool myself off and was heading down the hallway—clean undies in hand—when I heard Mr. Marshall, Ruthie's daddy, yelling, 'Tick, suppertime!' As I stepped into the bathroom, I spotted Tick through the window, wiggling out from beneath the forsythia hedge along the rear fence, next running frenziedly to the deck. He scrambled up the steps, skidded over the floorboards, and slammed into the back door. But no one was there to let him in. I swished the shower curtain aside, reached into the stall, and cut on the cold water just as Mr. Marshall began to call for Tick again. I caught sight of the little fellow halfway across the yard, pricking up his ears before bounding back to the house. Once more, no one opened the door for him. Curious now, I turned off the faucet and tiptoed down the hallway. 'Tick!' the voice rang out. 'Tick! Tick! Tick!' At the edge of the sunroom, I could see Tick plainly though the low row of windows, insanely scratching the door. I noticed Caruso on the other side of the sunroom, rocking with glee on his perch. And, right then, the culprit exposed himself, squawking loudly, 'It's suppertime, Tick!'"

"Wow!" Joe says. "I didn't know birds were so devious."

Devious, Caruso thinks. The gall of the man.

"No, just bored." Clarissa jumps in to defend him, and Caruso feels grateful for this scrap of support.

"Animals are a mystery to me," Joe says. "We never had pets when I was a kid. Mama thought they were dirty. Last summer, I stayed with a family in Mexico that had a lot of pets, but I wasn't there long enough to really get into their heads."

"And you..." she begins cautiously. "Do you feel like your mama does about animals?"

"Not really," Joe says after a brief silence. "I don't think they're dirty, if that's what you mean."

156

"You might change your mind if you experienced a molt. Now, that's a mess. Sheaths, powder dust, and feathers all over the floor. Those little pinfeathers are sharp when they come in. They drive Caruso crazy. So I remove the sheaths off those he can't reach since he doesn't have a mate to do it for him."

"It must feel itchy, like growing a beard."

"Uh-huh. He's miserable and cranky."

"Poor guy," Joe says, as though commiserating with him. "He's way too proud to put up with that."

"See, you're getting into your best buddy's head," she says.

"Like when I finally understood the eccentricities of my family really weren't that weird."

Joe will never understand his family of birds, Caruso thinks.

"Speaking of eccentric families—when would you like to meet them?" Joe asks her.

"Soon," Clarissa replies, "but, you know, I can't leave Rick at the height of the season."

"At the end of summer then?"

"I'd love that," she says.

Rattled, Caruso stiffens on his perch. She wants to meet his family— another step to the altar, he thinks, his legs shaking, his heart slamming against his chest. Suddenly, his anguish is so pure, his sense of prophecy so vivid, that they override his need to be in control, and, forgetting himself, he recklessly yanks out a feather—one in full view, from the center of his breast. Why is he doing this? he puzzles. In his secret heart of hearts, does he want her to find him out? Is he willing now to settle for her pity?

Sixteen

A WEEK LATER, she is pulling out his poop tray when she spots one of his perfectly formed wing feathers, which he plucked out yesterday. She finds another from his belly, a dozen from his shoulders, and five more from his breast until there is a nest of them in her palms.

"Caruso," she says, holding her hands up high, parting them. "My poor darling," she says as the feathers cascade like dandelion fluff to the floor. Catching her lower lip between her teeth, she looks guiltily at him. "I didn't know you were so unhappy," she says as she uncoils the wire from his cage door.

Her pity confuses him even more, and he emits a long, protracted cry. "Sad Caruso," she says, drawing the door open and presenting her arm to him. He steps up, his toes uncertain. She brings him out into the sunroom, turning him this way and that, her azure blue eyes scrutinizing his body, her hard stare belying the tenderness in her face. "What's this little spot on your breast?" she says, studying him carefully, then lifting his right wing. "Not under here," she mumbles to herself. She lifts the other wing and gasps. "My sweet boy, you've been busy, haven't you?" she says, concerned. She taps her shoulder, and he wobbles up the slope of her arm. She purses her lips for a kiss, but he holds back.

"Goodness, look at the two of us," she says. "Both of us acting like strangers. It's Monday. How about we spend a little time together?"

He answers her with a blank, watery stare.

"We'll take a bike ride, drop by Biff's, and see Beryl."

He remains still and silent.

"I'm calling Joe right now. Gonna tell him I'll see him tomorrow. Today, I'm all yours."

She returns him to his cage and pads down the hallway to the living room. He can hear her muted voice as she speaks and wonders if she'll keep her promise, but, true to her word, they leave soon after she hangs up.

When they pedal by a young woman in a sundress and an older man in cut-off jeans, Caruso can't decide if the two are friends or lovers. Nothing is clear to him these days. Except the cloudless, white sky. The sight of Silver Lake Harbor glimmering in the distance momentarily lightens his spirits, and he feels a reprieve from the sadness engulfing him lately—but then he hears a car horn blasting as a bright red convertible passes, almost forcing them off the road into a clump of southern sweet grass. He is unsettled again. "Damn dingbatters!" she says, jerking the handlebars to the right, regaining control.

They cycle on. In the library parking lot, three of the local boys are playing a game of Ringer, reminding Caruso of the old man's stories about his marble-shooting days. As usual, they wave at him, but this morning Caruso feels too low to flap his wings back. More cars pass, heat rolling off their fenders. The crape myrtles, all abloom, look like pink-flowered sunbonnets, but, though bright and cheerful, they don't delight Caruso like they used to.

Clarissa takes a few more turns, and presently they are cycling along Silver Lake Drive toward Biff's Dockside Store. In the harbor, the seagulls are shrieking behind the shrimp boats coming in to dock. Their voracious, insistent cries annoy him. All his life, he has snubbed this no-count bird. Moochers, wastrels, thieves, he calls them. Every seagull he has ever known was like this—the black-headed gulls digesting the putrid leftovers of men's meals in garbage dumps; the greater black-backed gulls stealing the eggs of razorbills and plovers from their nests on the edges of cliffs; all of the lazy seagulls swooping down to freeload on any escaping fish from the baggy bills of brown-feathered pelicans after they've surfaced.

When he first came to Ocracoke, Clarissa had read *Jonathan Livingston Seagull* to him every night. How he grew to resent the goody, two-web-footed Jonathan, bravely risking failure to make his dreams come true! He would have preferred a book about a cockatoo, and if not a cockatoo, then some other parrot—or even an oystercatcher, if she wanted the protagonist to be a seabird; at least the oystercatcher is industrious enough to do his own fishing, probing his long, orange beak into mud flats for mussels and then using it to smash their shells into pieces.

Watching the seagulls now, circling and screeching, Caruso thinks he might have judged them too harshly. Perhaps they're simply screaming for a little extra attention. Perhaps they feel rejected by the world, too. Lately he wants to throw a tantrum, yell and scream and cry like the seagull, like the little girl next door, but he does not dare because his powerful voice would drive the neighbors to distraction. And if they complained too much, Clarissa might be compelled to give him up.

One day, Caruso had looked on as Ruthie stomped on her mother's prized heirloom hollyhocks until she got the Popsicle she demanded. He could do the same with his beak—could blackmail Clarissa by wreaking destruction with it—but he tried that once with Theodore Pinter, who, without a word, had calmly retrieved the stuffing from the sofa pillow that Caruso had demolished and then ignored him. For three long days, the old man had shunned him, refusing to communicate with him in any way. Bored and lonely, Caruso had been forced to think about his bad behavior, ultimately replacing it with more subtle methods of manipulation.

"You're getting my undivided attention today," Clarissa says, slowing down as she veers onto the weather-beaten pier, the wheels of the bike thunking over the warped planks. At the entrance to Biff's, she comes to a stop. Kicking down the stand, she straddles off the seat and holds out her arm to him. He ascends to her shoulder, his heart definitely not in this visit. She skids open the pocket door. "Hey, girl," she says, poking her head inside.

"Hey, you," Beryl says, glancing up from the *Jacksonville Observer* next to the cash register.

"It's freezing in here," Clarissa says, sliding the door shut.

"I know. I set the air conditioner on high. I best cut it off for Caruso," she says, coming out from behind the counter.

"See how much Beryl loves you," Clarissa says.

"When ya gonna introduce me to your fella?" Beryl asks, the noisy rumble ceasing when she switches the unit off.

"Why, Beryl, you're looking right at him," Clarissa says, winking at Caruso, who crosses over her arm to the counter.

"And a very handsome fella he is, indeed," Beryl adds, scooting rapidly back to her spot beside the cash register.

"Not for long, if he keeps plucking out his feathers."

"I don't see any feathers missing."

"Look under here," Clarissa says, the muscles in her jaw tightening as she lifts up his left wing. "Did most of his plucking where I wouldn't be able to see it."

"*Nastysome*," Beryl says.

"Here's another spot," she says, pointing at his breast with her pinkie.

Embarrassed, Caruso bows his head.

"I had no idea," Clarissa says, "until I found the feathers at the bottom of his cage."

She has no idea about anything, Caruso thinks. For he constantly hides his true self from her. He plays the role of her clownish cockatoo, tirelessly climbing the bars of his cage, or turns himself into Rip Van Cockatoo after she goes to sleep. He is her thoughtful cockatoo, refraining from grinding his beak at night, so as not to wake her. Her grateful cockatoo, pretending to like the bland parrot pellets in his food dish. He keeps the instincts of his species in check—reining in his shrieking, never destroying her possessions with his beak, not once flying off, though he could if he chose to. He is always the companion bird—never the companion.

"He's never plucked before," Beryl says, scraping a fleck of oil paint off her middle finger with her thumbnail. "Why now?"

"It must be Joe," Clarissa says bluntly. "The vet in Wilmington gave him a clean bill of health just a few months back."

Caruso's mind drifts off, looking for solace in memory. After their visit with the avian vet, they had taken a lovely stroll along the river walk. "Fisherman's stew," she had said, stopping in front of a little bistro, breathing in. "Snapper," she said, with another noisy whiff, "lots of garlic, tomatoes, wine, and...what's that?" She sniffed again. "Fennel," she answered with a smile.

They moved on, halting beside a wrought iron fence around a

Spanish-style patio. She held up his carrier cage and pointed. "Look over there near the gate. They're eating she-crab soup. Smells luscious, doesn't it?" Then she pointed to the table in front of them. "Wow!" she exclaimed. "That's not shrimp salad. That's sculpture on a plate." Caruso eyed the shellfish. From a bed of watercress, the shrimp rose upward like a staircase. There were swirls of orange sauce around the plate. He remembers how much her enthusiasm had delighted him, how thrilled she was to see art on a plate.

Before this morning, she thought him magnificent. As beautiful as a statue by Rodin, she once told him. Now he has defiled his body with his beak. A bedraggled cockatoo, he is, his feathers ruffled this way and that.

"He's jealous," Beryl is saying when he comes back.

Yes, jealous, Caruso admits, with a long, despondent caw.

"Clarissa, did you hear that?" Beryl asks her. "He cawed like a crow."

A murder of crows. An unkindness of ravens, Caruso thinks. In no time, he'll be crying like a grackle—the saddest call of all.

"I heard him." Clarissa sighs. "Lately he confounds me, and I'm coming to my wit's end."

The two of them fall into a deep silence.

"I love to work with my hands," Caruso remembers her saying that day months ago as she had leaned against the wharf railing and had looked out over the river. "I like to feel the glossy skin of an onion beneath my fingers when I slice it. To snap broccoli florets off their stems. To mince plump cloves of tangy garlic. I like to taste mashed potatoes, soft as clouds on my tongue. To admire the texture of tomato aspic, sleek as a frozen pond. I like the smooth, clean crack of an egg when I break it against a bowl and the muted thump of a wooden spoon inside an iron skillet."

Upon hearing those words, he'd winced, envisioning himself as an egg in a nest of soft shavings in the hole of a gum tree, his parents keeping him warm and safe from hands like hers, casually cracking his shell against a bowl.

"I like to decorate plates with red nasturtiums and the sugar-frosted petals of a light-pink rose," she went on. "I like to create art on a plate. Work is what makes us happy, Caruso," she had said. "It makes us human."

At this moment, it dawns on Caruso that joblessness might be his problem. After all, he is a bird who has worked hard to make Clarissa happy, and now this is Joe's job.

With a quick snap, Beryl smashes a bluebottle fly lighting on her newspaper. Startled, Caruso jerks back. "Sorry, Caruso," she says as she scoops up the fly with the edge of the swatter. "I just can't stand—hey, Clarissa, look here," she says giddily. "Here's the answer to your problem." She draws her finger beneath a line of bold print and shifts the paper around for Clarissa to read it. "Right here," she bubbles.

"You think?" Clarissa says with an upward glance.

"What do you have to lose?" Beryl says. "Go ahead and give them a call. You can use the phone in Biff's office. He won't mind."

Clarissa takes the classifieds with her to the back of the store.

The Great Mother will sacrifice a fly to help Clarissa, Caruso thinks, but won't sink a surfboard and smash it into bits for him.

"You're a genius," Clarissa says, emerging a few minutes later. And then, before Caruso can squawk good-bye, they are dashing out the door, pedaling along Silver Lake Drive, and weaving down Fig Tree Lane toward their *once-cozy* cottage.

"I know I promised to spend all day with you," she says, unlatching his cage door. "I know I promised to give you my undivided attention, but something has come up."

Another broken promise, another betrayal, he thinks, slumping down on his perch.

"I'm taking the ferry to the mainland, and when I come in tonight, I'll have a great big surprise for you."

A great big surprise, Caruso thinks with a doubtful squawk. What could it be? he wonders. Why must she go all the way to the mainland to get it? His bag of parrot pellets is almost full, and she buys his seeds and peanuts here at Styron's. So why the mainland? Does she want to pick some willow twigs for him to gnaw on? He loves them, but willows don't grow on this tiny island. Or maybe she wants to buy him a gift of gum nuts, which can only be found in Wilmington.

"No feather plucking while I'm gone," she orders him. "Remember, Caruso, you're my main man," she coos before hurrying out the door.

The car sputters and grumbles as she backs out the drive. Is he really her main man? he thinks, his gaze inadvertently landing on the cage door. For the first time in days, she didn't wrap the thick rope of wire around it. Perhaps she trusts him, he thinks, remembering what the old man had said after the shunning was over and Caruso had learned how to control his destructive beak. "Love, Caruso, blooms in the wake of trust," he had told him. Staring at his cage door, free of the wire rope, Caruso wants to believe that love is abloom, once more, in the wake of her newfound trust.

Seventeen

CARUSO HEARS FOOTFALLS IN THE YARD beyond the upraised window. It's late afternoon, not quite sunset, when the heat has bullied its way into every living and nonliving thing. Who could it be? he wonders as feet thump up the wooden steps. The back door whines open, and Caruso freezes.

"Caruso, it's me—Beryl!"

She didn't have to say her name, he thinks, her familiar voice putting him at ease.

"Came to see how you're doing," she says from the doorway.

He greets her with a flap of his wings and a squawk.

"No way for Clarissa to drive to Camp Lejeune and back and not have to take the last ferry," she says, moving toward him.

She went *where*? he thinks.

"You aren't plucking, are you?" she asks, eyeing him from crown to tail.

He vehemently shakes his head.

She unhitches the cage door and peers inside. "No loose feathers and still plenty of food. How about some fresh water?" she asks him as she slips the container from its holder. She shuts him in and starts toward the kitchen.

He hears her twisting on the faucet, then hears water pinging against the metal bowl. She cuts the flow off and comes back. "Nice and cool," she says, opening his door, sliding in his water dish.

He lowers his head for a neck rub, and she obliges him with a paint-smudged finger.

"Powder dust," she says, raising her finger to her mouth, blowing the white film off. "It's everywhere," she says, glancing around. "Clarissa is definitely not into cleaning."

He bobs his head.

"Why don't I do a little dusting," she says. "Keep you company for a while. Kill two birds with one stone."

That aphorism is disturbing, he thinks with a shiver.

She latches his cage door and disappears into the kitchen. Several cabinet doors bang before she shouts triumphantly, "Hey, I found the polish!" She begins with the painted chest, dousing her rag with polish, vigorously buffing the top, until it sparkles spinach-green. After that, she moves on to the table and shines its base and legs and the two chairs beneath it, followed by the chaise longue's oak frame. "Dust free," she says, her tone pleased.

For the life of him, Caruso doesn't understand why she attacked his powder dust with such a vengeance. For he has observed sparrows, through these very same windows, flapping their wings as they bathed in the dusty driveway to rid themselves of parasites.

Without warning, the back door opens with a rasp. "Clarissa, you home already?" a voice shouts.

Joe, Caruso thinks glumly.

"Nope, it's Beryl!" she yells back. Recapping the bottle of polish, she puts it and the dust rag on the floor beside the chaise longue.

His sandals schuss across the linoleum.

"Joe Fitzgerald," he says as he passes through the doorway. "I've heard a lot about you," he says, thrusting forth his calloused hand.

"Beryl Gaskill—in the flesh," she says, taking hold of his palm and shaking it firmly.

The grip of an oyster shucker champion, Caruso thinks.

"Clarissa left a message at Blackbeard's," he explains. "She was going to the mainland and wouldn't get back until late. Wanted me to check in on Caruso."

"Yeah, that's what I decided to do, too."

"What happened?" he asks. "She up and left and didn't give me a reason why."

"It's a secret and a surprise," Beryl says.

"Can't you tell me?"

"I'd rather not say in mixed company," Beryl says, grinning and nodding at Caruso. "But she'll tell ya in the morning."

"Sure, I can wait," Joe says.

"His feeder was full, and I changed his water, but the good news is...no more plucked feathers."

"Plucked feathers? Clarissa didn't tell me about that." He looks hard at Caruso. "Where? I don't see any bald spots."

"Hidden beneath his wing."

"Poor little fella," Joe says, as though he means it. "He's never done that before. How come now?"

"Why do you think?" Beryl asks him. "It's been just the two of them in this cottage for two years."

"I feel like a home-wrecker."

"Ya think so, maybe?" Beryl says with a penetrating stare.

Joe meets her gaze. "I came here to wind down from law school, to surf and bask in the sun. The last thing I was thinking about was a serious relationship. I didn't plan on meeting Clarissa," he says in a calm voice.

"She didn't plan on meeting you either," Beryl says, crimping her lips into a smile. "Clarissa's my best friend," she goes on. "She and Caruso are like family to me. She's finally got some peace in her life, and I don't want that to change."

"I understand. You're her friend, and you want to protect her."

"The way I see it, she and Caruso complement each other," Beryl maintains. "He's her other half, and she is his. I don't want them hurt. So you best think long and hard about your intentions. You need to know where the two of you are heading."

"Could Ocracoke use another lawyer?" He chuckles.

"We already have one, and one's enough," she jokes back.

"Chapel Hill has restaurants, some good ones, too."

"That's exactly what I mean," she says. "A person can't be in two places at once. Right, Caruso?" She walks over to the painted chest and from the bottom drawer pulls out the baby blanket. "Bedtime," she says, draping it over his cage.

Their footsteps fade as the back door closes on their voices, so soft now he can't make out their words. Every so often he hears Joe laughing while they linger on the deck, quietly talking. He'd like to know what they're saying, but, same as a person, a bird can't be in two places at once.

Eighteen

"MORNING, CARUSO," SHE GREETS HIM as she takes the baby blanket off his cage and throws it over the back of the sunroom chair. Her voice is as cheerful as the sunlight flooding in through the open blinds. Last night, she had come in through the front door, seldom used, and gone straightway to her bedroom without letting him know she was home, and he is still miffed at her. Uncurling his leg, he yawns by stretching his left wing and leg downward, while spreading out the left side of his tail. He yawns again, boosting his body with another blast of oxygen.

"You ole sleepyhead," she says, her lips curling upward.

He gives her a dismissive glance and ignores her lovely face, even lovelier without makeup. Her silky arms are swaying gently against her thin yellow nightgown as she babbles sweet nothings to him. Finally she comes to a standstill, her features melding into a contemplative pose.

He fans his wings over his back and stills himself also, clueless as to what is going on.

She clears her throat, fixes her blue eyes on him, and says in a light, chirpy voice, "Your great big surprise is back in my bedroom. Wanna see it, Caruso?"

It would be surprise enough, he thinks, if she would just say that he is the only fellow she loves.

She oscillates down the hallway, the ruffled hem of her gown like a wave breaking around her toes. The bedroom door opens, and he hears a loud, nostalgic racket. Lowering his head, he glues his eyes anxiously on the wire-meshed floor.

"Look, Caruso," she says, her footsteps inching closer.

He breathes in. No whiff of gum nuts or willow twigs in the air, rather a scent from long ago. Confused, he raises his head and spots the small, round cage dangling from her fingers. Bright rays of sunlight bounce off its curved metal bars, blinding him, but in the next instant he clearly sees the pink-feathered chest and neck and the light-gray tail and wings. It is a Rose-breasted Cockatoo. He jerks his head back down, his yellow crest rocketing up in horror.

"A Galah," she tells him.

As if he doesn't know what kind of bird it is. As if she doesn't know that Galahs thrive by the thousands in his native land.

"I bought her because you've been lonely," she explains. "Her family was transferred to Germany, and she needs a new home. What do you think of her, Caruso?"

He closes his eyes in dismay. The word, Galah, means *loudmouth* in Australia.

"Her name is Matilda."

A wild bush cry flies from his throat.

"Okay. Okay," she says coolly. "You need some more time."

He flaps his wings in fury and blindly chomps the air with his beak, and the bird reacts as he expects. She elongates her neck and flattens her feathers in fear.

"Please be nice, Caruso," Clarissa says. "You're scaring her."

He harnesses every bit of his willpower and puts an end to his bad behavior.

"It's all right. We'll try this again later," she says, turning to leave.

He shuts his eyes tightly and doesn't open them until she closes her bedroom door. She has ambushed him, he thinks. Ambushed him, as surreptitiously as an owl snaring a mouse in the night. His legs fold beneath him. Dizzy, he slips off his perch, thumping against the wire-meshed bottom. Pawned him off on another bird, he thinks, because Joe is her main man now.

"I MUST MAKE SOME CHANGES in the cottage," she says, throwing the latch on his cage at Crab Cakes. "You can visit with the staff while I'm gone. They want to spend some time with their favorite fellow. Now, act nice," she reminds him as she closes the cage door. "And remember, no more feather plucking. Those bald patches look nasty," she says before she goes.

This morning, the Galah was forced upon him. This afternoon, the restaurant staff. One second, he's everyone's favorite fellow. The next, her embarrassment. So much for her great big surprise, he thinks bitterly.

"How are you doing, big guy?" Rick asks. Caruso swivels around to face him. "Clarissa says you're not up to snuff, but you look just fine to me. You wouldn't believe the Parmesan sauce I prepared last week," he says, his right eye floating delightfully toward Caruso. "It was my best yet. I began with a Sauce Béchamel—a rich blend of butter, flour, milk, and chicken broth..."

Caruso's thoughts wander as Rick describes every ingredient, every step of the process. Before Joe came into their lives, Clarissa would talk to Caruso in the sunroom after a long day's work. She would tell him what she had cooked, which dishes worked and which ones didn't, but with such vibrant energy that he never missed a word, never wanted to.

"...and then I tossed in the heavy cream, some finely grated Parmesan, a little salt, a dash of freshly milled pepper, a pinch of nutmeg, and my secret ingredient..."

Nothing is so annoying as a secret, Caruso thinks, recalling the banter of Clarissa and Joe over paella that evening of their first date—the secret ingredient in his scrambled eggs and tuna, in Granny's vinegar-raisin pie.

"Mace!" Rick says exultantly, as though he were giving away the most important secret in the history of the culinary arts. He nudges his blond bangs to one side with his fingertips, arches the black eyebrow above his wandering eye, and, in a blissful voice, adds, "Clarissa liked it, said the mace made the sauce much more interesting." A faraway look on his face, he stands there reliving his moment of glory, then fixes his eyes on Caruso and says, "You know, Clarissa's heart is big enough to love two guys at once." Spinning around on the balls of his feet, he retraces his steps over the patio and tugs open the kitchen door.

Caruso scoops up a beak of tepid water, tips his head back, and swallows. Clarissa's heart is only big enough for Joe, he thinks as he looks despondently at the birdseed in his feeder. It is sleep he wants, not food. He longs to draw a curtain on the world and fall into this endless dream:

Clarissa is a Sulphur-crested Cockatoo in the bush of Victoria. He spots her in a gum tree, preening her beautiful feathers. Erecting his magnificent crest, he screeches his love and catches her attention. With his beak, he widens a tree hole to demonstrate his skill at carving a nest. She flies over to inspect it, flaps her wings in approval. He shows his devotion by tenderly grooming her pinfeathers. She does the same for him until they are completely at ease with each other. Ready to mate, she dips down, with her wingtips lowered, and he presses his body against hers. During the brooding season of September, they separate from their flock to find a safe haven for their clutch of eggs. In the trunk of a eucalyptus tree, they find an abandoned woodpecker hole, which they enlarge with their beaks. The shavings fall into a soft nest at the bottom. They take turns keeping their eggs warm until they hatch, then raise their chicks together. In this way, they become paired forever—a couple of cockatoos in love.

"Hi there, Caruso," Pops says, ambling over the pathway from the bar. "What do you think about my new necktie?"

Caruso rocks forward on his perch, scrutinizing the bright yellow background covered with dark blue squares and circles.

"It's a Roaring Twenties tie. A classic. I found it in a consignment shop in Wilmington. Goes well with my suit, doesn't it?"

Caruso opens wide his beak and quickly snaps it shut.

"Yeah, I thought you'd like it. We're the same—me and you. We know what's important. The craftsmanship of a classic timepiece, an antique necklace, or the old stylists when they sing. I know you like Miss Peggy Lee. Clarissa told me. We both love that sexy, sultry voice of hers. Oh yes..." he says, closing his eyelids, as he begins to hum and sway. "'I stood there shivering in my pajamas and watched the whole world go up in flames,'" he says, wrapping his arms around himself, rocking from side to side. "'And when it was all over I said to myself, "Is that all there is to a fire?"'"

For the first time, Caruso fully grasps the meaning of this song, these lyrics he's listened to for years. Is that all there is to love? he wonders.

"'Is that all there is, is that all there is,'" Pops sings, his eyes now open, his voice full of feeling. "'If that's all there is my friends, then let's keep dancing/Let's break out the booze and have a ball/If that's all there is.'" And when he's finished, both he and Caruso are surprised to hear Devon giving him a round of applause.

"Awesome!" Devon says, shaking his head exuberantly, his thick braids flying.

"That was Miss Peggy Lee," Pops tells him.

"Never heard of her."

"One of the great old stylists. Won a Grammy for that song. Randy Newman did the arrangement."

"He's pretty famous," Devon says. "I can hear him in that song. It's—"

"Weird and wonderful," Pops jumps in. "I love it, although I don't feel about life that way. Life is still amazing to me."

The way it once was for me, Caruso thinks.

"What amazes you, Devon?" Pops wants to know.

"Kites," he answers instantly. "I love designing and building them, and then letting them fly."

"Good!" Pops exclaims. "Keep on doing what you love."

"Caruso, my friend," Devon says, coming over to him.

Caruso lowers his head, and Devon gently brushes his fingertips down his neck.

"Gotta party of twelve coming tonight," Pops says. "Wanna help me scrounge up a few extra chairs?"

"Sure," Devon says as they set out for the bar.

"Caruso!" Sallie calls, dashing through the bar door, brushing against Pops and Devon as she clomps toward him. "Clarissa told us about the parrot. Said she bought her for you because you're lonely."

Gingerly, she slips a fingernail between her teeth and nibbles on

176

it. "She didn't have to ask me to talk to you, Caruso. We talk all the time, don't we?"

He bobs his head and waits for the other shoe on her gigantic foot to drop while she spits out a sliver of nail, which sails into his water dish and floats there, light and poisonous as a jellyfish. "The way I see it," she says, narrowing her eyes to slits, "she has her hands full—Crab Cakes and Joe. So she got you a companion to keep you busy."

He cheeps anxiously.

"Didn't I warn you? Didn't I say three's a crowd?" She shoots him a critical look. "And if three's a crowd, what do you think four is?"

Squawkless, he is.

"Four," she says, emphasizing the word, "four makes a family. The two of them are the parents. You and that other bird—the kids."

"Claaa-risss-a," he says soulfully.

"Don't worry, Caruso," Sallie says, softening with the sound of approaching footsteps. "I'll be here for you. I'm still your friend," she says, shifting around to the sight of Manuel. "Your turn," she tells him before leaving, her shoes pounding loud as ever over the bricks.

Not Manuel, Caruso thinks wearily. On good days when he's clearheaded, he's unable to understand his Spanglish. How will he be able, with his mind in such a fog, to understand him now?

Manuel, small and brown as a wren, stops short of his cage. Smiling broadly at Caruso, he doesn't speak but instead begins to juggle the serving spoons in his small hands. They fly through the air, somersaulting above one another, as he agilely catches them. Laughing, he balances on one leg and tips precariously to the side, as though he might tumble over, but doesn't, and Caruso, forgetting his troubles for a moment, bounces with delight. Manuel pauses, pulls the red bandana tied around his forehead over his eyes, and begins to juggle again—the serving spoons like playful birds, dipping, diving, and tumbling—while he plucks them from the sky. When the performance is over, he pushes his bandana up, winks at Caruso, gives him a little bow, and bounds over the patio to the kitchen.

Caruso catches sight of Clarissa, back now, going from one station to another, coring and slicing a red bell pepper into strips on the worktable, stirring and tasting a sauce on the stove, then dressing several chickens on the counter beside the sink. He could be one of those poor chickens, Caruso thinks. Before long, he will be as denuded of feathers as they are and will feel as dead inside as one of their carcasses. And though he doesn't think much of their intellect, chickens deserve more respect than this. Once they were alive and free, not just meat.

Caruso turns his face away, but, seconds later, unable to control himself, he looks back to see Rick inching a spoon toward Clarissa, who, oblivious to it, glances up and points at him beyond the glass panels, her lips silently moving. *Poor Caruso, he's lonely,* he imagines her saying. Again, he turns away. He does not need her pity. Best to close his mind to her, he thinks, folding his leg up, tucking his beak into his back feathers, falling into a deep, dreamless sleep.

BEFORE HE CAN WAKE UP FULLY, she is removing him from the Victorian cage to take him home. Her Reeboks crackle through the desiccated grass. Bleary-eyed, he stares at a blur of yaupon shrubs in the adjoining yard. Mosquitoes buzz near his ear coverts. Close by, a tomcat—that stealthy butcher of birds—yowls. Yet Caruso doesn't flinch. Cats are the least of his worries these days.

She ascends the rickety steps to the wooden deck, pushes open the door, and goes inside. In the sunroom, she clicks on the overhead light. As soon as she unhinges the cage door, he whiffs the faint odor of Galah.

Wary, he eases himself into his refuge, his castle, his sanctuary—as she calls it—and spots beak marks, proof of Clarissa's betrayal, on the stale dog biscuit which he has been ignoring for weeks. She'll stoop to anything, he thinks. While the staff was courting him, she was courting Matilda.

"You know, don't you?" she says, watching him closely as he settles upon his perch. "Please don't be upset with me. Matilda needs to get used to her new cage."

Her new cage. How painful it is for him to hear these words!

"I'll be right back," she says, latching him in.

He pivots toward the long arm of windows and stares into the desolate night. The stars, it seems, have fallen from the sky and drowned themselves in the ocean. The moon is hiding his face in a hazy fog. Somewhere at the end of Fig Tree Lane, a dog yelps. He listens to her bedroom door, opening and closing, then opening once more, and, after that, her footsteps in the hallway, but he refuses to cast his eyes on her.

"Caruso," she says softly. "Turn around."

He feels her presence and detects the scent of bird.

"Look at me."

Reluctantly, he pivots in her direction. She is five feet away. With her right side foremost, she stands there innocently, the Galah's pink crown of feathers like an indictment behind her head. "I'm doing this for you," she says, shuffling sideways toward him, moving closer and closer as he puffs out his cheek feathers and frets on his perch. She twists her left shoulder slightly, and the Galah, crouched on her arm, swings forward. "Matilda's not going to take your place," she says reassuringly. "Good boy," she tells him as she slides one foot over the floor, then brings the other to rest beside it, again and again, until she and the Rose-breasted Cockatoo are inches from his cage. She continues to shift slowly, stopping only when the three of them are face to face.

He stares apprehensively into her eyes, next the Galah's, and is amused by the spectacle of its deeply colored eye rings and dull brown irises. He hadn't noticed this before. Such human folly, he thinks as a low-pitched chuckle escapes from his beak.

"You like her, don't you, Caruso?" she says, smiling. "Such a pretty little bird, isn't she?"

She, he says to himself, chuckling with irony.

"You'd better behave yourself, you naughty boy." She wags a finger at him.

He lets loose a rollicking hoot.

"I knew you'd come to accept her," she says, heaving a big sigh of relief.

Another duped Homo sapiens, he thinks, staring wide-eyed at the bird and bursting into a long, sustained laugh.

Matilda is a Matthew.

Nineteen

FOR SEVERAL WEEKS NOW, she has been moving Matt and him around in an endless game of musical chairs. In the early mornings, she puts him on the T-stand and Matt in the big cage. Minutes before she leaves for work, she returns them to their respective cages, now only a few feet from each other. Then, after work, she takes the Galah out and gives him a little taste of freedom while leaving Caruso imprisoned. All this commotion—so that they will become familiar with each other, she tells them.

Yesterday, he heard her bubbling in the living room on the phone to Beryl, saying that the Galah was a brilliant idea, that he and Matilda were becoming close, that Joe sends his thanks, droning on and on, numbing him down to his pinfeathers, and he had turned away from her voice to catch sight of the Galah flying audaciously off the T-stand. Teetering over the floor, he climbed up the leg of the blue chaise longue to perch on its cushioned seat—his pink-feathered chest swollen with self-importance.

Caruso glared at the bird through the bars of his cage, but Matt wasn't intimidated. Seconds later, with renewed confidence, he fluttered down and waddled over to the painted chest. Three times he flew upward and tried to reach the top, but his clipped wings failed to keep him aloft. Finally, on the fourth try, he made it, landing next to Granny's Wedgwood plate, at which he stared in wonder. *A cockatoo is an accident waiting to happen,* Caruso had often overheard the staff at the pet store say, and Matt, though a Galah, remains a cockatoo, his inquisitive nature making him as accident prone as Caruso. For a brief moment, Caruso hoped that Warramurrungundji would will a mishap, that gawky Matt would brush against the plate and knock it off. However, the Galah had returned to the T-stand without incident. It was then Caruso realized that he could not rely on the Great Mother to act. If he wanted something to happen, it would be up to him.

Caruso rappels all the way down to the bottom of his cage and picks up the dog biscuit reeking of the squatter's stink. He will act without restraint, he thinks as he ascends to his perch, staring hard at the Galah on the T-stand while eating the smelly dog biscuit with fake relish. Stealthily, Matt sidesteps toward him, covetous of what he believes is *his* dog biscuit. To goad him on, Caruso chews it even more energetically. The Galah extends his neck and makes a noise that sounds like a greedy grumble. Immediately, Caruso drops the biscuit, hurls himself against the metal bars, and latches onto them—ferociously flapping his wings and hissing. The Galah scoots to the opposite end of the T-stand, his body thin with fear.

At last he has been put in his place, Caruso thinks. Soon Clarissa will make them trade places again, but until then he will plot and scheme. For he is no simple-minded bird—no gullible, trusting parrot. From this moment on, he will be strong, will call things as they are, and will look at the world through clear lenses, unlike Theodore Pinter in his rose-colored glasses, transforming Olivia's every gesture toward him into something more meaningful than it was.

From the corner of his eye, far off in the distance, he spots a white carpet of ibises winging for the marshes near Ocracoke Village. Once Clarissa took him to see the flickering tongues of fire in the gaseous swamp, a place that reminds him lately of the hot anger he's feeling. The screen door clacks when she comes in from picking herbs. He hears water running, and after that a thunk on the worktable. Within seconds, she is passing beneath the archway and into the sunroom, flinging her white floppy hat like a Frisbee on the chaise longue. "Well, look at you two in your cozy cottage," she says, walking over. She opens his cage door and presents her arm. With sham collegiality, he steps up. "Good boy," she says, and he feigns a contented squawk.

Stay strong, he tells himself. The mask is doing its magic.

"Time for some major steps," she says cheerily. "First, a little taste of mutual freedom." She sets Caruso on the chaise longue before placing Matt on the floor near the table.

Caruso flutters off the cushioned seat. Putting on his best behavior, he puffs out his cheek feathers, coos, and waddles toward the Galah.

"What good friends you're becoming," Clarissa says when Matt moves forward. Just then, the telephone rings. Abruptly, Matt comes to a standstill. "I'll be right back," Clarissa says.

As soon as she passes out of sight, Caruso trills sweetly at the Galah, who rises to the bait and waddles toward him. Time for his own perverse tango, Caruso thinks. Time for the back-and-forth dance, the mixed signals, the pull and tug of war.

Lifting a menacing foot, Caruso seethes like a death adder. Matt freezes, parts his beak as if to screech, reconsiders, and snaps it shut. Caruso fakes a happy-go-lucky twitter. Uncertain, Matt rocks on one foot and then the other. Come to Papa, Caruso thinks, chirping benignly like a sparrow, and Matt teeters on the way to him. What is it with this bird? Caruso wonders. What compels him to risk disappointment over and over? What makes him think the outcome will be different this time? Is he dull witted? Naive? Crazy? Hopeful? No fight, flight, or acceptance for him. He is choosing an altogether different path. The path of *foolishness.*

Whipping boy, Caruso thinks, unleashing the full strength of his hot fury. With an aggressive flap of his wings, he charges at the Galah, who stops dead in his tracks. Caruso stares icily into the bird's dull brown irises. With a slow and deliberate motion, he raises his foot and brushes his claws gently over the bird's chest.

"I knew you two could get along without me," Clarissa says when she reappears and sees them crouching side by side on the sunroom floor. "Now, let's try something else—something even bigger," she says, offering each of them a forearm and taking them to Caruso's cage. "Such sweetness!" she gushes when Caruso steps up on the perch beside Matt.

On their bicycle built for two, he thinks acidly.

"Thank you, Caruso," she says, beaming fervently at him, "for making us one big happy family now."

Twenty

HE LISTENS TO CLARISSA SINGING while she washes dishes. Before, he loved the sound of her voice; lately, he hates her thin soprano. Those habits of hers that he once adored now grate on his nerves. Her giggle is as off-putting as the shrill cry of a magpie. The sway in her walk seems forced. He dislikes how she closes her eyes whenever she drinks tap water. The little moan she makes after eating something tasty annoys him. He hates the way she caresses the underside of her arm, hates the way she baby-talks him. Her sensuality is a pose, he thinks, false and phony.

But then she will do something, some new little thing—like slipping the tip of her thumb into her mouth—and suddenly he's a goner, tumbling and spinning through the air, grounded no longer. He eyes Matt on the perch beside him and feels only disdain. Yet he's confused about Clarissa. Does he love her or hate her? Can he feel both emotions for her at once?

"Love and hate are two sides of the same coin," the old man had said. "I love her, and I hate her," he confessed one cold, wet January day when they thought the rain would never end. Though early, it seemed as if the evening had swallowed the afternoon, and Caruso remembers that he

185

could see only a drizzling gloom through the study window. There was no birdsong—no sound of any living creature, just the pounding rain.

"I wish those raindrops were snowflakes," Theodore Pinter said, nudging his glasses against the bridge of his nose. "One winter, long ago, it snowed here. Not much, just a few inches of heaven." He rubbed the corners of his eyes and twisted his lower lip in memory. "Olivia and I were young, not quite teenagers, but even then she had begun to pull away from me. That day in January, we grew close again. As soon as it began to flurry, we dashed outside simultaneously—she from her back door, I from mine. *Snow!* we squealed, our voices mingling. We scooped up handfuls of it, washed our faces in the cold flakes with movements that were perfectly synchronized, as though we were dancing. We ran through the white fluff toward each other, coming to a standstill at the property line where our backyards met. We stared at each other and knew intuitively what the other was thinking. We leaned over and packed snow in our palms. Laughing, she pelted me on the nose, but I—forever the gentleman—would not throw snow at her delicate face and waited until she turned her back to me. That day, Caruso, we were fully present. We lost ourselves in the seamless whiteness of the moment. Snow," he murmured over and over before spluttering into silence. Meanwhile, the rain continued to fall.

"I love her, and I hate her," the old man said at last. "I love her because I've always loved her. I hate her because I've always loved her. I love her because she is what I am not. I hate her for the very same reason. I love her because I can't seem to move forward. I hate her because she has. I hate her because, while I suffer, she seems happy. I love her because the sight of her smiling face through this window makes me feel glad. I love her because she is someone without me. I hate her because I am nothing without her."

Sighing wearily, he reached for the drawstring to close the curtain, just as Olivia Greenaway materialized, like a beckoned spirit, in the lamplit living room across the way. That day, she was not smiling. She was sobbing, her shoulders heaving. "My darling Olivia," Theodore Pinter groaned, taking her sadness into his very being. She came toward them, pressed her forehead against the window—the raindrops trailing down the glass. "I'm here, Olivia," he said with a step backward, reaching behind him, searching for the chain on his desk lamp with his fingers.

Tug on it, Caruso thought. Illuminate yourself in our darkness. Let her see how much you care.

Caruso could hear the old man's inhalations quickening in his throat, see the lamp chain gripped in his fingers, and sense his desire to act. Still, he just stood there—motionless—in the dim room, while Olivia anguished in the light. Do it! Caruso thought.

"I can't," the old man gasped. "She'll see us. She'll see me and be so embarrassed. I can't take her dignity from her like that." And, letting go of the chain, he had dropped his arm like a weight beside him.

Caruso shifts toward the Galah and gives him another hard look. Had the old man ever acted spontaneously? he wonders. On that snowy day in Greensboro, had he really lived in the moment? It seems to Caruso that spontaneity should be a part of every present-centered act. If so, why had Theodore Pinter hesitated to throw the snowball until Olivia turned her back?

Clarissa cuts off the flow of water, then clinks a pan against the counter as she dries it.

Theodore Pinter's thoughtfulness had restrained him, Caruso reasons—had prevented him from acting impulsively. The trait of which he was most proud, the trait which he felt most distinguished him from Pascal, had kept Olivia from choosing him. Best to be selfish, Caruso thinks. Best to be mindful of tricks and division. Best to remember how to win the game.

From the bottom of the cage, Caruso retrieves a gum nut, which he has been hiding. He climbs back up to the perch, the gum nut in his beak, and takes a sidestep toward Matt, already crouching and flattening his feathers against his body, and, strangely, Caruso feels ashamed.

He misses the clarity of his life in Australia. He misses the simple things—the deep orange sun at twilight, the bush, the outback, the mountains, the rain forests, the beaches, pink Galahs in the blue-white sky. He pines for the warmth of his parents and mourns the life he could have had if he had not been stolen from them. The mate. The clutch of eggs. The chicks. The fledgling that looks and acts like him. He yearns for that feeling of interconnectedness that made him a part of something bigger and grander.

He hears her footsteps over the floor and instantly comes to his senses. He will stick to treacherous kindness.

"Oh, how precious!" she says from the doorway when he gives the gum nut to Matt.

Yet as he watches the Galah eat it, he's not gratified by his deception but experiences another emotion altogether. *Real* is how he feels, as though he's a part of something bigger and grander, the way his father must have felt while feeding him as a chick.

Twenty-one

"YOU SHOULD HAVE SEEN IT," CLARISSA IS SAYING to Joe in the kitchen. The rich smell of the sauce wafts into the sunroom, where Caruso is nibbling on a pinecone in the middle of the floor. "Right before my very eyes, Caruso gave Matilda his gum nut." She releases a whoosh of air that sounds like a grateful sigh. "My sweet ole Caruso is back, and he's stopped that awful plucking, too."

"That's the best news yet," Joe says.

Caruso drops the pinecone and waddles over to the kitchen doorway just as Clarissa stops stirring the sauce. Enough sauce in there to feed an army of boyfriends, he thinks mockingly when she lays the wooden spoon on a plate.

"You raise good parrots," Joe says.

"I know I do," she says, glancing at Caruso, who lets their flattery roll off his back.

"Yeah, Caruso's a decent guy at heart."

She smiles over her shoulder at Joe, then repositions the red lid on the pot so that there's a small slit through which the steam can escape. "This sauce has been simmering all afternoon," she says, shifting around to face him. "It has everything under the sun in it."

"I thought this meal was going to be light and easy," he says, laughing as he leans toward her.

"Hit's right hard for me to do easy," she jokes back, slipping into her mountain twang.

Joe plants his hand, as big as an albatross's foot, on her shoulder. "You're pretty intense about cooking," he says, giving her shoulder a little squeeze. "If a dish doesn't work, you're mighty hard on yourself. I wouldn't wanna be inside your head."

"You sure know how to compliment a gal," she says, shrugging his hand off.

"What I'm saying is...you don't give yourself a break."

"Well, that's obviously not your problem," she fires back.

"No, I guess not," he admits.

"All those doting sisters," she says, "hanging on to your every word. Letting you know how special you are, thinking that no girl is ever good enough for you."

"At least they don't bite."

"Maybe not with their teeth."

"What do you mean by that?" he asks, going over to the bench at the worktable, sitting down. "Okay...okay, I confess," he says moments later. "I'm a confident guy. My sisters love me. Don't expect me to feel bad about that. No sane person would want it otherwise. But my oldest sister never lets me off the hook. Jo Ann will give me hell if she thinks I deserve it. She's my moral backbone—my saving grace, so to speak."

"If you knew my family, you'd cut me some slack," she says with a reproachful look. She draws her mouth to one side, thinking. "I tried to be perfect when I was a kid," she tells him. "No matter how hard I tried, I never got what I needed from my parents. They were always tough on me. So I'm tough on myself. Learned behavior," she adds, sighing. "It took me years to understand why Randall was spared their criticism, why they treated him so differently. His flaws, I finally figured out, made them feel needed. His imperfections demanded their unconditional love."

Joe comes to his feet. "You're perfect to me," he says, reaching out and catching her hand. "I'm way too cocky for my own good. Always think I've done my best when I haven't, but you...you push yourself to do better. An exacting passion drives you, and I love you for this."

You'll change your mind when she's more passionate about her cooking than she is about you, Caruso thinks scornfully.

She lets her gaze linger on Joe, her lips half smiling. He releases her hand. She fills up a boiler with water, thunks it on the stove, and twists the flame up high. As soon as the water bubbles, she opens the cabinet, retrieves the sea salt, pours some into her palm, and spills it into the pot. After that, she adds the pasta. "Is al dente all right?" she asks, lowering the flame.

"You're the chef," he says as he comes up behind her and kisses the back of her neck.

My swan neck, Caruso thinks, averting his eyes. Seconds later, Matt patters over the linoleum past him to pause slightly beyond the doorway, near the worktable's leg. Fascinated, the Galah seems, by the clouds of steam rising from the pot of pasta.

Clarissa cuts off the burner and drains the pasta into a colander in the sink, then douses it with olive oil. She takes the lid off the pot of tomato sauce and puts it on the counter. "My Neapolitan ragù smells scrumptious," she says, leaning over and whiffing in deeply. "Oh," she says peevishly. "I forgot the parsley. I like to garnish with it. It won't take but a second," she says, starting for the back door, Joe following after her.

Caruso watches as they laugh and flirt near the herb garden. She has already set the small table on the deck with a bright floral tablecloth and matching napkins, her bone-white china, pearl-handled cutlery, and goblet wineglasses. A bottle of Italian red wine and a small vase of Catherine O'Neal's red zinnias rest in the center. The salad plates are filled. The bread is in its basket, loosely tucked into an embroidered tea towel. He looks for her again. She is bending over, pinching off sprigs of parsley.

He shifts to check on Matt, now mesmerized by the bright red pot and the tiny puffs of vapor drifting up from it. Caruso spots a rose-colored feather beneath the edge of the worktable. Serendipitous, he thinks, waddling over to retrieve it with his beak. This is the mishap he's been waiting for. A feather in the sauce. Her meal ruined. Her perfect evening vanquished by the squatter. Proof she needs to send the Galah packing.

He glances back at the two of them through the screen door, sees her dangling parsley, like mistletoe, over Joe's head. The die is cast, he tells himself. It's now or never.

Flapping his wings, he sails directly above the pot and parts his beak. The pink feather floats downward, vacillating on a breath of steam, before landing in the sauce. Right then, the sauce burps, sucking the feather under. Panicked, Caruso sails into the sunroom, hunting for another. He finds it, snared in the wire-meshed bottom of his cage, two times larger than the first. His heart bursting with adrenaline, he tweezes it out with his claws, clamps it in his beak, and flies back into the kitchen, just as Matt, with a downward thrust of his wings, rises upward and flutters unsteadily toward the stove. He hovers above the pot of sauce, the steam wafting around him, then plummets like a stone.

Caruso screeches, the feather falling from his beak. There is the faint sound of a frightened chick calling out, followed by a moment of terrifying silence.

"Claaa-risss-a!" Caruso cries, swooping over the worktable, vehemently slamming against the screen door. "Claaa-risss-a!" he cries again and keeps crying until she's running over the parched lawn toward him.

She takes the deck steps quickly and rushes inside, her eyes darting frenziedly to Caruso on the floor beside the door, to the worktable, to the lid on the counter, to the splattered, red-flecked stove.

"Please, dear God, no," she murmurs.

Twenty-two

WITH HIS HEAD DOWN and his hands shoved into the pockets of his jeans—the same hands that took Matt out of the pot because Clarissa couldn't—Joe drags his feet through the sandy driveway, rounds the corner, and disappears from view. From the deck comes his concerned voice asking her if she's feeling better. She bluntly tells him, "No." He insists that it wasn't her fault, that accidents do happen. "Whose fault was it then?" she says in a voice so choked and strained that Caruso wouldn't have recognized it had he not known she was outside. Joe argues that they were gone for just a few minutes. "Long enough for a cockatoo to get into trouble," she says back. He responds that if she has to blame someone, she should blame him for distracting her. She releases a startling, nervous laugh.

Abruptly their voices cease, and there is silence.

And yet the silence that Matt left behind still whispers from the Wedgwood plate on the painted chest, from the red pot inside the kitchen cabinet, from the dog biscuit at the bottom of his cage. Benumbed, Caruso moves through Matt's stillness.

Beyond the long row of windows, he hears footsteps again and turns just as Clarissa comes to a halt in the driveway, frowning and blinking. Joe runs his finger down her cheek. Immediately, she holds her hands over her face. To hide her grief, Caruso thinks, his eyes on her, her shoulders heaving while she cries. Joe hugs her, and they walk, their fingers woven together, to the end of the driveway and out of sight.

Before long, the screen door opens and closes. "My carelessness, Caruso, has caused us enough sorrow. I'm not taking any chances with you," she says, shuffling across the sunroom floor, double-checking the thick wire, looped once more around his cage and cage door. He notices the sheen of sweat above her lip and on her forehead and the ashen pallor of her skin. Her hands shaking, she slides out the poop tray and removes the soiled newspaper, spilling seed husks and filth upon the white linoleum. She rolls the newspaper up and unmindfully lays it on the table. "Me and my big reckless hands," she says, lifting them up and staring reproachfully at them. "I hope you can forgive me, Caruso."

As a girl, her large hands had been her shame, and she had kept them hidden from the eyes of others—tucked under her folded arms or else clasped behind her back. Yet she had learned to appreciate them when she began to cook, for they were flexible, coordinated, and strong enough to do a chef's work. Sadly, the self-rebuke in her voice now tells him that she's ashamed of them again.

More culpable than she is, he lowers his head.

"Why can't you look at me?" she asks him.

Sheepishly, he glances upward, afraid that his eyes will betray him. If she looks deeply into them, she might see through the many masks he has been wearing and know who he really is.

"I understand," she consoles him, their shared sorrow and guilt reuniting them at last.

"WE'RE GOING OUT," she says a few days later, nudging him off his perch. She deliberately takes the dusty lanes where the tourists seldom venture, all the while talking about her work, the way she once did after a long day at Crab Cakes. She complains about the cheese soufflés that fell last evening. She did what she always did, she says—even added an extra two egg whites for fullness, then baked them in a water bath to be on the safe side—but they fell anyway. "I'm distracted," she confesses. "Too much sadness inside me."

Distracted also, he listens to her halfheartedly. In front of him, a skeeter hawk rapidly whirls its transparent, net-veined wings. A pale yellow butterfly flits near a patch of daisies. They pause beneath a gnarled live oak, its leafy canopy a respite from the sun. "Hot as Hades," she mumbles as they saunter on. "Makes me miss the coolness of the mountains." And Caruso hopes for a summer storm to ease the August heat.

He hears a gurgling noise, and to his left, just beyond a low brick wall, he spots a stone sculpture of a heron, its upturned beak spouting water into a fountain. "An egret," she says, stopping to point it out. She should know her birds by now, he thinks, without a hint of judgment. Suddenly, a young robin bounces down on the pathway in front of them. "Look," she says gleefully, unaware of the tiger-striped cat crawling out from beneath a spindly bush. Instinctively, Caruso swoops off her shoulder and dive-bombs his furry back. Yowling, the cat runs off, and the fledgling flutters upward, his mother's *tuk tuk tuk* calling him from a nearby tree.

Hope is the thing with feathers—Caruso thinks as he watches the young robin fly away.

Twenty-three

"Joe," she says, "I love you."

Their lips are making little sucking sounds that come through the upraised window beyond which the full moon flowers in the dark night.

Don't love him, Caruso wants to protest. Blame him for Matt's death, for my feather plucking, for turning our cozy cottage upside down.

"I adore the sunsets here in May and June," she says dreamily, "but it is the August moon that dazzles me."

"The moon is a street lamp compared to your face," he teases her, and they kiss again.

"Let's go to the lighthouse," she says. "It's the perfect spot for moon gazing."

Our lighthouse, Caruso thinks despairingly.

"It'll look magical pirouetting in this pearl-blue moonlight," she says.

Our pearl-blue moonlight, Caruso insists.

"But you are my celestial planet," he says.

"We'll take a long, romantic stroll there," she says with a giggle, "and you can sweet-talk me all the way."

"Okay...my love...lead me."

She is his moon goddess, leading him with Amber Hands, just like the moon leads the sea, he thinks, as snatches of Emily's moon poem come back to him. "It's about Olivia and me," the old man would say after reciting it. "I follow Olivia like a docile boy, and, although she doesn't realize it, she follows me."

Has Clarissa ever followed him? Caruso reflects. And when had Olivia ever followed the old man? Illusions...illusions, he thinks. Loving someone you've lost.

Don't wanna lose her, he tells himself as she and Joe creak down the deck steps, their conversation fading as they cross the yard. Don't wanna lose her.

He moves with deliberation toward the thick rope of wire, loosens a strand of it with his claws, and champs down hard with his beak. The filament snaps in half. Don't wanna lose her. He unravels another strand and severs it, then another and another until he has bitten through every filament. He flies out into the sunroom and through the kitchen. The weight of his body springs the latch on the screen door, and he escapes into the night.

Don't wanna lose her, he thinks, soaring high above the backyard. With exhilaration, he rockets upward into the moonlit sky and for a moment feels joyful, the way he once did when he was learning how to fly. He looks down, searching for her on Fig Tree Lane and the pathways nearby, but she's nowhere.

Effortlessly, he veers right, flapping above an empty street. He wings past Crews Inn and the old church place, then banks right again onto British Cemetery Road, his shadow flittering batlike above the quaint, historic graveyard—its weathered, mossy headstones scattered among the sassafras and loblolly pines. He spots a white-footed mouse dashing from one clump of tall weeds to another and stares into the glittering eyes of a mink, but his red-headed Eclectus hen cannot be found.

He circles back onto Silver Lake Drive, rimming the harbor, and observes the diners in the courtyard of Barney's Café, eating seafood brought in on the fishing boats this morning.

I can't lose her, he thinks as he swerves left, gliding over the Halo Hair Studio and the Sea Maiden's Muse on Creek Road. On a bench in front of Albert Styron's Store, two men are smoking cigarettes, the glowing tips oscillating through the dark space like intoxicated lightning bugs.

In the near distance, the lighthouse, white and picturesque, beckons him. He heads toward it, the gusty wind off the water flattening his crown of feathers. Minutes later, he is winging over Lighthouse Road and the white picket fence that surrounds the lighthouse and the keeper's quarters with its red metal roof. The wind slows him down as he flits erratically above the walkway leading to the tower. He is almost there when a bank of clouds snuffs out the moonlight, but the beacon's steady beam is there for him to follow. A few seconds later, the clouds disperse, and the world below him is bright again. He notices the ocean's swells, slick and wet as the skin of humpback whales. With banging heart, he leans into the salty wind. Same as Joe, he has never cast his eyes upon the lighthouse at night. And when he comes upon it, it is—as she described it—a magical sight.

Descending, he circles to the right, seeking her out. A moan rides toward him on the robust wind. He follows where the sound takes him, and there she is—a dark form against the white curve of the tower, her arms high above her head, his hands pinned against her palms, her legs wrapped around his waist—as he kisses her face, her neck, her breasts. Held yet horrified by the sight, Caruso is a flash of white, zigzagging uncontrollably back and forth in front of them.

I've lost her, he thinks, the light from the beacon a laser beam in his breast. I've lost her.

He soars past them, his thoughts flying inward, but this time he can find no comfort in memory. For everyone he has ever loved, he realizes in a blinding moment of clarity, becomes lost to him.

Landing on the deck of their cottage, he pries open the screen door and teeters over the lunar radiance striping the kitchen floor. He pauses, closing his eyes on the world, but then the image of their entwined bodies rises up behind his eyelids, and he feels such numbing pain that had he shrieked out he would not have heard the anguish in his voice. He whips his eyes open, mining his memory for a time when he had made her moan like Joe. Not once, he thinks, his legs growing weak beneath him.

He stares at his breast, zeroes in on a feather, and jerks it out. Then, he gouges his bare flesh with his beak. Deserved pain, he thinks, as blood tattoos his plumage. Flying to the kitchen sink, he twists on the faucet and bares his red chest to the water. The Great Barrier Reef with its shimmering coral polyps is polluted and dying, he thinks, cutting the flow off. Ayers Rock is as weightless as one of his pinfeathers. He flutters into his cage and locks himself in with the mangled strands of wire. She is his illusion. A red-headed Eclectus hen can never be human, but a lover always is, he thinks, trembling on his perch. And most tragic of all, families are born of blood or passion.

BEFORE LONG, Caruso hears them kissing passionately on the deck and, after a brief moment, her footsteps as she meanders dreamily into the sunroom. "Hey, Caruso," she says, shifting in his direction, touching her swollen lips. The moon, through the open blinds, captures her in its spotlight. She shakes off one sandal, then the other, and moves toward him, bringing with her the loud, oppressive scent of Joseph Hampton Fitzgerald.

Unbuttoning the front of her dress, she pulls it over her head and flings it on the chaise longue. She steps out of her panties and leaves them on the floor. "I need a shower," she says, coming closer. Cringing, Caruso tucks his beak into his wing feathers to block out the smell of Joe.

"How about a shower?" she asks him. "We haven't done that in a long time."

He unsheathes his beak.

She smiles at him, oblivious to the maimed wire around his cage door as she untangles it. She leans over, her breasts milky white in the moonlight, her stomach round and soft. She presents her alabaster arm to him, and timorously he steps up. She holds him close as they start down the darkened hallway, the seaweed perfume of her filling his head.

She swishes the curtain aside and turns on the water. "My sweet Caruso," she says, drawing her fingertips over his tail feathers. A strange, powerful yearning permeates his body. Fervidly, he rubs himself against her skin, releasing his pent-up passion. Stepping into the stall, she closes the curtain behind her and puts him on the plastic shelf. She removes the sprayer from its holder and wets herself down. Taking the soap in her large palm, she runs it languidly over her body and then rinses the soap off. "Now you, Caruso," she says, shifting toward him, dousing his feathers. He squawks excitedly and does a gleeful shimmy. "Clean boy," she says, spraying him again.

He shrieks with pleasure, the warm water running over him, his heart soaring with love. Fluttering off the shelf, he lands on her shoulder, pressing his beak against the dark mole, his mole, on her neck.

"Caruso!" she says, startled, the sprayer plummeting from her fingers. Dangling at the end of the metal cord, it begins to swirl, shooting water against his wings, her face, the stall. She shields her eyes with her hands while he flits over her body, shyly at first and then boldly, reveling in the velvet softness of her skin, high on her conch shell odor. "Quit that, Caruso!" she says, pushing him away with her hands.

Yet, caught in the grip of Eros, Caruso cannot help himself.

He lands once more on her shoulder and entangles his beak in her wet hair.

"Please don't," she tells him.

"Claaa-risss-a!" he cries out.

"Enough," she says in a level, firm voice.

He yields to her.

Quickly she cuts off the water, wraps her long fingers around his torso, and gently eases him onto the shelf. "What's wrong with you?" she says, her blue eyes dark with worry.

My soul is sick with love, he wants to confess as she opens the curtain and steps out.

Twenty-four

THE FULL MOON IS GONE, erased from his sight, while Emily's moon poem lingers in his mind. After closing the blinds, she blew him a good-night kiss, carefully arranged the baby blanket over his cage, and went to bed, leaving behind the fragrance of talcum powder. Did he lose her tonight at the lighthouse when the moon was full? Will he ever be the moon pulling her toward him? He now remembers every word, every line of the poem, and the strange, contradictory mix of emotions he had felt that day in April when, for the very first time, he had gotten a different glimpse of Theodore Pinter through a crack in the mask he wore.

"What do you think?" the old man had asked him, waiting until noon when the sunlight was dancing behind the draperies before he drew them open. "Will April treat me kindly or cruelly this year?" Pausing, he took off his glasses and tucked them into his shirt pocket. "Kindly, I hope," he said. "For today, Olivia will see Pascal for the man he is."

He glanced up at the grandfather clock on the wall behind him. Then, catching Caruso's eye, he tapped his fingertips against the desk and went on, "I have a plan, Caruso. At noon precisely, her doorbell will ring. On her way to answer it, she will walk by these windows and pass out of sight. But I know who will be waiting for her on the front porch. A man from Duncan's Florist Shop with a box of twelve long-stemmed pink roses. Instinctively, she will lift up the lid, anticipating Pascal's name on the card inside, ready to forgive him for years of past neglect—yet my name will be there. HAPPY SEVENTIETH BIRTHDAY, MY DARLING! FROM YOUR EVER-DEVOTED TEDDY, the card will read, with Emily's moon poem in my bold script below it." Ardently, he began to recite the verses:

> The Moon is distant from the Sea—
> And yet, with Amber Hands—
> She leads Him—docile as a Boy—
> Along appointed Sands—
>
> He never misses a Degree—
> Obedient to Her Eye
> He comes just so far—toward the Town—
> Just so far—goes away—
>
> Oh, Signor, Thine, the Amber Hand—
> And mine—the distant Sea—
> Obedient to the least command
> Thine eye impose on me—

Finished, he stood there, tears in his eyes, but he quickly winked them back and said, "A perfect plan, isn't it, Caruso?"

Caruso vehemently bobbed his head while Theodore Pinter stood speechless, staring, it seemed, right through him. Caruso watched his chest rising and falling as he breathed steadily through slightly parted lips, his face tightening into a mask of resolve. He gripped the edge of the desk firmly, appearing to draw courage from the wood, took one last deep breath, and said, "Without fail, Pascal Robinson comes home for lunch at twelve-fifteen. Same as always, he'll pull his black Mercedes into the driveway. Same as always, he will have forgotten her birthday, but this time she won't suffer his thoughtlessness in stoic silence. No, this time she won't let him off so easily because this time she will be holding my gift in her arms." He grabbed the binoculars off the desk, pivoted around, and took a resolute step forward. Pressing the apertures against his eyes, he turned the wheels and brought them into focus.

It was then the grandfather clock began to chime. Caruso counted— once, twice, and then twice more. He shifted nervously on his perch as a stream of vehicles rumbled by—three sedans, an old battered farm truck, and a bright red sports car. "The van from Duncan's. Where is it?" the old man said, peering nervously over his shoulder at Caruso.

Five...six...seven. Caruso kept counting. "Hurry up...hurry up," the old man said, rocking from one foot to the other. By the tenth chime, he whispered, "Please." Seconds before the last chime struck twelve and "Ode to Joy" began to play, a tan delivery van rolled around the corner and groaned to a stop. "Thank you," Theodore Pinter said softly. A young man opened the door, stepped down, and headed for the back of the van just as Pascal Robinson drove up in his black Mercedes and got out.

"Sir!" the young man shouted, holding the box of roses up high.

With a bland face that conveyed nothing, Pascal Robinson turned toward the voice and waved the young man over. Slipping his wallet from his pants pocket, he took out several bills, tipped the man, and retrieved the box.

"No!" Theodore Pinter said, his voice deep and harsh.

Nudging the lid up with his thumb, Pascal Robinson fished out the card and read it. He pivoted toward the old man's window and, with a graceful, mocking gesture, raised his hand, disdainfully crumpled the card in his fingers, and shoved it into his coat pocket.

Caruso looked on as Theodore Pinter opened and closed his eyes at least a dozen times, as if he couldn't grasp what had just happened. "She will know they are from me...surely," he said.

THE OLD MAN had spent that afternoon in the kitchen. From his cage in the study, Caruso caught glimpses of him through the open pocket doors, nursing a glass of red wine while he cooked. Caruso listened to water running, to a knife thumping against a cutting board, to a rolling pin creaking over a counter. Once he smelled something burning on the stove.

"I'm going to bathe and dress," the old man said, coming into the study right as the clock chimed six. "I want to be my best for the dinner party this evening."

What dinner party? What was the old man thinking? Caruso wondered as Theodore Pinter started for the hallway. He had lost contact with his friends years ago. So who could be coming? Caruso craned forward on his perch, waiting for the whooshing sound of water. A moth batted its wings against the shade of the lit floor lamp beside the sofa. The grandfather clock ticked. Still, no rumble of water.

Bored, Caruso shifted toward the window and caught sight of Pascal kissing Olivia's cheek in the living room next door, after that of Olivia closing the curtains. Outraged, he whipped back toward the hallway and to the sudden sound of the shower's roar. Before long, Theodore Pinter rounded the corner.

"Well, what do you think, Caruso?" he asked.

Caruso liked the way he had parted his hair and neatly combed it back. He was dressed more sprucely than usual in a light-gray linen jacket, charcoal linen trousers, a white shirt, and a slate-blue silk tie.

"Impressive, huh?" he said, clicking the heels of his old wing tips together.

Caruso was surprised to see them polished to a high shine.

"I'd better check on the rib roast," he said, glancing at the clock. "Don't want to overcook it. It's best when slightly pink in the center, right?"

What does a cockatoo know about roast beef? Caruso thought.

Thirty minutes later, Caruso was in the dining room, perched on the back of the massive antique sideboard, admiring the splendid meal before him. In the center of the tablecloth was a rolled rib roast atop a Limoges platter, surrounded by a sea of pearly onions. Two pink candles glowed on either side of it, along with an array of steaming dishes.

"Please have a seat, my dear," the old man said, addressing an empty chair directly in front of him. He pulled it out. To the left of the place setting stood a single light-pink rose in a delicate cut-glass vase. "As you can see, I've prepared your favorite dishes. Roast beef and mushroom gravy, just the way you like it, creamy mashed potatoes, sugar snap peas sprinkled with toasted almonds, pickled peaches—I pickled them myself—and silver-dollar biscuits because I know how much you like them."

He stood there, his arms behind his back, rocking on his heels, perusing the meal he had laid out. "Ah, I know what's missing," he said at length. "Music. What would you like to hear, my darling?" Confused, Caruso stared at the vacant chair. "Gardel," he said all at once, loudly.

"Carlos Gardel." He made a frantic dash to the living room, and within minutes a melancholy Argentinian tango permeated the air.

"A taste of pinot noir?" Theodore Pinter asked in a calmer voice as soon as he came back. "Yes, my darling, I know—just a little," he said, bending over, taking hold of the bottle, pouring red wine into a fluted glass. He set the bottle on the table. "And small portions of everything," he said, spooning a little from each dish onto the gold-rimmed porcelain plate before him.

He walked around to the opposite side of the long rectangular table and filled up another plate, directly across from hers. "You love your Scotch and soda while I love my wine," he said, seizing the bottle again, pouring himself a full glass. He put the bottle down and raised high the wineglass. "Happy seventieth birthday, darling," he toasted, taking a sip, the candlelight bouncing off the etched stem. "You're still beautiful, my dear," he said somberly. "Age has not stolen any of your loveliness."

With those words, he pulled out his chair and settled gracefully into it. Cutting off a sliver of roast, he chewed it lavishly. "It's very nicely cooked, isn't it?" he said, dribbling gravy over his mashed potatoes, then tasting them. "Delicious," he said, swallowing. He dabbed his thin lips with his napkin. "I hope you enjoy it. I've had so much fun planning it. From your favorite meal to your favorite flower. No...no...it was no trouble at all, although I went to a half-dozen places before I found the candles. They had to be pink—not red, not white. 'Pink smells tender, the way it looks,' you once told me. There was no shade of pink you didn't like. Pink Pepto-Bismol, pink cotton candy, pink sunsets, pink lipstick. Remember the time I bought you cotton candy at the fair? Remember how you got it all over you—on the tip of your nose and in your hair? You were mortified, you told me, but I thought you were adorable."

Whipping up his fork, he stabbed a sugar pea and popped it into his mouth. "It's easy remembering the things you liked," he continued with a swallow, "but I also remember those things you seldom talked about. For instance, heights. You were afraid of high places. Whenever we climbed the staircase at your house, you would hug the wall. You doubted your intellect, although I've always known how smart you are."

He quit speaking and leaned back into his chair, sipping his wine and eating. "I'll never forget the year, the month, the day, the minute you were born, my love. I can recall every one of your birthday parties," he said as he laid down his fork and made a tent of his fingers, leaning forward, staring longingly into the face that wasn't there. "Your seventh is the one I remember best. Your mother brought out a three-tiered *dreamsicle* cake, covered with fleecy white icing. I had never eaten orange cake before. There were seven small pink candles on it, along with a big candle for you to grow on. Exquisite, that cake was! I can still taste the pungent flecks of orange peel and the honeyed citrus in it. When the Happy Birthday song was over, you blew out all of the candles with one long breath. I gave you a doll, I recall, and you said she was beautiful."

Draining his glass with a flourish, the old man announced that it was time for dessert. Rising quickly, he gathered together the dirty dishes and took them to the kitchen. A short while later, he reappeared carrying a large cake, ablaze with pink candles.

"Happy birthday, Olivia," he said, setting it on the table. After that, he sang the birthday song to her in a fragile but inspired voice. With flushed cheeks and feverish eyes, he vowed, "There will be no more games between us. We've been playing together for so long. At first, kids' games, then even sillier, adolescent games...all that back and forth during high school...still playing games, games, and more games. But I have no regrets because in the midst of all those ridiculous, pretentious games were the moments that felt real. For me, and I know for you, too. The talks we had, the tangos we danced, that kiss...those moments were real for both of us and have led us, like stepping stones, to this...to this moment when we are no longer pretending...no longer wearing masks."

Inhaling deeply, he blew out all of the candles. Next, he sliced off two thick wedges of the orange cake. "One for you and one for me," he said, sitting down, forking up a bite, and eating it with closed eyes, as though savoring the memory of eating it when he was a boy. Opening his eyelids, he tilted forward, his stiff shirt bunching against the table's edge, and said softly, "Remember, my darling, no regrets. Regrets are for cowards. No regrets, now. No regrets, ever. I've loved you forever, Olivia," he said, coming to his feet. "Back when we were souls waiting to be born, I loved you. When I was but a spit of vapor and you a morning star, I loved you. I loved you when I was a homely starling and you were a pretty yellow finch. Life after life, I've loved you, but always from afar. Today, though, my darling, I'll love you up close, in my arms. Shall we dance?"

Caruso could almost hear the *swish, swish* of the old man's blood pulsing in his neck, could almost smell the ardor of love on his skin, taste the hope on his lips, as he stood there holding out his hand. Caruso followed the birth of a smile on his lips, which grew into a grin, then collapsed into a frown—his eyes sinking into their sockets, as though the hard-earned lessons of his life were weighing them down. After that, his face changed again—his lips taut, his eyes dark and troubled, as he stared at some unwanted memory that had ambushed him. One second he appeared contented, the next depressed. Courageous, then cowardly. Unassuming, and after that, vain. Over and over, his features remolded themselves as he donned mask after mask, experienced emotion after emotion, until it seemed the masks were wearing him and not the other way around. The kaleidoscope of his feelings came to an abrupt end, and he simply stood there—his face so distorted by regret and rapture that Caruso had to look away.

Twenty-five

HE HAS DEVOLVED INTO AN ORDINARY CREATURE, no better than a dog really, waiting for his master to come home, grateful for a few pats on the head, Caruso thinks, shoving the carrot into his open beak as he stares into the darkness.

Birds cope with their fears by winging upward, by finding sanctuary in the sky, but not Caruso. Lately, he eats and eats and eats. Which makes Clarissa think he needs more protein in his diet. As a result, she gives him a hard-boiled egg each morning. She consistently brings him leftovers from the restaurant. One night, she served him a ramekin of cooked pasta. Not your typical fare for a parrot, and he drove himself to distraction looking for the hidden meaning in her gesture. Is he gradually becoming like the old man, seeing love in Clarissa's every overture to him? he asks himself, the thought so disturbing that he frantically scans his cage, hunting for more food. This constant eating keeps him from thinking.

Where is she now? he puzzles, his worst fears taking over as he envisions the two of them holding hands, passing by the row of empty rockers on the porch of Blackbeard's Lodge, a smile capturing her face as they step inside the lobby and climb the staircase to his room. He tries in vain to shut his mind off, but once the images begin it's hard to make them stop. Panicked, he prods through his food dish with his beak, searching for vegetables. He finds a half-eaten corn cob and gobbles down the milky kernels. Still, as soon as he's finished, another vision of the lovers rushes in—Joe's body pressed against hers—and he must look for something else to eat. He spots a wedge of pomegranate hidden among the scraps in his feeder and swallows it down, the red juice staining his feathered chest. Relief is what he feels—the same relief that plucking once gave him.

What if he could substitute eating with a more mindful activity? he wonders. Perhaps he could find a vocation that would fill the empty hours of his days, now that he is no longer the one responsible for making Clarissa happy. He could become a poet, like Emily Dickinson, he thinks. He could write about life and, in this way, cope with his heartache. The difference is he would not write about the moon, the sea, and human love but about bird love. Poems not only about birds but also for them. Birds will be his audience, he thinks. But what species of bird will he write about first? Who will be the *birdsona* of his verse? Not a cockatoo, he decides, for he needs some distance from his subject. A sparrow? A pelican? A kookaburra? No, no, no, he thinks, as the distance between them and him is too great. A parrot it must be. A parrot who suffers from lovesickness, same as he. A parakeet? A lovebird? A macaw? A lory? He swings his head—no. A quetzal? A trogon? A lorikeet? All no.

But who, who? he asks himself. For a long while he ponders the answer until—out of nowhere—the *birdsona* of his poem emerges from some mysterious place deep inside him. The kakapo, the largest of all the living parrots. Flightless and near extinction, he clings to the hope of love and still believes in it, though he lives a life of utter solitude in the mountains of New Zealand.

Yes, the kakapo will be the voice of his poem, Caruso thinks, as words upon words, images upon images present themselves like gifts to him, as though Warramurrungundji Herself is whispering them in his ear:

The kakapo digs a shallow grave—
No Wings to carry him to Love,
Booms a call into the dead of night
Counterfeit cry of the Namaqua dove—

It ricochets off the mountain ridges,
Lonely Echo in the empty Dark—
Enchants no female to him,
A desolation of his Parrot Heart—

Driven by a pure blind faith,
Not enslaved to any single mate—
He puffs out his chest once more
And blows Hope against the face of Fate.

Even though hope is only a flight of fancy to him, Caruso longs to believe the final line. Didn't the Great Mother whisper the words to him? On the other hand, what did Theodore Pinter's hope give him? Caruso can see no difference between the old man speaking across a dining room table to an empty chair and the New Zealand kakapo calling out for love from the ridges of Fiordland into a void where females no longer dwell.

No, he'll stick to truth. He has lost Clarissa. He will take the path of acceptance. No more fighting, no more fleeing. This love cannot be saved.

He imagines two kangaroos boxing their affection, a pair of platypuses swimming side by side, his parents pairing in flight.

It is then that the same old argument begins to run like a tape inside his head. Hope—without risk—is impotent. Truth—without hope of success—lives a woeful life. He remembers how he felt as he dropped grapes into Clarissa's mouth, how her eyes smiled as she gave the plumpest ones to him. No, he will not—cannot—accept a loveless life. Not even in the name of truth. For isn't it also true that some hopes are worth fighting for, some loves worth saving?

Worth saving the birds of Australia—the kookaburra with its rollicking laughter, the colorful rainbow lorikeet with its brushy tongue for removing a flower's nectar. Worth saving the odd-looking black swans and the black-and-white feathered pelicans. Worth saving the Australian stork, fish eagle, sacred ibis, and heron. Worth saving all of the birds on this spinning, swirling planet. Worth saving their efforts at procreation, their mates, their chicks, their meaningful, connected presence. Worth saving even an old, tiresome, romantic cockatoo like Caruso. Isn't he worth saving, too?

A wave of hope washes over him, and he holds fast to the memory of Clarissa stroking his neck, his heart brimming with devotion. And so, unable to control himself, he surrenders to the *hope of her* and booms his call of love into the desolate night.

Twenty-six

AWFUL DREAMS HAVE BEEN PLAGUING HIM lately. In the beginning, they came like ghostly visitations in the night. Now, they come whenever they please. Perhaps they're products of his constant eating, he thinks. This morning, she gave him some leftovers of baked mackerel and coleslaw, and at noon, when the heat is most brutal and the sunlight most blinding, he had a dream. No, a nightmare, he corrects himself.

In it, the Great Mother finally hears him and wills an earthquake off the shore of Ocracoke Island. Beneath the ocean, the sand shifts slightly, the plates of the planet groan, and the waves begin to crest just as Joe paddles away from the breakers, his face eager, his arms strong, his body ready to ride the swells. Which are growing bigger and bigger, higher now than their cottage on Fig Tree Lane. They tower over Joe and crash down upon him, sending his surfboard downward, shattering it against the ocean floor. When Caruso parts the waves with his beak and stares into the deep, dark water, he feels not the relief he's been waiting for but only horror at the sight of Joe, half-buried in the sand, and Clarissa, lifeless beside him.

Startled, he awoke, gasping for breath.

Now, he dreads the long hours ahead, fearful that these nightmares will continue. He is definitely not her sweet Caruso anymore, he thinks, bracing his eyelids open.

Inexplicably, she appears like a specter gliding over the dry grass toward him, and, stunned by this vision of her, he blinks in confusion. Is this another dream? he wonders after the screen door bangs and she breezes into the sunroom. "Too much solitude is bad for a bird," she carols, unlatching his cage door, presenting her arm to him. "Truth is, too much solitude is bad for anyone."

Could too much solitude be the cause of his bad dreams? he muses, stepping upon her arm, ascending to her shoulder.

"My, my...you're heavy," she says, eyeing him from top to bottom. "A plump little butterball you've become."

He is no turkey, but he may be soon, he thinks cheerlessly.

She puts on her floppy white hat and sunglasses. "I'm taking the rest of the day off," she announces. "Have saved a month of vacation days. No reason why I have to work. We're going to Beryl's studio."

They head out through the kitchen door. He inhales the warm air, feels it flowing through his lungs and into the tubes that fortify the rest of his body. From that single breath, he can extract more oxygen than a mammal with its baggy lungs. She takes the sandy back lanes until they come upon Beryl's studio—a small wooden structure built by her brothers—separated from the family home up front by a thick row of tall beach grasses. Clarissa opens the screen door, crosses over the porch, and briskly knocks three times, then waits a few seconds before knocking once more. The secret code of blood sisters, she has told him. "I'm letting myself in!" she yells, taking off her sunglasses, tucking them into her shirt pocket.

She passes beneath the doorway and into a sunlit place of wonder with two walls of continuous windows as well as a skylight in the center of the roof. Hanging from the white rafters are Tibetan prayer flags in vibrant colors of pink, orange, red, blue, yellow, and purple. Baskets of every make and kind are lined against the interior walls. There are intricate baskets from the islands of South Carolina; rustic wicker baskets from Haiti; round double-weave grass baskets with stripes of cream, red, and black from Ghana; and sturdy, square baskets from Amish villages in Ohio. All of the baskets are filled with tubes of oil and acrylic paint, brushes of various sizes and thicknesses, mineral spirits, rags, smocks, palette knives, and art books about famous painters piled up crooked, or *catawampus*, as Beryl would say.

"Hi, there," Beryl says, pitching them a smile over her shoulder. "I saw ya coming through the window."

"Me, too," comes a voice from behind an enormous canvas.

Caruso doesn't have to see the face to know that it's the nice waitress who brought him the dish of fresh pineapple that day at Iris's Coffee Shop.

"Caruso!" the girl bubbles when he releases an excited squawk.

Clarissa sidesteps away from the canvas. Sure enough, it is the koala bear girl, sitting on a stool, tilting forward with her arms around her waist.

"Hey, Sam," Beryl says, loudly tapping her paint brush against the edge of her easel. "You lost the pose again. That disgruntled look I wanted. Now, get it back."

"I'm tired," Sam moans. "Been disgruntled almost an hour now, been holding that look for days."

"Don't say I didn't warn you," Beryl says with a grin. "Okay...okay. Let's take a break and visit some with Clarissa."

Sam slides off the stool. Wiggling her shoulders, she scrunches up her nose, pulls her chin down, opens her mouth wide, and yawns.

As addled-looking as an emu, Caruso decides.

"This modeling stuff is hard work," Sam says to Clarissa. "Much tougher, I bet, than taking care of a parrot, especially one as sweet as Caruso."

"Remember, Caruso? Sam here brought you a plate of pineapple," Clarissa says, looking up at him.

She should know he never forgets an act of kindness, Caruso thinks, fixing his eyes on Sam.

"Y'all go sit down," Beryl says as she positions her palette beside a jelly jar of mineral spirits on a small table next to the easel, then dunks her paintbrush into the jar. Lacing her fingers together, she raises them high above her head and cracks her knuckles. "I'll be back in just a minute. Gonna fetch us some lemonade and a plate of gingersnap cookies," she says, disappearing into a small kitchen tacked to the back.

At once, Sam moves ahead of them toward a raspberry-pink table. She slides out a matching raspberry-pink chair with powder-blue roses painted on the back slats and slumps down. "I like what Beryl has done to this place," she says brightly. "She ain't no sissy when it comes to color."

"She's channeling Frida Kahlo," Clarissa says, plopping her floppy hat on the seat of the chair beside her. Caruso wobbles sideways along her arm to perch on the top of its slatted back, at which point Clarissa eases out a chair and sits.

"Who's Frida Kahlo?" Sam asks.

"A great Mexican painter," Clarissa says. "If Beryl's not channeling her, she's channeling Gauguin."

"Yes, ma'am, she's been going on and on about him since I got here."

"*Ma'am?*" Clarissa repeats.

"Sorry," Sam says. "A habit. I even slip up with my sister, and she's only twenty-one."

"Well, I'm not a whole lot older than she is," Clarissa says.

A curtain swishes, and Caruso inches around to see Beryl pattering rapidly across the floor. Forever in a hurry, he thinks, noticing a new streak of red in her coal-black hair. "Here we are," she says, setting down a metal tray. "Some pink lemonade," she says, handing each of them a glass. "And you can help yourselves to the cookies."

Caruso is crestfallen when he spots nothing on the tray for him.

Clarissa picks up a gingersnap, tosses it into her mouth, and crunches. "Not bad for store bought," she says, taking a sip of lemonade. "Amazing," she adds. "This is tasty, too, and I'm sure there's not a drop of lemon juice in it."

"You can thank the Martha Stewart in me," Beryl wisecracks.

"Bottoms up," Sam says, dribbling a dark wet spot of lemonade on her halter top as she swallows.

"Wondered when you'd add some color to all that dreary black," Clarissa says, pointing at the red stripe in Beryl's hair.

"Black, dreary? I love black," Beryl says thoughtfully. "Black is honest, true to itself. It never plays games and is way more interesting than other colors. Whenever a ray of sun hits a crow just right, the purple, blue, and red hues in his feathers shine. I decided to create the same effect, so I got out the dye."

"Why don't you add a blue streak?" Sam suggests, taking a bite of her gingersnap cookie.

"Yeah...the wings of a crow...purple, blue, and red alongside each other," Beryl says.

"My hair is boring brown," Sam says.

"I could change that for you," offers Beryl with a laugh.

"No way—no, ma'am—my mama would kill me."

"There you go with *ma'am* again," Clarissa says, shaking her head.

"Sorry," Sam says. "Like I said, I've been slipping up with my sister, too. She came home this summer to work for Daddy, but there was a problem, and she moved to Roanoke Island to work in his agency there."

"Did they butt heads?" Clarissa asks.

"Oh no, not at all," Sam says. "Daddy's a sweetie."

"Who's your daddy?" Beryl says, swallowing a mouthful of cookie.

"Garland McKenzie. He's the State Farm agent here."

"Oh, you're Garland's girl—Maggie's little sister," Beryl says, surprised. "I haven't seen you in years. Didn't recognize you. Just assumed you were from the mainland, spending the summer on Ocracoke with your parents."

"I'm away most of the year," Sam tells her, "at boarding school in Greensboro."

Trudy Fenton pops into Caruso's mind.

"Ocracoke School did okay by Maggie. She got into a good college, but Daddy wanted something different for me. Don't ask me why."

"Maggie was a couple of years behind me," Beryl says. "I ran into her at Styron's a few months back. She's still drop-dead gorgeous. She's at Duke, right?"

"She was real happy at Chapel Hill, but Daddy kept insisting on Duke."

"Parents are like that," Clarissa says. "They think they know what's best for us without taking the time to find out what we think."

"Yeah, that's Daddy."

"So why did Maggie leave?" Clarissa asks.

"It's complicated. Loads of drama and heaps of hurt."

"Must be a guy." Beryl sniffs.

"You bet," Sam says. "He's studying law at Chapel Hill. They dated hot and heavy for almost a year, but she felt one thing and he another."

"He was feeling something between his—"

"Beryl," Clarissa interrupts, "let Sam finish her story."

"If a man from elsewhere and Ocracoke are in it, we already know the plot," Beryl says. "It'll hang on the foolishness of men and the stupidity of dingbatters."

Clarissa groans.

"Or maybe the stupidity of men and the foolishness of dingbatters," Beryl amends.

"Both," Sam says, stressing the word. "I mean, this guy really tore up Maggie's heart. Then comes here to apologize, but acts like the mindless dingbatter he is. 'What you been up to? I'm here to surf,' he said."

A silence, thick enough to drown in, engulfs the room. Caruso glances at Clarissa, whose cheeks have lost their rosy color; at Beryl, whose green eyes are warning Sam not to say another word; at Sam, nervously biting her bottom lip.

"What was this guy's name?" Clarissa asks, her voice uncertain.

"Joe Fitzgerald," Sam mutters.

Clarissa places her hands firmly on the table and rises to her feet. "I best get—"

"Yeah, I know," Beryl rushes in. "Crab Cakes. I'll call you later."

Clarissa offers her arm to Caruso. Jittery, he gently presses his beak against the back of her hand to gauge his balance and steps up. Seizing her floppy hat, she walks stiffly to the door and mechanically draws it open, the hot whiteness of the day a kick in the gut.

Twenty-seven

AFTER LEAVING BERYL'S STUDIO, they head home in silence. Clarissa clutches her floppy hat in her fist and walks dully along while he perches rigidly on her shoulder, afraid to move lest she might split in half should he disrupt the eerie composure holding her together. He has never seen her like this. Even her hair seems different—the rich, deep red faded by the sun.

For the first time ever, she locks the kitchen door after they go inside. Unmindful, she puts him on the worktable. He flutters to the floor and waddles behind her into the sunroom, hotter than usual with the overhead fan off and the air conditioner set to click on sporadically. She lies down on the blue chaise longue, crosses her hands over her chest, and stretches her eyes wide, as if she is trying to expel her feelings through them. Still as stone, she is, except for her parted lips, quivering with the intake of short, shallow breaths.

It's not long before the phone rings. Caruso expects her to answer it, but she doesn't.

"Hey, it's me," Beryl says on the answering machine. "Sam just left. We should talk about this. I know you want some time to mull it over, but we both know you'll start brooding and blow everything out of proportion. So call me the minute you get home."

"You must be there by now," Beryl says on the machine fifteen minutes later. "I promise I won't talk hard at you. I'll shut my big mouth and listen. Please, call me back."

"Clarissa, I'm worried," she says, after another five minutes. "Please, pick up. Pick up the phone. Pick up..."

Finally, Clarissa heaves herself off the chaise longue and trudges down the hallway with Caruso at her heels.

"Pick up, or I swear I'll come right over...I'll..."

"Beryl," Clarissa says coldly into the receiver. Her profile is a puzzle, while Beryl whooshes panic at the other end of the line, but then Caruso notices her mouth, moving silently, rehearsing her response.

"I'm fine," she says the instant Beryl quits speaking. "No need for you to worry. Really. I *am* fine. Need to think, that's all. I'll call you later. I promise..." Her face impassive, the phone loose in her hand, she listens some more before replying stonily, "No, I haven't heard from him." She takes several short breaths, holds the phone away from her ear as Beryl begins talking. "Bye now," she says, cutting her off. "I love you, too," she says and quickly hangs up.

After that, she punches in the number for Crab Cakes and tells Rick that she is sick and wants him to cover for her tomorrow. She places the receiver in its cradle and lets her hands drop to her sides, passing through the living room, down the hallway, and into the sunroom. She assumes the same pose on the chaise longue—her hands crossed over her chest—though this time she closes her eyes and talks to herself, her words thick and unintelligible.

Alarmed, Caruso flitters up and keeps watch by her feet. Soon, her utterances come to a stop, and her face appears calmer, except for the sheen of perspiration washing down her forehead.

Flying into the kitchen, he lands in the sink and twists on the spigot. He squats beneath the water until his feathers are soaked, cuts the flow off, and waddles back to the chaise longue. Scaling up its leg to the top, he vigorously flaps his wings and cools her off with a spray of water.

She whips up. "You insufferable creature," she says, wiping her face with her hands. "Can't you ever leave me alone?" Plunking her feet on the floor, she stands quickly. "I hate this damn house," she says, her skin reddening with rage. She seizes a pillow from the chaise longue and flings it down. "I hate my life. I hate myself," she says, sobbing, tears rolling down her cheeks and falling onto the white linoleum. "I'm not doing this anymore." She grabs another pillow. "I'm not feeling this anymore." She wheels around and hurls it like a javelin. It hits the painted chest with enough force to send the Wedgwood plate toppling over. The blue porcelain breaks into a dozen fragments against the floor. He ducks his head in case she decides to throw another, only she slumps down.

"Oh, Granny, Granny," she moans, wrapping her arms around herself, folding her body over. "Granny...Granny...Granny," she repeats. Her shoulders shake as she rocks to and fro. Minutes later, she is crawling over the floor toward the broken pieces, picking them up. She comes to her feet and tenderly piles them on the painted chest.

The phone rings again. A short, soft, high-pitched call emerges from her throat, reminding him of the *seet* call of a hedgerow bird, not a shrill alarm that would attract a predator but a delicate signal to warn the other birds of an approaching sparrow hawk. Caruso releases a *seet* call in turn, doing what a hedgerow bird does to pass the alert along.

"Clarissa, it's me," Joe says. "Only calling to let you know I'm taking the ferry to Hatteras. The surf is up, and I wanna catch the waves at Rodanthe. This is my last chance to do some serious surfing. Wish you could come, but know you can't. I'll be away a couple of days. Will call you as soon as I get back."

"Will call me," she says dispiritedly, setting out for the kitchen with Caruso following her. She flings open the top cabinet door beside the sink, pushes the canned goods aside, and retrieves a fifth of Booker's—a small-batch, cask-strength bourbon, 127 proof—which the owner of Crab Cakes gave her months ago and which is almost full because she sips it sparingly. "In case of emergencies," she says. She pulls out the cork, puts it on the counter, and grabs a juice glass from the drainboard. She fills it halfway. "A toast to my never-changing life," she says, a note of self-pity in her voice, and takes a sip.

She gazes at the smoky, amber-colored whiskey and sips again. "You must think I'm stupid," she says, glancing down at him. "You tried to warn me, but I chose to ignore you. Why?" she asks, staring beyond him into space. "Mostly because I *am* stupid and because, after all, you *are* a bird," she says bitterly, drinking the Booker's on her way to the sunroom. "But you're a whole lot smarter than I am." This time, she gulps down a mouthful. "Wow! My, my," she says. "I better pace myself, or I'll get into trouble." She drinks a little more and keeps it in her mouth a few seconds before she swallows. "The water back home is what makes this bourbon so smooth," she says. "Maybe I should've stayed there."

She drags a chair out from beneath the table and sinks down. He climbs up and squats on the chair seat beside her, studying her face while she drinks in silence. "If I had feathers, Caruso, I'd pluck them out like you do," she says after a little while. She breathes in deeply, her nostrils quivering, and murmurs, "I'm sorry, Caruso."

But she need not apologize. He is putty in her hands whenever a man hurts her.

"It's not about Maggie," she says. "It's that he didn't tell me about her. He picks and chooses the details of his story, so in his mind he's not lying."

"Law...yer," Caruso squawks.

"Yeah," she agrees. "You're my sweet boy," she says, sipping. "A loyal cockatoo. A truthful bird. I wish more of us humans were like you." She stares sadly through the windows, and he looks where she is looking. "Insipid pink blossoms," she says when a breeze ruffles through a stand of crape myrtles.

Her words give him a start. He thought she liked pink, as much as Olivia had.

"I like hydrangeas better," she adds, slugging the bourbon down, "'cause their blossoms are snowy white, fat, and brazen."

He doesn't know her as well as he thought he did.

She drains her glass and tilts it to one side. "Empty. Time for another," she says, pitching tipsily against the table as she straightens up.

Back in the kitchen, she spills more Booker's into her glass and lifts it to the afternoon sunlight shining through the window. "Nut brown," she says, taking a swig, going over to the refrigerator, and opening it. She peers inside. "Just like a chef. Nothing much in here." She finds a brick of cheddar cheese, so old her best German knife won't cut through it. She tosses the cheese into the trash can. "But there's some fruit for you," she says, glancing over her shoulder at him. "Are you hungry, Caruso?"

Amazingly, food is the last thing on his mind. He shakes his head.

"No, huh? Me neither."

She meanders back into the sunroom. Her foot grazes against the antique plate holder, and she stumbles, spilling bourbon on the floor. "I forgot about that," she says. Extending her arm out to her side, the drink in her hand, she remarkably maintains her balance as she squats to pick it up. She sets the holder on the bookcase and returns to the chaise longue but doesn't sit.

"Beryl's right," she suddenly declares. "Order your life. Order your mind. Gotta clean this mess up."

Downing the rest of her drink, she starts toward the kitchen. He hears the closet door opening and closing, water gushing and ceasing to flow. Within minutes, she is back with a mop and bucket and a handful of paper towels. She wipes up the spilt liquor in one fluid motion as though she's not been drinking, after which she wads up the paper towels and makes straightway for the trash can in the kitchen. When she comes back, she zealously mops the dirty floor around his cage and then splashes water into every corner of the sunroom, scrubbing the linoleum with a vengeance. Her movements are fast and furious, as if she's punishing the cottage for getting dirty.

She moves on to the kitchen. From atop the worktable, he watches her sponging grime off the refrigerator and stove until their white surfaces glisten, whereupon she cleans the counter, then takes a rag to the glass top of the back door until he can see the sunset glowing vividly through it. Sighing, she reaches for her empty glass beside the sink, pours herself more bourbon, and gulps. "What...can I...do, Caruso?" she asks, turning to face him. "She's prettier...smarter...and he got tired of...her. Am...no...Maggie," she slurs. "Betcha he'll be bored with me real soon." She takes another swallow and frowns into her drink.

Sliding out a bench, she sits down—all the while drinking and talking, her speech becoming more garbled, her features more bleary as she finishes off the glass. There are tears, he notices, along her lower lashes. Drunkenly, she shakes her head and flings them off.

"Sleep...how'll I sleeeep?" she mumbles in a voice so pitiful it makes him wince. She plunks her drink on the worktable and teeters to her feet, the bench rocking behind her as she staggers up. Moving unsteadily toward the long kitchen cabinet near the stove, she draws open the door and lurches forward, grabbing a plastic vial of pills from off the bottom shelf. A doctor on Roanoke Island had prescribed them for her, Caruso remembers, after a particularly awful phone call with her parents, and she had taken one at bedtime every night for a week to help her sleep.

She pushes on the plastic cap with the heel of her palm and tries to twist it open, but it won't budge. "Stuuupid, chile-prooof cap," she mumbles, turning the container on its side. She rummages through the counter drawer and takes out a small mallet. Wielding it like a hammer, she cracks the vial in two. She tweezes up two pills with her thumb and middle fingers, throws back her head, tosses the pills into her mouth, and swallows them with the last bit of bourbon. Next, she plucks up the remaining pills and deposits them in the spoon rest on the counter. She reels back toward him, opening and closing her mouth like a fish. With a startled blink, she takes a clumsy step forward, lifts her empty glass, and says, "To Caruso, the on...ly un who loves me."

She stumbles to her bedroom, smacks the glass down on the nightstand, and falls into bed. Fluttering up, Caruso settles on the pillow next to her face, counting her every breath.

Twenty-eight

THE TOILET FLUSHES. WATER GURGLES from the faucet as she washes her face. She seizes a hand towel on the vanity, but just as she is about to dry off, she lets out an agonizing groan, drops the towel to the floor, and staggers to the toilet. Her arms hugging its porcelain base, she retches violently into the bowl, then dry-heaves for several more minutes. Using the top of the commode like a crutch, she rises on shaky legs. When he steps aside for her to pass into the hallway, she says not a word, only presses her large hand against her forehead. "My head, my head," she moans before collapsing onto the chaise longue. He climbs up to be with her, and she tells him how bad she feels. He turns his face away from her stale, acrid breath. Before he can turn back, she is swaying upward, floundering toward the kitchen.

"My head is splitting," she says, unlatching the long cabinet door beside the stove and seizing a container. She flips the lid off with her thumb, spills three red pills into her palm, and swallows them. "Water," she rasps, moistening her dry lips with her tongue. She heads to the sink, reaches for a tumbler on the drainboard, cuts on the faucet, and rapidly swills down two glasses of tap water. She sets the glass on the counter and begins to weave back and forth. "Ohhhh!" she says, dropping to her knees, then sprawling out on the linoleum. She lies there on her back, breathing heavily with her mouth open, Caruso crouched by her shoulder.

"Hair of the dog," she mumbles, her gaze veering upward, landing on the half-empty bottle of bourbon on the counter. Using a bench for leverage, she maneuvers to her feet, grabs the Booker's by its neck, reaches for the tumbler, and splashes some in. "Relief—please," she says, sipping it on her way to the sunroom. "It's hot in here," she mumbles, flicking on the fan.

She sits down on the blue-cushioned seat, and he squawks up at her.

"Come to me," she says, and he does as she asks. "My sweet boy," she says as he nestles against her thigh. She tastes a little more bourbon and wipes her mouth on her shirtsleeve. The same shirt she had on the day before. The same shirt she slept in last night. The same seersucker pants.

She's a disheveled, smelly mess, he thinks, whiffing a sour odor. No food in her stomach since yesterday. No toothbrush. No bath. No baby powder. But at least her rampant red hair, flushed cheeks, and swollen eyes have replaced the drunken blur of her face and made it distinct again.

"I thought he would call me from Rodanthe, but he hasn't," she says, slewing her eyes around the room. "Looka there...spotless," she says, amazed, as if she doesn't know who cleaned it. She brings the glass to her lips and sips. "I thought he'd miss me, but he doesn't."

Her poor-pitiful-me tone annoys him. Where is his spunky Clarissa, who can whip up a soufflé without thinking, watch the same soufflé fall, and laugh about it while she whips up another? He wants that Clarissa back.

"You love me, don't you, Caruso?"

He bobs his head and coos.

"My main man," she says, curling her legs up on the chaise longue, rolling over, and drifting off.

"SHIT," SHE GRUMBLES several hours later when the Cedar Island ferry announces its arrival with five humongous foghorn blasts.

He chitters encouragingly while she struggles to sit up.

"Poor baby...we didn't eat last night," she says, all of a sudden remembering. "Come on. Let's get some fruit."

From the refrigerator, she takes out a navel orange, a Red Delicious apple, and two kiwis. She washes and slices the apple, peels the orange and divides it into sections, and cuts the rind off the kiwis. Even with a hangover, she arranges the fruit so that it looks pleasing on the plate. "A little nourishment," she says, setting the plate on the worktable, lowering herself onto the bench.

Ascending to the tabletop, he tweezes a chunk of apple between his toes, brings it to his beak, and crushes the mellow-flavored flesh with his strong, dry tongue. She wolfs down two wedges of apple and then pinches up a section of orange but doesn't eat it. "I'm feeling queasy," she says, giving the orange to him. She wobbles as she stands and moves shakily over the floor, her head disappearing into the frosty space when she opens the freezer door.

"Chocolate ice cream," she says, bringing out a quart of Edy's and putting it on the counter. She leans into the door as she closes it and opens the other side. "Great," she says, finding a carton of milk behind a large bottle of marinade. Leaning over, she retrieves the blender from the bottom cabinet, plunks it on the counter, and plugs it in. She removes the lid from the glass pitcher, scoops up some ice cream, and plops it into the container. She adds the milk, snaps the lid back on, and throws the switch, the loud sound of the machine making her grimace. Taking the lid off, she raises the pitcher to her lips and swallows, each gulp lasting longer than the other. "As good as one of Granny's remedies," she says, thumping the almost-empty pitcher on the counter. "Oh, yes, much better...much better," she says, nodding. "I need more hair of *this* dog, but first a shower. I stink," she says, scrunching up her nose, breathing in.

She returns the milk and ice cream to the refrigerator before starting toward the bathroom with Caruso in her wake. Midway there, the phone rings. Her body rigid, her features frozen, she peers down the hallway and waits.

"Hi, Clarissa, it's me," Joe says.

A strange gurgle skips from her throat.

"I'm catching the early ferry back tomorrow morning. How about lunch at the Treasure Chest—around eleven—before your day gets too busy? Will meet you there. Can't wait to see you. Bye now."

She swallows hard, staring blankly in front of her.

"You can't wait to see me," she mutters after a minute of stony silence. "But what will we see when we look at each other?" She pauses for another moment and asks, "Will I see someone I can trust?"

She is equivocating, Caruso thinks fearfully.

"Someone I can trust to change?"

Don't go, Caruso thinks.

Wrapping her arms around her waist, she girds herself and states, "I've gotta see him. At least I owe him that."

Disheartened, Caruso cries out.

"Oh, sweetheart, trust me," she tells him.

He trusts his instincts only. If she meets Joe for lunch, she'll give him another chance. "Lunch at eleven, then," she says, setting out again for the bathroom, the door closing behind her.

This time, she must trust her bird companion, Caruso thinks as the water from the showerhead pings against the stall.

Caruso hops through the sunroom and into the kitchen. With a determined pulse of his wings, he flies up to the counter, takes a pink pill from the spoon rest, and drops it into the melted ice cream at the bottom of the glass pitcher. He goes back, tweezes up a second pill, and drops it in. He scrutinizes the contents of the blender. Like a gambler, he weighs the odds and considers every unintended consequence. This is his last chance. No mistakes this time, he vows. Resolved, he plucks up another two pills, lets them fall into the chocolate slush, and returns for yet one more—a guarantee that she'll sleep through her luncheon date with Joe.

When she comes out, he is crouching beside the bathroom door. "I feel better," she tells him, her gait steadier on her way to the kitchen. He looks on, steely eyed, while she prepares another milkshake, the arm of her white robe swishing as she scoops up more ice cream and pours in more milk. She snaps the lid on the blender and turns the machine on—any incriminating trace of pink disappearing into the swirling chocolate mass. She drinks it all.

Meandering back into the sunroom, she lies down on the chaise longue beneath the schussing fan. Within minutes, she is sleeping. He flies up beside her.

Time passes. The sunset is replaced by a myriad of stars. In the moon's gauzy light, he watches her chest rising and falling, her belly undulating with each intake and release of air, and feels the gentle brush of her breath on his feathered cheeks. Her skin is smooth again, as satiny as a baby's, the lines erased along with the worry, and once more she is his lovely red-headed Eclectus hen. "Claaa-risss-a. Don't go. Sleep," he says, the words spoken softly into her ear.

Tomorrow, at noon, Joe will realize that she's not showing and that she doesn't trust him anymore. Then, Caruso will kiss her lips with his beak and wake his Sleeping Beauty from her deep repose, and together they will create their own happy ending. The rhythmic sound of the whirling fan calms him, and before long he has joined her in a deep, dreamless sleep.

Twenty-nine

THE BRIGHT SUNLIGHT WAKES HIM WITH A START. He jerks himself upright, the hot, wet air wrapping itself around him like a towel. Inhaling a blast of oxygen, he vigorously shakes his torso, preparing for battle, only to realize that he has already won the war. For the intense heat belongs to midday, not morning. She slept through her luncheon date with Joe.

Flapping his wings, he cries out in victory. He cranes his neck to look at the one he loves. She seems too still. Too peaceful. He moves closer to her face, listening for her breath, but her lovely lips aren't parted. Climbing upon her chest, he extends his wing, like a scarf, in front of her mouth and nose and notices his feathers trembling. She is fine, he thinks, and would have shrieked out in relief but hears the click, click, click of the rotating fan blades, feels the breeze wafting down from them, and realizes that they are ruffling his plumage.

Panicked, he destroys their fairy tale ending with a screech. He presses his ear covert against her chest, longing for a heartbeat. Oh, yes, sweet Great Goddess of Creation, it is there. "Claaa-risss-a," he says, thrusting his beak against her lips, feeling her erratic, unsubstantial breath against his face.

He shrieks loudly, his cry caroming around the room. "Clarissa!" he wails. "Clarissa!" But she does not stir.

He flies from the chaise longue into the kitchen and turns on the faucet. Again, he drenches his plumage in the gushing water. Cutting the flow off, he scales down to the floor, totters back, and awkwardly maneuvers his soaked body onto her chest. He flutters his wings, raining droplets upon her cheeks. Still, she doesn't react.

Screeching, he flaps wildly, the water flying, and swoops off the cushioned seat and darts toward the windows. He clutches the blinds with his toes and ferociously shakes them. "Clarissa! Clarissa!" he cries, all the while asking Warramurrungundji to help him. "Claaa-risss-a!" he screams as he hurls his small body against the panes of glass.

Three houses down, he catches sight of Joe, the Great Mother's answer to him. He shrieks his name over and over until Joe hears him and starts to run down the sandy lane, his strong legs propelling him forward, and—for once—Caruso is grateful for his strength. Sprinting down the driveway, he races past the long row of sunroom windows as Caruso follows him, lunging from one panel of blinds to the next, until he disappears around the corner. Caruso sails into the kitchen and lands on the worktable just as Joe clips up the deck steps, flings open the screen door, and bangs his hand against the glass top. When Clarissa doesn't answer, he grinds the doorknob. "Clarissa!" he yells, twisting the knob again and again. With an anguished cry, Caruso suddenly remembers that the door is locked. Whipping off his T-shirt, Joe wraps it around his fist and shatters the glass. Reaching in through the empty space, he flicks the lock and rushes in.

"Clarissa!" he calls, starting for the sunroom with Caruso in flight behind him. "My God," he groans when he sees her still body on the chaise longue. "Wake up," he says, his strong hands clutching her shoulders. "Wake up," he insists, shaking her hard.

He pulls her down until she is lying flat on the cushioned seat. Tilting her head back, he opens her mouth, sticks two fingers inside, and sweeps them around. "Steady pulse," he says, after pressing his index finger against her neck. He holds his hand in front of her nose. "Breathing," he says, "but gotta get her moving."

He makes straightway for the kitchen. Screaming, Caruso flies ahead of him, gliding through the doorway, settling on the counter, just inches from the spoon rest of pink pills. He flaps his wings and hisses.

"What has she done?" Joe says, coming over. He picks up one of the pills and holds it up to the light. "Xanax," he mutters and puts it back. Seizing a dish towel from the counter, he cuts on the faucet and wets it. After wringing it out, he dashes back to the sunroom with Caruso following behind him.

"Clarissa...Clarissa...wake up," he says, gingerly wiping her face. "Wake up. Wake up. Wake up," he repeats, hooking his hands beneath her arms. He pulls her off the blue-covered seat, the muscles in his chest and arms straining. "Clarissa, wake up," he says, his voice urgent. "Please, wake up."

Her eyelids flitter, and she slurs something incomprehensible before closing them again. "Time for a shower," he says as he wraps his arms around her chest. Like a lifeguard rescuing a swimmer, he drags her down the hall, her heels bumping over the floor. They are almost to the bathroom when she opens her eyes and, in a clear voice, insists that he *stop*, and then immediately falls silent, shutting her eyes once more. With a deep breath, Joe gently lays her down.

Caruso hears him banging cabinet doors in the bathroom. Within minutes, he is on the floor beside her, taking the cap off a bottle of rubbing alcohol, splashing some into his palm, and patting it on her cheeks and beneath her nose.

She grumbles and slaps blindly at him. "Don't," she says irritably, plinking her eyes open. He stops. "What...goin'...on?" she asks in a heavy, drugged voice.

"That's what I wanna know," he says back. Neither speaks for several seconds. Then Joe says, "I saw the bourbon and the pills. What were you thinking?"

"Not sure," she murmurs, her eyes struggling to find him. "I only took two." She pauses, and Caruso can tell from the baffled look on her face that she's trying to figure it out. "Yesterday, I was sick to my stomach. Drank two milkshakes." She yawns, her gaze falling on Caruso, stationed by her feet. "And felt better," she adds thoughtfully. "After that, I don't remember." She glances up and smiles weakly at Joe.

Caruso savors every inflection of her sweet voice. Thank you, Warramurrungundji, for sending someone to help her, he says to himself, his breath quickening, his heart torn, because this someone was Joe.

Thirty

"GONNA KEEP MY EYE ON YOU TONIGHT," Joe says, catching her eye and winking.

"Uh-huh," she says as he puts his palm under her elbow and guides her toward the bedroom. "But we've gotta talk in the morning."

"I'll be right here. You know, I love you."

"Really?" she says.

Nearby, Caruso is eavesdropping. The bedsprings creak as she slips under the sheet, but she doesn't speak again.

Back in the sunroom, Joe changes his water, finds the bag of parrot pellets, fills his food dish, and eases him onto his perch. "Thank you, buddy," he says, before retrieving the baby blanket and covering his cage.

Caruso listens to him padding around the room, shutting the wooden blinds, then shuffling down the hallway. The living room sofa whines when he sprawls out on it. He releases a noisy yawn and, almost at once, begins to snore—his snores as intrusive as blasts from a ferry's foghorn. Caruso doubts he'll be able to sleep but in no time falls into a restless slumber. At dawn, he wakes with a shriek that sends her running to him.

She whips the baby blanket off. "What's wrong, Caruso?" she says, right as Joe stumbles drowsily into the room.

Even he if could, he wouldn't tell her what he did, would never confess to what might have happened if he had put all of the pink pills in her milkshake. How could he describe in mere words the horror he felt last night as image after image of her still, lifeless body drifted in and out of his nightmares? How could he ever be honest about the reckless choices he has made for love?

She unhitches his cage door and reaches for him. He lurches back, undeserving of her touch.

"Don't worry, sweetheart," she reassures him. "I'm all right."

She makes him a better parrot than he is, he thinks, hanging his head in shame.

"Let's have a look," Joe says, coming over. With his fingertips beneath her chin, he turns her face toward him. "Yes, you're my beautiful Clarissa again," he says softly.

Caruso steals another glimpse of her. It's true. Her features show no trace of yesterday's sickness. But then he remembers the pills in her milkshake. "Claaa-risss-a," he says remorsefully.

"My sweet boy," she says, and he lets her rub his neck.

"You need to get back to bed," Joe tells her.

"No, I'm up," she says firmly, en route to the kitchen with Joe following after her. Water rumbles into the coffee pot. Next, she taps coffee into the perforated drum.

"You really do look better," he says.

"I feel better."

"A remarkable recovery, considering…"

"Considering…" she repeats, deliberately. "Considering you broke the glass top of my door."

"That's trivial considering how much...you..."

"I drank a chocolate milkshake," she insists. "Not a sin in my book."

"What about the bourbon, the pills?"

"That was the night before," she says. "I took two pills. That's all."

"Why?"

"I couldn't sleep. I was upset."

"About what?"

"Maggie," she says quickly.

"Maggie?"

"You know, Maggie McKenzie, the girl you dated on the mainland."

Caruso catches the spur of accusation in her voice.

"Oh, yeah, Maggie. I dated her for a while. She's from here."

"Yes, that Maggie," Clarissa says. "Why didn't you tell me about her? Did you come to Ocracoke to patch things up with her, and when it didn't work out, settle for me? Is that what happened, Joe?"

"No," he says bluntly.

"Then why did you come here at all? The surf is better at Rodanthe."

"I picked this place to relax, like I told you, but also, truth be known, to apologize to her."

"Well, that's not what her sister said."

"I don't care what her sister said," Joe snaps back. "I went to Maggie's house to tell her I was sorry for the way I acted. Nothing more."

"You stopped dating her months ago. Why now?"

"Because I *do* care what *my* sister thinks of me."

"Your sister?"

"My older sister, Jo Ann. The only one who'll put it to me straight, who won't mollycoddle me."

"Lucky for us," she says.

"Lucky for me," he adds. "She called me a solipsistic, entitled toilet seat. Told me I led Maggie on. That, regardless of my decision to break it off with her, she deserved better from me. Said I acted like a jerk."

"I bet that made you mad," Clarissa says.

"Look, Clarissa. For as long as I can remember, Jo Ann and I have knocked heads, and, for just as long, I've ignored her. Convinced myself she was jealous of me. But this time, I couldn't shrug off her words. They dogged me for months, and then—out of the blue—I got it. Her truth cut through my denial like a razor blade, and I wanted to do the right thing. So I came here."

"Elaborate. Just how big a jerk were you?" Clarissa wants to know.

"The worst kind. A coward and a liar," Joe admits. "I lost interest and simply quit calling her. Then let myself off the hook by pretending she wasn't really interested in me. I've lived my whole life like this. Eating the last piece of pie without asking if anyone else wanted it. Rationalizing my gluttony by believing I was sparing my sisters the calories. I want to save the environment but act like the world revolves around me. Yeah, that's me. I treated Maggie badly and, as always, rewrote the story."

"Shitty," Clarissa says. "And did you tell her everything you just told me?"

"I tried. Said I should have talked to her, face to face, should have spelled out my intentions like a gentleman. But halfway through my apology, she shut the door on me."

"You could've driven to Roanoke Island when you were at Rodanthe and tried again."

"I did. I knew she was working at her father's agency there and took off one morning, but she refused to see me. So I left. What else could I do?"

"Come on, Joe. You know," Clarissa says. "You write her a letter of apology, spell out every rotten thing you did, and tell her you're sorry—but that would require some real honesty, some genuine regret, wouldn't it?"

"Maybe," he says.

"That would be too real, right?"

"Yes."

"Still a jerk," she says.

"I'm trying not to be, Clarissa. I wanna change, but change doesn't happen overnight. It takes time."

"And me?" she says, any brashness in her tone disappearing. "Are you bored with me now? When you go back to school, will you stop calling? Will you do to me what you did to her?"

"I can't even imagine that," Joe says, his voice quivering.

"And why's that?" she asks.

"'Cause I think about you constantly," he says. "'Cause we click. 'Cause I adore every little thing about you. 'Cause I've got you in my eye."

And then they are quiet.

Caruso listens to cups clinking against saucers, to coffee being poured, to spoons tinkling. He can hear them sipping and whispering—next, the benches scraping over the floor. He thinks they must be kissing. The Great Mother's revenge on him—or perhaps Her blessing, he reasons.

"What are you smiling about?" Joe says.

"About you...the jerk I'm letting back into my life," she tells him. "About me allowing my own foolish adoration to let you off the hook. About how I'm always overreacting. I need to change, too. Need to learn how to go with the flow, how to accept life gracefully."

"And us? What are you thinking about us?"

"We are special together," she says. "And we both know it."

"Special enough to live with each other?" he asks.

"Possibly."

"In Chapel Hill with me?"

"That's a big step."

"How about a little step, then? A trial run during the off-season?"

"Maybe," she says, "but I think I should have a serious conversation with Jo Ann first."

He begins to chuckle. "I'll give you her number, and you can call her while I fix the door."

"Later," Clarissa tells him. "Right now, I need to call Beryl and tell her I'm okay."

Okay. Such a tiny word, promising so much hope for the two lovers, Caruso thinks, his heart wavering between sadness and joy for them. *Okay.* He will never be okay again. But what if...what if he had someone like Joe's older sister, someone like Jo Ann? And what if that someone could care about him, even with all his flaws? What if she loved him enough to point them out to him? And if she should exist—somewhere out there in the vast universe—would he be willing to listen to her wise, true words?

Thirty-one

WHAT IS A LITTLE BIRD TO DO should the veil be ripped away from his heart and he—at last—sees into the darkest part of him? What is he to do if he should go there? Could he live with such a truth? It is true, Caruso thinks, that he has plotted and schemed to win Clarissa's heart, but any destructive consequences of his actions were unintentional. He has made mistakes, yes, but he never wanted to hurt anyone.

For he is not a calculated killer. No bird of prey, is he, who coldly kills his victims to provide food for himself and his offspring. If he had chicks, he would never choose to feed the eldest chick more, all the while knowing that he would grow strong enough to murder and eat his weaker sibling. Caruso would never do this, not even to guarantee the survival of his species.

Without warning, a voice inside him whispers, *Cain preying on Abel.*

No...no, Caruso thinks, quickly reconsidering. Birds are not like that. A bird of prey is simply following his instincts. Killing is in his nature.

It is the nature of jealousy, replies the faint voice in his head.

Jealousy is what humans feel, not birds, Caruso counters.

People love birds because they see themselves in them. Same as humans, birds can be timid or outgoing, tender or cruel, steadfast or disloyal, trusting...or jealous.

Birds are not jealous, Caruso objects.

Two harrier hawk chicks in a nest, the older one killing his younger sibling. Is that not like the "mark of Cain"?

Spiritual words written for human beings, not for birds, not for him.

What about "selfish jerk"? the voice says.

He cringes, remembering how he felt when Clarissa called him that. Did she really speak the truth? he wonders.

Yes, Clarissa hurt you with those words. But later, you felt better. She made you and Joe equals.

I must protect my nest...my mate, Caruso thinks. I love my red-headed Eclectus hen.

You and Joe are the same. He eats the last piece of pie. You eat the last grape. Both of you pretend you're eating it for her, satisfying her need to be loved.

Love is about sharing—what birds do, he thinks, justifying himself.

Make up your mind. Is it "survival of the fittest" or "breaking bread"?

No...no...it's the way of love—one for her, one for me, one for her, one for...

You claim to love the natural world, but how can you when you have such disdain for your feathered friends, when you act as if you are the center of their universe?

What is a little bird to do?

Or a little bird who fancies himself a human being? Her voice, once more, intrudes.

His mind is stunned by this painful truth. Is this the voice he's been waiting for?

Get out your binoculars, rotate the focusing wheels, look at yourself a little closer, the voice tells him. *See yourself clearly. Remember who you are.*

I am just a parrot, he thinks. I don't believe all the other birds revolve around me.

Are you sure?

Yes, because birds accept their place in the world. They are not proud.

Isn't the lesser masked weaver bird proud of his tightly woven nest?

Yes, but...

The bower bird is certainly proud of his decorating skills.

Still, though...

The peacock is proud of the eye in his tail feather.

"Proud" isn't an adjective used to describe a bird.

What about "proud as a peacock"?

A simile for a human being.

What about "proud as a cockatoo"?

Yes, but it's right that we feel proud.

I know...I know. In 1250, the Saracen Sultan gave you as a gift to the Emperor of the Holy Roman Empire of the German States. This makes you a bird of importance.

The truth cannot be ignored, he thinks.

The truth is your hubris compelled you to abandon your birdness. Which you did, as effortlessly as a preened pinfeather.

"No!" Caruso says.

Pride cometh before the fall.

"No, no!" he insists, fighting back.

It is your pride that did you in.

Not true, Caruso thinks. I can laugh like the kookaburra, decorate like the bowerbird, long for love like the kakapo. I don't put myself above them.

Well, what about the seagull? the voice asks him.

He is squawkless.

Jonathan Livingston and the other slackers.

I tried to empathize with them, he thinks.

Letting the humans do their fishing for them.

"No pride at all!" Caruso shouts.

While you are soooo prideful, the voice says, catching him in the net of Her words, *your pride egged you on. It led you to the precipice of your false human ego and pushed you over, didn't it?*

"The power of pride," he tries feebly.

The architect of your destiny, the voice boomerangs back.

He emits a thin, weak squawk of protest. It wasn't all my fault, he thinks, excusing himself. I was stolen from my parents, snatched from the sky, and locked into a cage on the other side of the ocean, thousands of miles away from home.

That's true, the voice, softer now, gives him. *It qualifies as a reason.*

I was scared and alone.

I know, the voice says.

I wanted to be loved.

Don't we all?

What I did was only natural.

I believe you believe that.

What I did was only human.

Yes, only human, She repeats in a firm voice.

Faint, Caruso wobbles on his perch. Stretching out his wings, he presses them against the sides of his cage and braces himself up.

Be honest, Caruso, She tells him. *Years ago, you began this long, arduous process of trading in your birdness for humanness.*

"No," he puffs, shaking his head in denial.

You refused to befriend Matt because you wanted Clarissa for yourself.

"Caruso loves Claaa-risss-a," he chokes out.

GWYN HYMAN RUBIO

And in your desire to have her, you led him to his death.

"An accident," he says.

The pink feather in the tomato sauce.

I didn't mean to hurt him. I never drew blood with my beak.

The pink pills in Clarissa's milkshake.

Only to make her sleep.

But it was a dangerous, selfish act, She says.

"Clarissa loves Caruso!" he cries out.

Yes, She says triumphantly. *That is what you want, what you've always wanted, and you've done everything in your power to get it.*

"Caruso loves Clarrissa!" he corrects himself. "I acted out of love."

No, not out of love, She says, *but out of some vast emptiness, as deep as the ocean, inside you.*

Out of love, he persists. Love is eternal hope, isn't it?

Hope is the thing with feathers.

Yes...feathers let me fly. I fly in hope. I fly for love.

The truth is...not always.

What do you mean?

Hope kept Theodore Pinter whole...almost 'til the end.

But the old man couldn't remember anything.

He remembered Olivia's birthday.

What good came of that?

The only thing that matters, Caruso, for birds or humans—another chance.

That's all this bird ever wanted. I deserve another chance.

So did the old man.

He quit trying.

But he did get another chance, didn't he, Caruso?

What could a little bird do?

You are no longer a bird, She says. *Even the flightless cassowary kept his wings, but you have abandoned your birdness.*

"Not so," he says, vehemently shaking his head.

Without your birdness, you won't be able to fly.

I still have my birdness, he thinks, his eyes darkening in anger. And to prove it, he erects his crown of gold, throws back his head, and delivers the long, sustained, ear-splitting shriek of the Sulphur-crested Cockatoo.

Yes, that's it, Caruso, the voice says. *Embrace your birdness. Embrace the truth. But embrace all of it.*

Thirty-two

"I'M NOT TRYING TO MOMMUCK YA, SWEETIE," Beryl says, interrupting Clarissa's energetic chatter about a tropical storm gradually gaining strength as it heads north toward them, "but ya two should be sailing leisurely toward your future, not racing there."

Apparently, Beryl is intent on talking about Joe and Clarissa, Caruso thinks. He has been obsessing over the lovers for days now, and each new tidbit of information about their relationship confounds him further. He longs to live in the present like a parrot, but this speck of humanness in his parrot heart won't allow it.

"I'm not racing anywhere," Clarissa tells her, thumping down a mug of peppermint tea, so strong he can smell it from his cage in the sunroom. "Except off this island if a hurricane blows our way."

"If ya move to Chapel Hill, you will be."

Clarissa clears her throat and in a hurt voice says, "You don't want me to spend the off-season with Joe, do you?"

"It's not that," Beryl says after several seconds. "I like Joe. I'm happy that you two have worked things out. Really. I mean, he seems nice enough, but living with a guy hain't the same as dating him."

"I know that," Clarissa says defensively.

"What if he surprises you again?"

"I know who Joe is, especially now," Clarissa says. "Anyway, I'm tired of flipping hamburgers at Howard's Pub when the island shuts down."

"Chef Louie might keep the Treasure Chest open this winter."

"I wouldn't line-cook for that sleazeball if that was the only job around."

"Well, then, what about Caruso?"

"We're taking him with us."

"But he's never liked Joe."

"His attitude is changing."

"I could take care of him while you're gone."

"Leave Caruso?" Clarissa says, her tone incredulous.

"For just a few months," Beryl says. "He'd keep me company."

"I'd never do that."

"Still..."

"No way I'd leave him behind."

"Ya sure don't mind leaving me."

"Oh, so that's where this is heading."

"Who will I talk to?"

"Let's see—your huge family, the Art League crowd, and every person on this island you've known since you were a kid."

"Hain't none of 'em you," Beryl says in a pouting voice.

"Other than art school in Savannah and the trip you took to Mexico, you've never wanted to be anywhere else but here."

"True, but here won't be the same without you."

"I'll miss you, too," Clarissa says.

"You'll get bored," Beryl warns her.

"No, I'll get to know him better."

"He'll be away a lot—studying."

"Beryl, there *are* restaurants in Chapel Hill. I can work, you know."

"Well, I want a letter a week from ya, when the mail's called over."

"And I'll be coming back every few weeks to check on the cottage. We'll be seeing each other all the time."

"Ya gonna marry him?" Beryl asks, out of nowhere.

"He hasn't asked me," Clarissa says.

"If he did, what would ya say?"

"A few days ago, I would've screamed *no!* Today, I think *yes*, but you're moving way too fast for me, Beryl."

Yes, Caruso thinks. That simple word rains down on him, waterlogs his feathers, and renders him as flightless as the kakapo. If Clarissa says *yes* to Joe, what will become of him?

"I'll be right back," Clarissa says when someone knocks loudly at the front door.

Rap. Rap. Rap. This sound has been weighing on Caruso lately.

She blows him a kiss en route to the living room. "Hey, Rick," she says seconds later. "What brings you here? What's going on?"

"Hurricane watch," he says. "Emily's official now. Wanted to make sure you'd heard."

"No, I hadn't," she tells him.

"Could be here by this weekend."

"Tropical storm one second, hurricane the next. I guess she's finally made up her mind," Clarissa says, laughing.

As always, they discuss their plan. She'll talk to his uncle. Rick will pick up the supplies at the hardware store. The staff will batten down Crab Cakes. For it is the way of humans to prepare for storms, to listen to forecasts, to decide if they'll stay or leave. Their nature demands a game plan.

Caruso sends his thoughts back to his homeland—to the brilliant scarlet wings of Australian king parrots and the green wings of their hens streaking west across the sky, to the feathered tribes of Major Mitchell's Cockatoos winging toward the outback, to the white flocks of Short-billed Corellas flying away from the paddocks. All birds are intuitively aware of approaching storms. They send out a universal shriek of alarm and immediately head inland—seeking shelter beneath cliffs and in forests—anywhere far from the water. For it is the way of birds to trust their instincts—to fly away from dangerous weather.

Thirty-three

"I PLAN TO RIDE THIS ONE OUT," Skeeter says, revealing a newly acquired tattoo of a blue mermaid on his upper right arm.

In his cage beneath the sprawling live oak, Caruso watches the staff's ebb and flow as they crisscross one another's paths, looking more like worker ants than human beings.

"Uh-huh, and have you even been through one before?" Pops asks, a touch of ridicule in his voice.

"No, this will be my first," Skeeter says, hoisting up two patio chairs in the crook of each elbow.

"It won't be exciting, if that's what you think," Pops says. "You'll be bored one minute, terrified the next, and if you survive it, you'll never want to do it again."

Although Skeeter has no comeback, Caruso can tell from his locked jaw that he's determined to stay and from Pops's annoyed face that he thinks Skeeter's a fool.

Sallie clumps past Devon, who is shuffling through a stack of plywood sheets in the middle of the patio. "Are you worried about the hurricane?" she asks Caruso, peeking into his cage.

He greets her with a squawk.

"I overheard the two lovers talking. Said there's no way they're gonna stay here. Gonna slip you into the back of the van and catch the ferry to the mainland. I don't blame them. A category three, maybe. Hundred-mile-an-hour winds," she says, whistling through her teeth.

She didn't have to tell him that Clarissa would leave. Time and again, she has vowed never to ride out a hurricane, regardless of its strength. Last year, the instant she finished boarding up, they had taken an early ferry to Cedar Island and then driven inland.

"Guess she'll see how y'all get along," Sallie says, craning her neck toward him. "Just a little experiment before she moves to Chapel Hill. What do you think about that, Caruso?"

He gives her a wary, upward glance.

"Naturally, she'll take you with her," Sallie goes on. "No matter what, Miss Goody-Goody will do the right thing, but it won't be like it is here on the island. Chapel Hill is a big city, with rules and regulations, and life there will be different." She runs her long fingernails across the bars of his cage. "What will you do with yourself when they leave you for hours all alone? What if she likes it there and decides to stay? What if they get married?"

Uneasy, he looks away.

"She's in a tough place, Caruso. She loves Joe but feels responsible for you." Sallie hesitates for a second, breathing heavily through her nose; then, in a soft, secretive voice, she says, "But I know what she could do."

He faces her again. She pauses, her eyes as round as magnifying glasses burning through him. "She could give you to me," she says. "We get along pretty well, don't we? This way, you could stay here, right here on our little island, and Clarissa could visit you anytime she wanted."

He fidgets on his perch, swings his head—no.

"I mean it," she says, her tone earnest. "I could speak to her right now, if you like."

Caruso hears the pleading in her voice.

"Think it over, Caruso. I could be your new Clarissa."

"I heard that," Devon says, making his way toward her with a plywood sheet beneath his arm.

"Heard what?" Sallie sniffs.

"We're all working our asses off," Devon says. "All you do is torment that poor bird."

"That's not true," Sallie says, raring back her shoulders. "I really would take him."

"But Clarissa didn't ask you, did she?"

"I only wanted to help," she says as he starts for the side yard.

"Don't mistreat him then," Devon says over his shoulder.

"I'd never hurt an animal," Sallie says, her eyes crackling with emotion. "'Specially not Caruso. I love him."

"I know you do," Pops says, walking over.

"Devon never understands me," she says in a wounded voice.

"That's because he hasn't known you for as long as I have," Pops says, squeezing her shoulder. "We need you back in the kitchen."

"Okay. Okay," she says as they retrace their steps to the glass-paneled door, leaving Caruso alone.

He listens to the anxious scritching of sparrows flying above the patio and to the buzzing of a drill as Joe and Clarissa hang the metal shutters up front. Hammers pound as nearby businesses nail plywood over panes of glass. Winches grind while sportsmen secure boats. Cars grumble in line to board the ferries. Every O'cocker is battening down his island home.

Swooping above the harbor, the seagulls shriek shrilly, aware of the changing weather. In the distance, the wild ponies whicker and neigh. How will they manage? Caruso wonders, although he knows they've been enduring these storms for years. Back when Blackbeard sailed the waters, they survived shipwrecks, swam to shore, and thrived in the saltwater marshes and scraggly woods, digging beneath the sand to find pockets of rainwater, a lifesaving gift from the same storms that threatened them. Weaving through all of this racket, as clear and pure as Jean Ritchie's voice, is the chiming of the church bells on Sunday.

"You've done enough. You should leave tonight," Clarissa is saying to Joe when they round the corner.

"Not before I board up your cottage," he says.

"Beryl's brothers always help me."

"We're gonna load my van, and the three of us will leave together," Joe insists. "I won't have it any other way." Wrapping his arms around her waist, he plants a kiss on her forehead.

Just like lovebirds, Caruso thinks.

"You're so damn stubborn," she says, laughing, pulling away from him. "Why can't you behave like all the other tourists?"

"They don't have you," he says.

On tiptoes, she kisses his cheek.

Radiant in love is she, Caruso thinks, his heart bittersweet.

The two of them start walking once more, every few steps pausing to kiss in the hazy sunlight. Caruso lifts his head and sees Jorge, Amelia, and Sallie stashing pots and pans into cabinets, just as Rick whisks by with locks looped around his middle fingers. Next, Caruso shifts toward the dining room and, through the bushy hedge, spots Manuel with a stack of tablecloths. Behind him, Pops is carefully removing two large oil paintings of Pamlico Sound. After a few seconds, Pops draws open the barroom door, pokes his head out, and yells, "Clarissa, where do you want me to put these paintings?"

She turns in the direction of his voice. "Hang on," she says, setting out toward him. "I'll help you with them." Meanwhile, Joe squats beside the plywood sheets.

Caruso closes his eyes and breathes in the scent of salt, much stronger now. The crape myrtles rustle in the short bursts of wind, and the limbs of the live oak rasp above his cage. From the bakery next door comes a thunderous crash, followed by a rush of curse words. Somewhere, a door slams, and a child begins to wail.

Caruso fixes his eyes again on Clarissa, who once more has her eyes on Joe as he sorts through the stack of plywood, choosing the biggest sheets to nail over the fragile panes of glass.

Life from beginning to end is a struggle, Caruso thinks. Mates loving and protecting each other, mates loving and protecting their young. From the bottom of inland cliffs, the barnacle geese of Greenland call to their chicks, and they respond fearlessly, skidding down the rock face, toppling head over heels between boulders, dropping off the edges of bluffs until they reach their parents and follow them to the nearest brook. Baby grebes climb atop the backs of their mothers, who upraise their wings to prevent them from falling off as they glide through the water. A robin will sacrifice itself to protect its offspring.

Life is a struggle for every bird on this planet, Caruso muses, for every living creature, for every human being. Life is fraught with danger but also, he believes, made bearable by love. Sallie wants to take care of him because she longs to love and be loved. And Caruso knows now that Joe loves him—that, like any other creature protecting its young, he will do what he must to keep him from harm, to keep Clarissa's tender heart from breaking.

Thirty-four

"I'VE NEVER CUT IT THIS CLOSE BEFORE," Clarissa says, nervously biting her bottom lip.

Earlier this morning, she and Joe had boarded up the replaced glass top of the kitchen door and about half of the windows in the sunroom before she had suddenly realized they were running late.

"Don't worry," Joe reassures her. "This storm is moving like frozen molasses. Besides, there'll be more ferries leaving later on today."

Clarissa stares over his shoulder beyond him into space. "I've dealt with tornadoes my whole life," she explains. "They're hit and miss. Might skip over you, might not, but hurricanes are a different kind of animal. They spare no one."

What kind of creature might a hurricane be? Caruso wonders. Not like a lone shark—stealthy, quick, and focused when it attacks. More like a school of sharks—high on the scent of blood, frenzied and unstoppable, when they strike. But then, what does Caruso know? Once he had compared Joe to a shark simply because he resented the man. Blinded by self-deception, Caruso had spared no one but himself.

"Look," Joe says, thrusting out his rough but steady hands. "Am I nervous?"

"Nope," she says with a faint half-grin.

"Emily's two hundred miles away."

"So?"

"So...we've got plenty of time."

She eyes him dubiously.

"Trust me," he says with authority. "The ferries will only stop running when the wind gets too strong...hours from now."

From his cage, Caruso watches as she gathers together a box of keepsakes—the photograph of her grandmother from the bookshelf, the fragmented pieces of the Wedgwood plate carefully wrapped in tissue paper, along with her favorite cookbooks and parrot books. She hurries over to the table, from which she grabs his almost-depleted bag of parrot pellets, his yellow rattle, and two pinecones. "Here," she says to Joe.

"How about a Ziploc bag to put these in?"

"Sure," she says, making a beeline to the kitchen.

Caruso listens to the grating of wood against metal as she opens and closes a counter drawer.

"Big enough?" she asks from the doorway, a gallon-sized bag dangling from her fingers.

"Yeah, that'll do," Joe says, shambling over. He takes the bag, brings her hand to his lips, and kisses it. It is an elegant David Niven gesture. "You're soft everywhere," he says dreamily. "When you're ninety, you'll still be soft."

"Right now, I'm not sure I'll be around next week," she jokes back.

"Oh, ye of little faith."

"Oh, ye of too much," she counters, flashing him a big smile.

Holding hands, they cross over the threshold into the kitchen. "I'm not about to leave my cast-iron pot," she says, thumping it into a box.

"It could survive anything," Joe says with a laugh.

"And certainly not my knife."

Caruso envisions her meticulously folding a tea towel around its ergonomic handle and blade of German steel.

"Now, what else?" she asks moments later. "Let's see...the deck furniture should be locked in the toolshed. Doggone it!" she says. "Where did I put that lock and key?"

"In a very safe place, I bet," he says ironically. She asks him to guess where it might be, and he says, "Tucked away with your extra house key."

"Maybe," she says as they come back into the sunroom. Going over to the painted chest, she eases out the bottom drawer, shuffles some papers, and brings up a manila envelope. Opening the flap, she thrusts her hand in and fishes out the house key along with a delicate silver bracelet that Caruso has never seen before. "I've been hunting for this since last summer," she says, swinging it from her index finger. "But no lock and key," she sighs, giving the envelope a shake.

"On a hook inside the shed," he offers.

"I'll check," she says, putting the envelope back, leaving.

"She needs me to balance her out, doesn't she, Caruso?" Joe says after the screen door bangs.

Erecting his crown of feathers, Caruso squawks.

"Whenever she's cooking, she never forgets a thing, never misses a detail, no matter how small, how trivial, but the rest of the time, she's a big-picture kind of gal."

But she remembers every little detail when it comes to me, Caruso thinks proudly. Pride cometh before the fall, he recalls and immediately admonishes himself.

"I'm the detail guy," Joe says, his tone thoughtful. "I guess what they say is true—opposites do attract."

He'll get no argument from me, Caruso thinks. After all, isn't he, a parrot, attracted to a human being?

"It's our differences that make us work," Joe goes on. "I'm easygoing, while she's intense. I'm happy with myself, but she's always wondering if she did the right thing. I don't ask too many questions, whereas she can't stop asking them. And you, my fine feathered friend, are a perfect blend of the two of us. So, taken together, we're a trio—a healthy whole."

A trio...a healthy whole, Caruso thinks dolefully.

"I love Clarissa, and you love Clarissa," he says. "She loves both of us, and she and I love you."

Aren't we right back where we started? Caruso thinks, confused. Another human game plan—choosing the proper role for him in their relationship, defining his essence, determining his fate.

"I found it!" Clarissa yells, her voice booming through the open window.

"Duty calls, buddy," Joe says on his way to the back door.

Through the windows, Caruso sees them carrying each chair into the tool shed, and after that the small patio table. Clarissa waits beside the shed door while Joe departs again and then returns with the heavy wooden lounger. Together they maneuver it through the empty space. No sooner do they step outside than she ropes her arms around his waist, leans in, and kisses him, her red hair flying in the blustery wind. A pang of jealousy nips at Caruso, and he turns away from them to see blossoms of crape myrtle whipping through the air like white and pink confetti. Plywood sheets are nailed over the windows next door, and the car is not in the driveway, letting him know that Ruthie and her parents have already left. Caruso wonders if Skeeter is hunkering down, if he stocked up on plastic gallons of water and tins of food, if he bought a flashlight and a battery-powered radio. Yesterday he asked Clarissa if he could take a few hours off to secure his bungalow. When he came back to Crab Cakes, he was wearing a cap with No Fear stitched above the brim. "Let's see how fearless you are when the wind blows the water out of Pamlico Sound," Pops told him.

Caruso lowers his eyelids and looks inward. Fear. There is danger all around. What will become of him? Pet or family member? Feathered friend or unfulfilled lover? Captive he remains and has been ever since he came to this continent and was thrust into their human world. If he's not careful, her kind voice, her sweet smile, her gentle touch will capture him once more. If not careful, he could lose the little bit of birdness that remains inside him.

"Most of the locals are staying," comes Joe's voice from the kitchen. "The desk clerk at Blackbeard's is keeping an eye on the lodge for the owners."

"Rick won't stay at the restaurant, but he'll check on it afterward," Clarissa says, smiling at Caruso when they pass beneath the doorway. "Beryl and her family will be here also. And a hurricane has never chased Catherine O'Neal off the island. She's a fearless old salt."

Unlike Catherine O'Neal, Caruso isn't fearless. Yet it is not the hurricane that frightens him, rather the thought of living without love.

"There used to be a pattern to hurricane season," Clarissa says, "but nowadays the storms blow in all the time. Look," she says, pointing. "The sand is a flying carpet."

"Go pack your clothes, and I'll board up the rest of the windows,"

Joe tells her. "After that, we'll load the van."

Once she loved him the way she loves Joe, Caruso thinks, keeping his eyes on her as she hastens down the hallway. She still loves him, but now her love is different. Or maybe she loves him the way she always did, he decides, more than she would love a pet but never as a partner. Earlier Joe called them *a trio—a healthy whole.* They are a triangle, Caruso thinks, except their sides aren't of equal length. While Joe's and Clarissa's are equal, his is shorter. Caruso is loved, but not as much as they love each other.

Loss and longing, Caruso thinks wistfully. These are the constants of life. Past loss, future longing. Over and over until one's life is over. What if he could learn to live again in the present with love and hope in his heart? Then what? he wonders.

WITH ALL THE WINDOWS boarded up and the power off, Caruso watches them in darkness through the wedged-open doors.

"Is there enough room for these old vinyl records?" Clarissa asks.

"Sure," Joe says, picking up one of the crates beside her feet and sliding it into the back of the van, parked now behind the deck. "Where are your clothes?" he asks as he slides in the other crate.

"Here," she says, stepping to one side, revealing two large, bulging suitcases.

"Come January, we'll need to rent a truck," he says with a mischievous grin.

"What makes you say that?"

"Sisters," he quips.

"Will I get to meet them this trip?"

"That depends on Emily," he says, shoving each suitcase between the two crates. "If she makes a big mess, you'll want to come right back."

"Yes," Clarissa says. "But at least I'll see your place."

"Typical student apartment," he says. "You know, mattress on the floor, beanbag chair, makeshift bookshelves, tiny kitchen with a dozen takeout menus on the wall."

"Apartment?" she says, as though she has never considered this.

"We've never talked about it, have we?" he says after a moment's thought.

"Not really," she says. "I just assumed you had a house. Caruso can't live in an apartment."

"And why not?" he says stiffly.

"You're kidding, right?" she says with a disbelieving smile.

"People have pets there."

"Yeah, dogs, cats, gerbils, parakeets—pets like that—but no right-minded owner of an apartment building is gonna rent to someone with a parrot."

"Caruso's well behaved."

"You've heard him shrieking."

"Yes, but—"

"How do you think your neighbors would feel if he did that?"

"Truthfully, I didn't give it much thought."

"Yeah," she mutters, her face clouding over. "Maybe Beryl's right. We should be leisurely sailing to our future, not racing there."

"So I'll find another place. An old farmhouse out of town, where Caruso can scream all he wants."

"Wouldn't that be expensive?"

"I'll scrimp and save."

"What about your lease?"

"I can deal with that."

"Leases are contracts, Joe," she reminds him.

"Don't do that," he says testily. "I know contracts are serious business."

"That's right, Joe. The l-a-w is serious business. When you least expect it, it comes back and bites you in the butt."

"Well, it won't bite me," he says. "'Laws, like the spider's web, catch the fly and let the hawk go free.'"

"Well, Mr. Joseph Hampton Fitzgerald," Clarissa fires back, "a hawk like you can get away with everything, I guess, while shit just happens to us flies."

"Whatever you say," he says, grinning. "I'll be a hawk if you want me to be."

"No, thank you," she says briskly. "I've already got the bird I want in my life." Pausing, she swallows hard and stares into space, her face expressionless as she thinks. "Did you tie down the propane tank?" she finally asks him.

He nods.

"Clean out the gutters?"

"Not if we want to catch the last ferry at five."

She walks past him, moving to the left toward the front yard.

"What are you doing?" he calls out after her.

"One last check," she says. "I'll take this side, you the other. We'll meet up front. Whatever's left out we'll lock in the shed."

At this moment, Caruso wishes he were some inanimate object so that they could lock him in the toolshed, too, forget about him, and go on with their lives. *Their lives*, he muses, the full meaning of those words, at long last, sinking in. He could fly away, he thinks, just like

Clarissa had flown to her grandmother's house when her life became too unbearable at her parents'. He could start over, same as she. Sometimes a journey to find oneself becomes a loving gift to others. But with whom could he live? he wonders. Certainly not with Sallie. The Great Mother wouldn't have such a twisted sense of humor. With Beryl, yes. With Beryl, that's who, he thinks, his heart thumping with the possibility, his mind reeling with a thousand different thoughts. Hadn't Beryl offered?

He nudges up the latch with his beak and steps out of his cage onto the worktable. With a determined flap of his wings, he sails through the wedged-open door and into the yard. The strong gusts of wind push his small body back, but he is determined to move forward. He flies over the crape myrtles and wings toward the oleander hedge along the perimeter of the restaurant's terrace, landing beneath the whistling branches of the live oak. He focuses his gaze on the roof's overhang and follows it until he comes to the corner where the kitchen and dining room meet. Beneath the gutter, he spots the dark round hole through which he has witnessed many sparrows coming and going. Once, he even saw a cat stealing in to raid a nest. His breast leaning into the gale, his gold crest whipped flat, he lurches across the patio toward the crevice. When he is directly below it, he flutters upward through the empty space and into the darkness. There, he crouches, his mind still racing.

Time passes, and the weather worsens—the wind roaring, the rain pelting against the eaves. The water in Silver Lake Harbor slaps against the dock pilings. The foghorn of the Cedar Island ferry sounds its last call, and he can imagine their van *kerthump*ing over the steel ramp and onto the deck. In his mind's eye, he can see her distraught face, can hear Joe saying that it wasn't her fault, that they had looked everywhere, had waited until they could wait no longer. They will be better off without him, Caruso thinks. He must learn from his mistakes.

With five deep, mournful groans, the ferry announces its departure. Loss and longing, Caruso thinks as the boat grumbles through the choppy swells and recedes into the distance. Loss and longing. Love and hope. No creature on this planet can avoid the pain of living, he reflects. No living creature can avoid the pain of his decisions.

Somewhere nearby a loose gutter is banging against a wall. *Rap. Rap. Rap.* What does that sound mean? *Rap. Rap. Rap.* The sound of last chances, he thinks. Of choices made. Of consequences. The Morse code of his mistakes. What is the voice of truth trying to tell him? At last, Caruso allows himself to remember:

It was two weeks after Olivia's birthday, two weeks after Pascal had appropriated the box of pink roses that Theodore Pinter had sent her, two weeks after the old man had failed to win Olivia back. Upon rising that morning, he had taken the coverlet off Caruso's cage, and, like the other fourteen days, had not spoken a word to him or opened the draperies, only gone back to his bedroom and closed the door, as if he were trying to escape from the world, to run from the loss he was feeling. Lulled by the old man's snoring, Caruso had shut his eyes and drifted off. *Rap. Rap. Rap.* The sharp tapping on the back door whipped his eyes open. Unlatching his cage, he fluttered down, the urgent sound of the rapping drawing him to the kitchen, where he saw Olivia's face pressed against the glass door. She was sobbing.

Caruso listened for any movement in the old man's bedroom, checked to see if he might be coming. No.

He glanced back at Olivia, kept his eyes on her fist pounding against the glass, and noticed the small card, Theodore Pinter's birthday card, trembling in it like a time-worn dance card from her youth. "Teddy!

Teddy! Teddy!" she called, banging and banging. "Teddy! Teddy! I know they were from you."

And although he should have done something, should have gone to the old man's bedroom and woken him, Caruso could not do it.

"Caruso!" Clarissa cries, her voice as clear and real as the clamor of wind and rain outside his hiding place. "Caruso!" she cries again.

Claaa-risss-a! he thinks, recalling, at that moment, everything he has ever loved about her. Her sweet soprano singing "Summertime" to him. Her fingers dropping white grapes into his mouth. The smell of lavender rising off her skin. Her infectious giggling. Oh, how well she has loved him!

He hears something large and metal slamming against a wall. One of the limbs of the live oak groans and then snaps in half. He freezes, makes not a sound, as he listens to Joe—insisting they go back to the cottage and wait there for him. Next to Clarissa—insisting she won't go back until she finds him. The wind howls around his cubby hole. The furious pounding of the waves echoes in his head. Seconds later, their voices become sharper, spiking upward, surfing on crests of wind that rise up to him. Now, she is telling Joe to leave, shouting that she does not love him, and he is yelling back that he's staying with her no matter what.

Everywhere there is chaos and turmoil, compelling him to make a choice. The right one, this time.

Being loved or loving. I choose loving. I choose you, Clarissa, he thinks, soaring through the gap and shooting upward, like a white bolt, into the dusk. The gusts try to shove him back; the rain stings his eyes. Though he promised he wouldn't, he must see her for one last time. Fiercely fluttering his wings, he looks down. And there she is in all her glory—her long neck thrown back, her alabaster arm raised high, her blue eyes following him in flight.

Thirty-five

THE STORM PUSHES CARUSO WESTWARD, away from Silver Lake Harbor. Below, the flagged red cedars are whipping to and fro. He spots the Island Grill, its silver shingles ripping off and cartwheeling in the wind. He flaps his wings and goes on, gliding by the Old British Cemetery. A tree limb cracks and falls, and he worries about those buried beneath the mossy, weathered gravestones. Does the sound of the roaring gale frighten them? He hopes the animals are hiding in places that will keep them safe from harm.

He shuts his eyes tightly against the stinging rain, searching for Warramurrungundji in the lonely void inside him. He wonders if She will rise up from the water and empower him with Her strength. Will She do it now that selfless love, not selfishness, fuels his wings? When he opens his eyes again, he is flying above Oyster Creek, the wind pushing him into the abyss of Pamlico Sound, where the waves surge upward like gigantic nets trying to snare him and pull him down. Why won't the Great Mother speak to him?

Far below, the moored boats resemble inebriated sea monsters rocking on the five-foot swells, slamming relentlessly against the shore. He breathes in salt, feels it circulating through his body and crystallizing in his feathers, already heavy with rain. Once more, he asks Warramurrungundji to help him, to bless him with powerful, stalwart wings. He listens for Her voice in the raging wind. Nothing. He searches for Her spirit shining in the darkness above the waves, but She is not there. She has forsaken him, and he will not ask again.

Lowering his head, he fights the storm alone. If Warramurrungundji will not come to his aid, will any power greater than he intervene?

His body weakens with fear as he imagines Clarissa and Joe, unable to return to the cottage, riding out the hurricane inside Crab Cakes. He pictures them crouching between the large refrigerator and freezer in the storage room, the wind ripping the metal shutters off the front windows, panes of glass shattering in the air. In his mind's eye, she is crying—not for herself and Joe—but for him.

The foam clings like life buoys to the towering breakers as they roll backward, emptying out Pamlico Sound, leaving behind its sandy, pockmarked bottom, as stark and empty as the outback of his native land.

The past and the future fuse together, and he listens to the truth of the now. *Trust in love. Trust in hope*, a voice deep inside him whispers. *You are her guardian.*

With all the stamina he has left, he breathes in deeply, fills his lungs with oxygen, and sends it into the air sacs at the rear of his body. He brings his wings down, and his body rises up. If he wants to save her, he must become a powerful bird of flight, as mighty as the wedge-tailed eagle. He breathes in again, and with each breath he takes, his wings become a little stronger, his air sacs a little bigger, his lungs a little more forceful. Buffeted by the rain and wind, he hovers stationary in the tempest. His spirit falters. How can he perform the miraculous, when he is such a flawed creature? he thinks. Why would any Being bless such a despicable bird?

That is not you. I know you, comes the voice of Warramurrungundji from out of the darkness. *Take off your masks,* She says. *See who you really are.*

He recalls his many selves. A cockatoo, from the top of his crest to the tip of his tail. A fledgling who loves the bush of Australia, his hole in the tree, his parents, his flock, his birdness. Then the net falls over him, and he is born again into a cage crowded with birds he doesn't know. All he wants is to escape from this cold metal jail—to fly home to his parents. Day in and day out, he grieves. Day in and day out, he nurses his grievances, feels disdain for his birdmates and a grudging admiration for the Homo sapiens who water him, feed him, and clean out his cage. A Sulphur-crested Cockatoo he remains, but one who is angry, vindictive, forever plotting.

Theodore Pinter steps in and saves him from a life of parrot mills and misery. Over the years, Caruso learns to like, if not love, the old man. He learns to appreciate Olivia Greenaway, to understand why Theodore Pinter loves her, but he also doubts the old man's lack of action—his life of dreaming about romance behind a wall. Still, he sees the card in her fingers, her fist rapping against the glass door, her voice calling—*Teddy! Teddy! Teddy!* He should wobble the few steps to the old man's bedroom and wake him. He should shriek out. Do something. Anything. For hasn't Theodore Pinter earned this moment of joy? Haven't he and Olivia traveled a lifetime to get here? Yet he can't. His body is frozen. Why? he wonders. Is his brittle heart so filled with bitterness that he is unable to do right by the old man? Is this the truth of who he is?

Look deeper, the voice of Warramurrungundji tells him.

His heart fearful, he does what She demands and pulls off another mask. Caruso deeply loves the old man and is afraid of losing him. Just as he was afraid of losing Clarissa. Through the years, he has made one bad choice after another. Each in the name of love. The same mistake over and over because he was too fragile to see the *real* bird behind the false mask he had created.

Be brave, Caruso, Warramurrungundji says. *Take off the last mask now.*

Trembling, he tears it off, and it flies through the air, spinning away from him.

You are the sum of everything you've ever been, the Great Mother tells him. *No better, no worse than any other living creature. I bless you with My love.*

With newfound strength, Caruso shoots through the slanting wind and rain, away from the shoreline and toward the vast, dark sea. His powerful wings push onward. Every time he flaps them, he takes some of Emily's wrath with him. For he will not let the hurricane have Clarissa.

Focusing his energy into the center of his being, he breathes in deeply. The oxygen shoots through his body and propels him upward, and he steals even more of the tempest's fury. Then, with one final effort, he transforms his wings into a million beating oars and adamantly drags the hurricane away from Ocracoke Island.

Subdued now, Emily follows him. He orders her to ride on his back as he soars high above the Atlantic Ocean, where the two of them dance in the sunny tranquility of the eye wall. Guided by pure love, he breaks free of Emily's embrace and sails into the realm of *Dreamtime.*

There, he rests his eyes upon a flock of cockatoos, perched in a casuarina tree on the bank of the Murray River. "Home," he says aloud as he flies toward the Great Barrier Reef and glances down, but its million coral polyps do not shimmer like they used to. He circles the continent, unable to find the radiant glow that once sustained him. The

Great Mother, now one with him, leads him to Ayers Rock.

In the outback's fading light, he speaks her name, "Claaa-risss-a," even though he vowed to let her go. He looks down, sees her lying atop the sacred monolith, her red curls gleaming as they cascade to the scorched brown earth below. He glides toward her, nestles his crest in her tresses, and senses the warmth of her love. Gently, he spreads his wings over her—their bodies, a white, powdery snow dusting the face of Uluru in the *Everywhen*.

Epilogue

From the *Jacksonville Observer*, September 2, 1993

JACKSONVILLE, N.C.—Yesterday, the fringes of Hurricane Emily skimmed the lower villages of Hatteras Island in the Outer Banks of North Carolina, causing considerable damage with 100-mile-per-hour winds, heavy rainfall, and surging seas.

Island residents from Avon through Buxton and on to Frisco and Hatteras saw water levels up to five feet inside their homes, the highest levels since the hurricanes of 1933 and 1934, according to the National Weather Service. Especially hard hit was the village of Buxton, at the southeastern tip of the island, where locals awoke to uninhabitable houses, destroyed docks, and overturned boats. The stench of overflowing septic tanks and rotting fish filled the air, along with the fresh smell of pine needles from thousands of downed evergreens. Songbirds flew erratically in the sky.

Yet most people along the coast considered themselves lucky. If Emily's gaping eye—headed straight for Cape Hatteras—had not made that propitious shift to the north, she would have unleashed her fury over the island, then moved up Pamlico Sound, causing further devastation. As it was, the tiny island of Ocracoke and other areas were spared.

Catherine O'Neal, a lifelong resident of Ocracoke, has never left her house during a hurricane. "She was a fickle one, ya know," she said about Emily's path. "One day a tropical storm, then a hurricane, then back and forth a couple more times." She nodded and smiled. "Just like a woman, she couldn't make up her mind. Was she fixin' to hug ya or push ya? But she must've loved us some. A godsend, it was, when she turned *away*."

Acknowledgments

I want to thank Jane Gentry Vance for encouraging me every step of the way through the ups and downs of writing this book. Her helpful suggestions, insight, and optimism kept me focused and made the struggle less arduous.

I am grateful to my agent, Susan Golomb, who offered constructive and invaluable feedback as I revised the manuscript, and also to her associate, Krista Ingebretson, who remained determined, hopeful, and efficient as she searched to find the right publisher for this book. My heartfelt thanks go to Midge Raymond and John Yunker for having the vision, passion, and talent to establish Ashland Creek Press. As innovative publishers, they are courageous enough to do things differently, and I admire them for taking the risk.

Without Steve Duffy's amazing computer skills, this novel would not have found its way to any publisher's desk. His generous nature and expertise came to my rescue more than once. In addition, I'd like to thank Harck Pickett for his abundant patience and technical assistance during my moments of panic.

For the inspiration and comfort they've given me these past years, my gratitude is extended to the following people: Sherry Holley, Ginger Ford, and Cindy Bloch for their unwavering support of this book and for Sherry's enthusiastic love of birds; Jean and Allen Porter for the *dreamsicle* cake every Christmas; Cathy and George McGee for chocolate brownies, Irish humor, and constant kindness; Heike and Irwin Pickett and Carol and Steve Duffy for the many wholesome meals that nourished my body and spirit; Connie and the late Andy Ryan for cocktails and conversation; Jo Ann and Mark Gormley for allowing me to use the names of their family members as the names of characters in my book; Judy Cooper for her genius and empathy; Dotsy and Mike McGown for the loving calls from Germany; Charlotte and Pete Pfeiffer for their support throughout my writing career; Doretha Burton for her sweet words of reassurance from the start; and—above all—Angel, my compañero—for his unflinching belief in Caruso. He has been by my side every step of the way, working with me on revisions, coming up with solutions to problems whenever I was stumped, and following through on the tedious details that had to be resolved before publication, especially the pursuit of permissions. Thank you, my love, with all my heart.

Finally, I am grateful to the authors of the many books I read before I ever put pen to paper. Their knowledge assisted me in creating the *other world* of my book. The authors and their books are as follows: Mattie Sue Athan, *A Guide to Companion Parrot Behavior*; David Attenborough, *The Life of Birds*; Georges Bernanos, *The Dairy of a Country Priest*; Bill Bryson, *In a Sunburned Country*; Petra Deimer, *Parrots*; Bonnie Munro Doane, *The Pleasure of Their Company: An Owner's Guide to Parrot Training*; Bonnie Munro Doane and Thomas Qualkinbush, *My Parrot, My Friend: An Owner's Guide to Parrot Behavior*; John O. Fussell III, *A Birder's Guide to Coastal North Carolina*; Ruth Hanessian, with Wendy Bounds, *Birds on the Couch*; Chris Hunt, *A Guide to Australian White Cockatoos: Their Management, Care & Breeding*; Werner Lantermann and Susanne Lantermann, with Matthew M. Vriends, *Cockatoos*; Thomas Merton, *The Seven Storey Mountain* and

New Seeds of Contemplation; Veronica A. Parry, *Kookaburras*; Helmut Pinter, *The Proper Care of Cockatoos*; Marilynne Robinson, *Gilead*; Roff Martin Smith, *National Geographic Traveler Australia*; Donald and Lillian Stokes, *Beginner's Guide to Birds* and *Beginner's Guide to Shorebirds*; Irene H. Stuckey and Lisa Lofland Gould, *Coastal Plants from Cape Cod to Cape Canaveral*; Zeke Wigglesworth and Joan Wigglesworth, *Fielding's Australia*; Walt Wolfram and Natalie Schilling-Estes, *Hoi Toide on the Outer Banks*.

About the Author

Photo credit: Hayward Wilkirson

Gwyn Hyman Rubio is the bestselling author of *Icy Sparks*, a Barnes & Noble Discover Great New Writers selection and a 1998 *New York Times* Notable Book. A national bestseller, the novel was praised as "vivid and unforgettable" (*New York Times Book Review*) and "a combination of fire and ice that will take your breath away" (*Atlanta Journal-Constitution*). Her second novel, *The Woodsman's Daughter*, was published in 2005 and applauded as "richly atmospheric and engrossing" (*Atlanta Journal-Constitution*) and "set in a world wondrously created and mastered" (*Louisville Courier-Journal*). A Book Sense Pick by the independent bookstores of America, it was nominated for the PEN/Faulkner Award, was the finalist for the Kentucky Literary Award, and was listed as one of the ten best books of the year by the *Louisville Courier-Journal*.

Gwyn's work has been nominated for a Pushcart Press Editors' Book Award and has appeared in literary magazines around the country. She is a winner of the Cecil Hackney Literary Award as well as a recipient of grants from the Kentucky Arts Council and the Kentucky Foundation for Women.

Gwyn grew up in Cordele, a small town in south-central Georgia. Her father, Mac Hyman, wrote *No Time for Sergeants*. Published in 1954, it was a national and international bestseller and was adapted as a play and a movie, both productions starring Andy Griffith. Gwyn now lives in Versailles, Kentucky, with her husband, Angel, and their rescue dog, Fritz.

Ashland Creek Press is an independent publisher of books with a world view. Our mission is to publish a range of books that foster an appreciation for worlds outside our own, for nature and the animal kingdom, for the creative process, and for the ways in which we all connect. To keep up-to-date on new and forthcoming works, subscribe to our free newsletter by visiting www.AshlandCreekPress.com.